SILK

THE COMPLETE TRILOGY

Daryl-Jarod Entertainment
www.daryljarod.com

This is a work of fiction. The characters are fictional
and any resemblance to actual persons, living or dead,
is purely coincidental.

Manufactured in the United States of America

Cover Design: Designran

First Trade Paperback Edition February 2017

ISBN: 978-1-945748-00-4 (pbk)
ISBN: 978-1-945748-01-1 (ebook)

SILK

THE COMPLETE TRILOGY

DARYL-JAROD

CONTENTS

Thanks so much to my beta readers, Casey, Kelly, Amber, and Jarvis. Without you, "Pink Fortress", would've never seen the light of day!

Many thanks to everyone who asked and pushed me to release this print edition. This one's for you!

Silk

The rain softly falls down from a darkened sky onto my windowpane. The soothing sounds relax me as I sigh deeply. Lavender scented candles surround the king-sized bed I lie in. The light flickering from the candles, along with the magnificent scent they provide, adds even more pleasure to my relaxed state of mind.

He snores softly beside me. His head is planted on my chest as my fingers roam through his curly locks. I lift my head up from the pillow in order to kiss his forehead. A tiny smile forms at the corner of his full, succulent lips.

I allow my head to fall back onto the pillow. This feels perfect. My man lies comfortably in my arms after a passionate session of lovemaking that transpired only an hour ago. I've experienced pleasure from many men in my lifetime but no one has ever been able to explore my body the way this man has.

Everything about my love is just right: the way he holds me almost always causes chills to run down my spine; the way he kisses me sends bolts of energy flowing between my legs; the way he makes love to my body leaves me speechless. No one can ever amount to the love this man shows me, both inside and outside of the bedroom.

I soak in the enjoyment of this perfect moment a

while longer before I come to the terms of reality with our complex situation. I love him with all my heart and soul. He loves me also. But the love we share is not what I desire it to be. We remain in the shadows while other couples display their commitment and affection in public. I can't see him every night, although my body yearns for him constantly.

We live in two different worlds, each longing for the day when our lives can forever become one. He is not mine. And I am not his. Although he is the only man I've ever truly loved and my soul cries out whenever he's not near, the truth continues to whisper softly in my ear: he belongs to someone else.

The ceiling fan hums softly above the bed. It sends cold air to my naked body, but it's not cool enough to settle the heat that develops between my thighs. My heart begins to beat faster as thoughts of tomorrow begin to develop in my head. These never-ending thoughts haunt my brain like an evil ghost.

My mind needs to settle down. I can't continue to focus on what tomorrow will bring, for tomorrow I will once again be alone. I need to focus on this moment. I have him here with me now and in two hours he'll be gone.

As my brain continues to ponder on these issues, my hand travels down his chest, caressing each pack of muscle that makes up his well-defined six-pack. It continues to travel down to his thick dick. Even on soft, it still amazes me how long and extremely thick it is. I massage it gently in my hand. It takes no time at all for it to lengthen to its max of ten solid inches. It pulsates and feels hard as a brick in my grasp as I begin to stroke it.

Soft moans escape from his lips while his sticky nectar oozes from the slit of his enlarged member. In a matter of seconds, I place him on his back and my tongue slowly licks his precum. I moan in excitement, allowing the delicious taste of him to travel down my throat.

His strong hands find my head. They grasp a handful of my hair, silently urging me to continue. I obey with pleasure. His body jerks as my tongue circles around his shaft and his dick becomes prisoner to my throat. I take all of him, inch by inch, until his entire dick is surrounded by the canal of my throat.

Slowly, I tease him by squeezing his balls and pinching his nipples. He looks down at me, smiles, and then throws his head back into the soft pillow. He's never had anyone make sweet love to his shaft the way I do. No one has ever grasped, sucked, rode, and soaked it up with hot and sticky juice that can only come from passionate sex, like I have.

I lick his balls and then place them both in my mouth. His hands tug at my hair as I tighten the lock my strong jaws have on his jewels. I tease him a bit longer before placing that beautiful monster back inside my thirsty mouth. It only takes a few minutes of passionate sucking and vigorous head bobbing for him to feel an orgasm on the rise.

He lifts my head up; putting an end to the playful game my mouth had so much fun playing. He pulls my body onto his. My tongue travels inside his mouth, allowing him to taste the precum I devoured from his dick.

I giggle as he forcefully throws me on my back. His strong muscular arms have no trouble at all in opening my legs as wide as they can go. He softly kisses me before placing his head between my legs and gently licking my center. I moan out loudly. My thrills of pleasure are loud enough for my neighbors in the apartment suite next door to hear. He does this again, this time more slowly. My hands reach for the pillows while my legs tremble, begging for him to fill me up; for our bodies to become one.

He senses this. He knows my body so well he can figure out exactly what it whispers to him. Our eyes meet. This is only for a second, due to the pleasure his three thick fingers bring to my insides, causing me to tilt my head back. Those fingers roam inside my tight playground for a moment before they forcefully hit my g-spot in an upward motion. I scream as he continues to hit that spot with a huge grin plastered over his face. Before I can even come to terms with what's going on, I find myself erupting like a hot volcano all over his fingers.

He slowly eases them from my scorching hot vagina and inserts two fingers inside his mouth. His tongue flickers around them, consuming my pussy juice. After ensuring that he has sucked and licked away my remains, he brings the third finger to my mouth so I can taste the sweet fulfillment he brought onto my body.

He then proceeds to place his magnificent body on top of mine. My legs wrap tightly around his firm buttocks. He leans over me so closely that I can smell his sweet breath. Our eyes meet. They talk to one another since our mouths can't summon any words to express. His eyes tell me that he's ready. Ready for round two; the final show of the night. The throbbing of his dick against my hardened clit teases the hell out of me.

Time is limited. My body is anticipating him to fill me up with all ten inches and make me scream while my pussy pulsates and throbs. I tighten the grip of my legs around his waist and push him into the slippery wet sea he loves to dive in every chance he gets. We both sigh in unison as he finds his home; the place inside of me no other can touch.

We have made love on a plethora of occasions but it has never felt as intense as it does at this very moment. His every touch, every kiss makes my body twist and turn. He starts with a slow rhythm at first, allowing the tightness of my walls to adjust to his length. When he feels my body preparing to erupt, he speeds up the pace. The bed rocks so much, I swear we could break it any minute now.

An eruption so hard, so powerful, overtakes my body. My legs shake uncontrollably as I have just experienced the most invigorating orgasm of my life. My lover chuckles while continuing to pound me, beating my pussy hard like a drum.

I began to see stars and bright flashing lights! I can feel another orgasm rising with quickness at my core. I scream as I erupt yet again, this time ten times more powerful than before. He continues to invade me as deep as his dick will allow. The headboard beats violently against the wall.

He moans and increases his already rapid speed as he releases a thick and heavy load inside of me. Sweat drenches us from head to toe. Our bodies are exhausted from the most passionate night of our lives.

My love remains inside of me a moment longer

until his dick returns to its soft, but huge form. He kisses my forehead before pulling out of me and entering the bathroom to shower.

As he washes away our evidence of love, I remain in bed. His cum drips from my hot pussy. I insert two fingers inside of my core and taste his delicious flavor. I wish things could always be this way, but he has to get back to his life. I know tonight will be lonely yet again since I will not have him by my side. I'll only have myself. Just me and the memories we have created inside of my silk sheets.

Sexual Tension

It's late. Eleven forty-two to be exact.

They have been here all day and there is still so much work left to be done. They are exhausted from a long, hard day at work and eager to get home so comfort can be found in their beds.

Despite their tiredness, sexual tension is in the air. This sexual tension causes a brick-hard erection to develop at the crotch of his pants. It causes her juices to flow like the Nile River. Jermaine stares at her as her head is buried deep in paperwork for the latest case the firm has spent two months diligently working on. She works so hard for what she wants. He admires that trait in a woman.

Jermaine's eyes have a mind of their own as they travel down to her succulent and juicy breasts. She wears a tightly-fitted shirt that leaves very little to one's imagination.

He wants to jump across the table and pounce on her like a lion, hungry for its prey. He craves what lies between those thick, but nicely toned thighs. He has had it once. He knows he can have it again.

The wedding band on his ring finger reminds him of his dilemma. He is married. He has been for six years. He has two little angels despite the doctor's predictions of his wife never being able to bear children.

Yes, he has it all. He has everything a man could ever desire. He knows men who would kill for a loving spouse, two beautiful kids, a two-story home that's already fully paid for, and expensive cars. To top that, he has a profession he has dreamed of succeeding in ever since he was a child.

But all of these things couldn't possibly be enough for a man. Here he sits fanaticizing and lusting for a woman who isn't his wife.

He wants her. He craves her. He wants her to scream out his name over and over again while he takes her to her sexual peak.

She's aware of his desire. She wants him also. Madison can feel Jermaine's eyes staring down at her breasts, as he pretends to be reviewing a document. She enjoys making his mouth water. She knows he would move mountains in order to pop one of her nipples in his mouth.

Madison almost giggles with delight at the game they play with one another. He is well aware of how much she wants him. And she notices how much his body craves her, just by observing the thrusts from his dick through his slacks.

If only he weren't married. Madison promised herself a long time ago that married men would not seduce her any longer. Jermaine's sexy, dark chocolate body made her renegotiate that promise as soon as she saw his face six months ago when she began working as the firm's new secretary. Everything about his body screamed "sex appeal". He had the body of a model and the brains of a genius.

He flips a page of the document, still pretending

that he is reading. His muscles make Madison's river wetter than ever as it drips down from her canal, sticky and wet. She wants to run her fingers over his well-toned six-pack abs. She desires even more to smack his juicy ass as he tongues down her nipples.

Madison places her pencil down and stretches back in her chair. Out the corner of her eye, she catches the slight glimpse he gives her. He is fighting everything inside of himself not to sex her right there on the conference table.

She resumes her position in the chair and continues her work. He follows her lead and does the same. He silently coaches his member down below to chill so his excitement won't be so easily noticed. This method fails incredulously. He is still erect and hard as a brick.

The sexual energy shared between them drives her insane. She wants him to give into her. She wants to be his.

Madison brings her cup of coffee to her lips, only to purposely spill some of it down her shirt. She quickly places the cup down and is greeted by Jermaine, who jumps over the table to hand her a napkin.

"Thanks. I'm just so damn clumsy," she says, with a sneaky smile as she retrieves the napkin from Jermaine and pats her chest.

"You're welcome," Jermaine replies, grinning from ear to ear.

The cold liquid exposes Madison's hardened nipples through her shirt. It is clear that she isn't wearing a bra.

"Here, let me help you," he says, grabbing

another napkin and rubbing it slowly across Madison's breasts.

"Oh, thank you so much Jermaine. I don't know how I can ever repay you," she replies, with naughty thoughts heavily invading her mind.

She stands up and reaches for another napkin from the table, bumping her elbow against Jermaine's erection. Jermaine wastes no time in standing behind her. He grasps her waist with both hands and pulls her ass to his neglected penis.

She does not fight this. She smiles to herself at how easily she has gotten him to give in to her. They don't speak for a couple of seconds. She closes her eyes as she feels his erection pulsate on her ass.

"I want you, Jermaine. Jermaine...now," she mumbles in a soft whisper.

With that said, he quickly turns her around and lifts up her shirt. He eagerly sucks her nipples as if they are his last supper. Madison moans as her shirt is slipped off of her head and tossed to the floor.

Jermaine's mouth finds hers and locks on for a passionate kiss filled with lust and desire. Their tongues dance with one another, as she is lifted up onto the conference table by Jermaine's strong arms.

He knocks over paperwork, in order to stretch Madison's body over the table. He admires her beauty. She is gorgeous. Her body is heaven-sent, if only for tonight.

Jermaine climbs on top of her and tongues down her breasts once again. He alternates between each pink hardened nipple with his thick tongue. Each nipple is shown the same love and affection. Madison lets out soft moans, while caressing Jermaine's dick through his jeans.

He lifts his shirt and throws it across the room. It flies out of an open window. He proceeds to unbuckle Madison's belt and quickly slides her tight jeans from her thighs. The only thing separating him from his prize is her panties. He rips them off within a few seconds.

Her secret place is no longer a secret. It is ready to be eaten and devoured. He is ready to suck and lick.

He slowly glides his index finger into her folds. It is hot, wet, and so tight that it causes his mouth to water. He pulls his finger from her beehive and sensually sucks away her sweet nectar. His thick finger reenters her walls once more, only to exit again.

His finger enters her mouth for tasting. He wants her to taste how sweet she is. He wants to ensure she knows the power of the golden fruit between her thighs.

She eagerly accepts the sample. Her tongue circles around his finger, licking up every bit of her essence.

Jermaine brings both his hands down to Madison's soft breasts. He squeezes them together, causing Madison's moans to become louder.

"You like that baby?"

"Ooh, Jermaine. Yes!"

"You ready for me to eat that pussy?"

"Yes! Go on and eat that pussy!" she encourages.

He wastes no time in bringing his tongue to her clit. He licks her hard core lightly, while his fingers pinch her nipples.

"Mmm...yeah claim this pussy! This pussy has your name written all over it baby," she coos, while rubbing his head.

Jermaine moves his hands down to her wet clitoris. He pinches it while his thick tongue explores her insides. The deeper his tongue explores, the harder he pinches Madison's clit.

"Aww...I'm about to cum!" she whispers within the next few minutes.

Jermaine pulls his tongue out and quickly climbs on top of the table. He finds his cup of water he threw to the floor minutes ago. He brings it to the table and repositions himself back on top of it. He opens the lid and pulls out a piece of ice from the cup. "Open your legs."

She obeys with no complaints or hesitations. Jermaine places the ice on Madison's clit. She moans. He smiles. He rubs the cold ice up and down and side to side on her already heavily teased clit. She arches her back and grabs his head, as if she is holding on for her life.

"Oooh!" she manages to say between whimpers and moans.

"That feels good, don't it?" he questions, through slurps on her core.

"Yeah...that feels...so good!"

He slips the ice inside of her vaginal walls. She moans his name louder. His smile widens. Jermaine uses his index finger and thumb to fish out the piece of ice. It's rapidly melting, due to the fire burning inside of her.

He lets the ice continue to fully melt on her clit. When it has melted completely, he leans in and blows on her ice-cold center. She sighs and rolls her eyes to the back of her head as she explodes.

She cums.

She cums all over his face.

Cum lingers on his chin.

He gives her a moment to recuperate before tonguing her down and climbing off the table.

Lust remains in her eyes as she seductively locks eyes with him, while pushing her breasts up to her mouth and softly licking her sensitive nipples. Lust remains in his eyes as he licks his lips, while unbuckling his belt and dropping his pants down to the floor.

She extends her index finger toward him, summoning him to finish what he started. He removes his shoes and tosses them across the room. They fly right out the open window. The lovers chuckle for a moment, before Jermaine steps out of his pants and walks over to Madison.

She is so beautiful. Just one look at her causes his already stiffened dick to lengthen even more.

She sits up, knowing it's his turn to receive. She is willing to give him her all tonight.

The huge imprint protruding out of his boxers makes Madison's mouth water with delight. She can't wait to have his chocolate Hershey's bar melt inside her warm mouth. She wants him to lose himself with her. She wants to be the only one to bring him pleasure. She knows his wife can't do it as well as she can.

She proves this to him by pulling his boxer briefs down to his thighs and gulping his huge penis down her throat in one smooth stroke. He moans. She smiles in satisfaction.

Her tongue softly licks around the head and her fingers gently squeeze his big, hairy balls.

"Damn...Madison...girl you bout to make me bust one," he moans, while holding onto her head.

This motivates her to work harder. This causes her head to move faster. This drives his body so wild that he loses control and ejects his warm goo down her throat.

"Damn!" he says, as he catches his breath. "That's the quickest I ever came. Damn! Girl you give better head than my wife."

Madison does not respond. She does not verbally give a thank you. Instead, she continues to suck and lick his penis until it is hard enough for round two. She gives her throat muscles a break and uses her right hand to stroke his long, thick erection, while her mouth gobbles up his balls one by one.

Jermaine can't believe the spell Madison's mouth has over him. They had never performed oral favors for one another until tonight. It is now oblivious that it was well worth the wait. "I wanna fuck you," Jermaine spits out in ecstasy as his balls receive love and much needed attention.

She stops and kisses him with a passion she has never given any man before. "What are you waitin' for?" she asks. "Go on and get it. It's yours."

He picks her up from the table in his arms. He then proceeds in carrying her over to the window. Her cell rings. It is tucked in the pocket of her Ralph Lauren jeans on the floor. He ignores the loud ringtone and pretends it is music to their lovemaking.

Jermaine places her on her feet and roughly inserts his tongue into her mouth. She can feel his passion and desire. She wants him now more than ever. "Give it to me Jermaine."

He takes this as an incentive to make her cum hard and strong. She'll be calling him Daddy by the end of the night. Jermaine pulls back the curtains to the window, exposing Madison's beautiful ass to the world. He turns her around and forcefully pushes her body into the window. Her full breasts are pressed so tightly against the window that the pressure on her nipples arouses her even more. Her head turns to her right shoulder so her tongue can meet up with Jermaine's.

He decides to give it to her from the back. He has never had the pleasure of experiencing anal sex, but knows now is the perfect time to try it out.

He slips his tongue out of her mouth as easily as it slipped in. His right hand travels down to his shaft. He pushes it inside of Madison's wet vagina. He has to get it wet and ready for anal action.

He strokes his hard shaft inside her walls a couple times, with his legs bent to help assist him in the position. Jermaine's member is now soaked with Madison's love. He takes it out and slowly, slowly pushes it inside of the tiny hole above her vagina.

"Ohhh, Jer...Jermaine," she whimpers in pleasure.

"Shit!" he mumbles, as he extends inside of her deeper and deeper.

It feels so good. It's like a rollercoaster ride. They are slowly rising higher and higher, anticipating a rush of ecstasy.

Madison's phone continues to ring. The smooth vocals from Usher only make the experience more enjoyable.

Pleasure and pain is exactly what Madison feels

at this very moment. It hurts, but feels so damn good buried deeply inside of her ass. Jermaine pulls Madison's body an inch away from the window without losing his stroke.

"Look at the cars below us baby," he grunts into her ear. "Let's give the people a show."

She obeys and focuses her eyes below. She knows no one can see them but the thought of being seen excites her.

Usher continues to sing "Trading Places" on her phone; extending the soundtrack to their lovemaking.

With time, Jermaine's thrusts go deeper. His stroke is fiercer. He moves in and out of her so fast, like the speed of lightening.

She moans. He moans. His finger slips inside of her mouth. She bites.

"Fuck…yeah!" he shouts, driving his dick through her like a tractor. His left hand pulls her hair. His thighs meet up with her ass at a speed that could start a fire.

Jermaine feels that sensation he knows very well as it develops in his stomach. Their rollercoaster is coming down. Before he has a chance to react and pull out, he explodes.

He and Madison hold their positions until they regain their composure. They share another passionate kiss before walking over to their clothes. Jermaine silently begins dressing himself as Madison answers her ringing phone.

It's her soon-to-be husband who has been blowing up her phone. She tells him a quick lie with ease, gives Jermaine a kiss goodbye and is off on her way home to her faithful fiancé.

Mrs. Santiago

I'm the dude ya mom and pop warned you about when you first began datin'. I'm the dude that'll look good on ya arm and have all ya girls creamin' their panties 'cause they want a taste of me. Yeah, I'm the dude that can tear ya walls down while makin' that tight lil' pussy milk out that sweet nectar all over my thick, chocolate stick. Hell yeah, that's me.

I stand at six-foot-four, weighin' 210 pounds. My body's rock hard and full of solid muscle. My skin's the color of honey brown with dark brown eyes, full lips and sparklin' white teeth. Can't forget about my twelve inches of thick dick that can fill even the loosest pussy up, guaranteed or ya money back!

Don't mean to brag but God definitely took his time craftin' me. I'm every woman's fantasy and every nigga's nightmare. When niggas see me at the club or at a jumpin' party, they try their hardest to distract their women from makin' eye contact with me. No lie, 'cause when niggas turn their back, their chicks be all up in my grill talkin' 'bout how they can't wait to ride this long stick. And when I break they backs out, they be ready to leave their men and be stressin' a nigga 'bout lettin' them taste this dick on the regular. But that's a definite no-no in my book. Hell no! A nigga like me don't want no commitment. I do the "no strings attached method". Just fuckin'. Open ya fuckin' legs, let a nigga bust a hot and heavy load, then keep it movin'. I'll be on to the next pussy before you can count to three.

A nigga like me loves some tight pussy, but I hate when the sex is over and a sprung broad wanna blow up my phone, talkin' 'bout I played her, even after I told her what the deal was from the jump. It just makes me wish I had jacked my meat off instead. Now don't get me wrong. I ain't on none of that homo shit. Ain't got nothin' against the gays but that pipin' another nigga down ain't my cup of tea. But whatever floats ya boat, you know. I'm just defendin' myself 'cause every time a nigga say he wished he hadn't fucked a nutty broad, she wanna go 'round sayin' a nigga must be gay and shit. That ain't hardly the case. I just hate when my dick fucks some good pussy, but the chick turns out to be fuckin' crazy.

I believe love is for the fuckin' birds. You can keep that shit. I been there, done that, and no matter how much my heart loves a girl, my dick will still crave to jump inside another. Guess it's true when they say a dude's dick thinks for a man instead of his brain 'cause when I see a juicy pussy, best believe my big-ass dick gonna strap up and knock that shit up 'til she beggin' me to stop. My sex game's bananas! Ain't being cocky, just confident.

I've only been on this earth for twenty-one years, but I've been inside enough pussy to know there are three types of women. The first type are the ones who grew up without the love of a father and expect me to buy them shit, take 'em out to eat and then make love to them. Hell the fuck naw! All I'ma do is dig deep in them guts and toss ya sad ass out. I ain't 'bout to be nobody's daddy outside the bedroom. See, these types of broads have low self-esteem. Even if you tell 'em they just a mere one-night stand, they still gonna blow ya damn phone up and wanna know who you fuckin' and why you fuckin' 'em. Bitch please! My own mama never kept tabs on my whereabouts, so I'm damn sure not 'bout to let some chick I fucked a few times control me. That's when they become blocked; including their text messages and phone calls.

The second type of women are the stuck up "I don't need no man 'cause I got my own fuckin' money" type. They can tell that lie to any other nigga that'll listen 'cause I know betta. These are the women who tell their girls that men ain't no good and it'll be a cold day in hell before they settle for a broke-ass triflin' nigga. I just shake my damn head 'cause these the same broads that be stressin' a nigga 'bout bein' official. This the type that'll take me on shoppin' sprees, suck the meat off my dick and then claim they in love 'cause a nigga like me dicked 'em down so good. I tell 'em to get real. They knew what the deal was comin' into this shit. I ain't 'bout the settling down crap. I fuck 'em then keep it movin'. However, dependin' on how wet and gushy the pussy is, I may keep some of 'em as a backup when I feel like explorin' them walls again. Type two definitely could never be wifey material either.

The next type of women are the "go with the flow kind". They understand I mean business when I say no strings attached. It doesn't bother them if another chick blows my phone up while I'm fuckin' their pussy 'til it's black and blue. They love the fact that I've been with many women 'cause it lets them know a brutha's experienced on how to please a woman in the bedroom. This type of woman is confident that she can get any man she desires. She will not stress a nigga out if he ain't givin' up da dick 'cause it will not be a problem finding more. Just talkin' 'bout the independent type makes my dick rise. Hell, I didn't even know these women existed until two and a half years ago. From my past experiences, I thought all women were either insecure or just plain annoying. But I opened my eyes when I was first seduced by a woman who pursued me and let me know straight up that she wouldn't be stressed if I didn't toss her dick daily. This woman blew my fuckin' mind.

The crazy thing is I didn't meet this chick at a bar or club. Didn't run into this sophisticated lady at my job or on the street. I had actually known her for quite a while. My whole life to be exact. This woman is my best friend's mother.

I know some of y'all probably frowin' ya noises up at me, but to be quite frank, I don't give a damn. Shit, I enjoyed the time I spent up in those sugary, wet walls. In my opinion, seasoned pussy is some of the best. I can't describe how good it feels when that pussy swallows the dick entirely and milks my joint so damn good that a nigga gotta control himself.

Now that I think of it, my best friend's sister wasn't half bad either. Hell yeah, I hit that shit too! But she knew what it was from the get-go so I didn't feel a bit of sympathy for her when I started bangin' her mom's back out. I can't turn down good pussy, so as I stated earlier, a relationship definitely won't work for a guy like me.

When Mrs. Santiago first began to hit on me, I found myself completely flabbergasted. But now that I ponder on it, I should have seen that comin' a mile away. It was in the way she eyed my lips and muscles when they were exposed through my wife-beaters. It was in the way she studied the budge that would protrude through my basketball shorts. During basketball games between her son Evan and me, she'd often bring us homemade lemonade to help cool us off from the hot summer heat. It never fazed me when she would sit on the front porch and watch us as we ran down the court, with my dick bouncin' up and down, swingin' side to side. One time I did catch her eyein' my dick after shootin' one of my famous three pointers, but shit, I'm used to chicks undressin' me with their eyes so I paid Mrs. Santiago no mind.

I ain't gonna lie though. The woman had a bangin' body for her to be in her early forties. She didn't look a day over thirty because her Latin skin remained flawless and her tits didn't show a single sign of saggin'. My best friend used to get teased a hell of a lot in school 'cause niggas couldn't keep their eyes off his mom's stunning appearance and her perfectly-round ass. The long jet black hair added an additional plus to her already Grade A features.

I didn't begin to notice Mrs. Santiago's attraction towards me until one hot summer's night. Evan and I were in the process of preparing for college, you know buyin' shit for our dorm rooms and purchasing new outfits. We did most of it together, so it was only natural that on most occasions I would spend the night, since my house was forty minutes away.

Evan slept hard usually, so since it was so damn hot in that house, even with two fans on, I decided to strip my clothing and allow only the thin sheet to cover my nakedness. Evan slept comfortably in his queen-sized bed while I attempted to get comfortable on the hard carpet. His snoring drove me nuts so I threw one of my pillows at his head. It stopped the snores temporarily, but I knew he'd start back up in five minutes or so. I turned on the TV to an episode of MTV's Jackass. It was my lucky night 'cause MTV was showing an all-night marathon.

The show entertained me for a few minutes until my eyes became heavy and sleep overtook me. I hadn't been sleep long when I felt the covers being pulled back. I kept my eyes closed. It definitely couldn't have been Evan admiring my magnificent body, so I figured it was Amber, his sister. It had been a hot minute since my dick throbbed between her legs. Just the thought of it brought my dick to life.

Instead of opening my eyes to discover if it was actually Amber, I made my dick jump without the slightest touch of my hands. My goal was to tease her. I knew she'd been dreamin' about this dick ever since I started ignoring her calls when she began to annoy the fuck out of me. Yeah I wanted her mouth to water and pussy to drip for just one taste of my delicious dick. Hell, I was startin' to get horny, so I had already made up my mind that I was gonna fuck her right then and there with her brother snoring peacefully in the same room.

My body was engulfed in pleasure as small but soft hands made contact with my swollen member. The hands stroked me softly up and down as if they were attempting to figure out how many inches I actually was. I had already told Amber my dick was a full fuckin' twelve inches. Shit! What did she have to measure me for? I wanted those lips kissin' my dick and that throat chokin' on my joint.

It was almost as if she could read my mind 'cause she licked my dick from the base to the tip and then greedily swallowed its entirety down her throat. This had taken me off guard a bit. Amber was good at suckin' dick, but damn! She had never been this good. Usually I could only manage to get about six inches down her throat before she started gaggin' and shit. Most girls couldn't handle swallowin' all of my monster. But that night...that night she had to have been on some other shit, I figured as her head bobbed up and down in swift motions.

I swear I almost nutted right then and there when she slid my dick down her throat until her nose touched my pubic hairs and her throat began to hum. The vibrations from her throat made my body flinch and toes curl. I had no idea who Amber had been practicin' on, but whoever the dude was, he got mad props from me 'cause she was doin' the damn thing.

She moaned while cuppin' my balls in one hand. Her other hand was occupied at the base of my dick, jackin' it off while continuing to suck and slurp on the top half. She then removed her mouth from my joint, but made sure she created a poppin' noise while doin' it. That shit drove me crazy. I loved it when chicks sucked the dick like it was the last piece of dick they'd ever get. I got off on the fact that girls enjoyed worshippin' my dick.

Her wet mouth found my balls and sucked them one by one. She sucked them gently at first and then increased the pressure on them while jackin' my dick that was fully saturated with her spit. Yeah, I had died and experienced heaven on earth. No one had ever made love to my jewels like this before. A moan escaped from my mouth as she managed to insert both of my huge balls into her mouth at the same time. Yeah, a nigga ain't ashamed to say she had me moanin'. That shit was spectacular! Let's see y'all get some brain like that and see if y'all don't be moanin' like a lil' bitch. I guarantee it!

This chick was suckin' my shit like she wanted to suck the black off it! I opened my eyes and looked down. I wanted to witness this grand event in history when a woman gave me, Dewayne Terius Williams, the best head of my life! But I couldn't see her lips 'cause her long, silky hair was in the way. I lifted it as an attempt to expose her face and those wonderful dick suckin' lips, but I failed miserably at my task. The light from the TV screen along with the sensations developing in my body, made it impossible for me to remain focused long enough to watch her. My head fell back onto the pillow while her head continued to bring me to ecstasy.

The shit felt too damn good for me to just lie there like a lil' bitch. I wrapped my fingers into her hair and began to lift my hips forward every time her head came down. I fucked her throat slowly at first, then extended to quick thrusts. She continued to amaze me as she didn't let out a single gag. I wanted to see just how much she could take before choking, so I began to thrust faster and faster. She didn't miss a lick. She met each stroke willingly, continuing to hum as I filled her wet mouth up.

I spent countless hours jackin' my dick as a teen. All those hours had paid off 'cause it helped me become a pro at controlin' my nut. I knew how to retain it and make it cum quick for occasions when a chick's pussy felt like fuckin' sandpaper. But on this occasion, all that time I spent touchin' myself went to waste and out the damn window. I managed to hold off on nuttin' twice but when she kept goin', I couldn't contain myself any longer.

"Oh shit! I'm 'bout to nut," I mumbled through moans. This was my warning for her to stop and jack me off 'til I exploded like a hot volcano into her hand. But she didn't take the hint. She kept suckin' my shit like a cherry lollipop.

My body froze in the air as the sensations multiplied within me. She bobbed her head faster and sucked harder. "Fuck!" I moaned as my cream escaped from my dick like a flood and down her throat. She sucked every last drop until I was completely empty.

I laid there exhausted as fuck, tryin' to catch my breath. She licked the slit of my dick and then traveled up my stomach with wet kisses. "Damn girl," I cooed. "I don't know what's gotten into you, but I love it! Amber that shit blew a nigga's mind, real talk."

After I expressed my gratitude, she released the tight grip her hand had around my semi-erect dick and licked my earlobe. "Amber can never suck ya dick like I can Terius. Don't you ever forget that."

My eyes popped open. Terius? No one called me that except for…except for Mrs. Santiago! *Oh shit*, I thought. I could now see the image of her body in the darkness. She kissed me softly before putting her robe on and exitin' the room, closin' the door softly behind her.

I laid there stunned. Speechless. Mrs. Santiago

had just swallowed my dick. My nut too! Fuckin' Evan's sister was one thing, but gettin' nasty with his mom was another thing! I didn't sleep a wink that night. Those soft lips, that deep throat, and soft wet tongue; they all continued to race through my mind.

I found it quite awkward sittin' at the breakfast table with Mrs. Santiago only seven hours after she blew my fuckin' mind. Evan was still in bed; he usually slept until twelve or one in the afternoon. Amber finished her grits and eggs and left the table to go to her room.

Mrs. Santiago and I sat in silence. Our eyes met briefly before I shifted my eyes around the room nervously. She chuckled to herself as she stood from the table and walked over to the sink. She then began to casually wash dishes.

My dick stood up hard and stiff as I watched her big, round ass jiggle. Damn she was fine! It never crossed my mind how much of a dime she actually was until that moment. I mean, I knew she was attractive, but I never thought of her sexually 'cause she was in fact my best friend's mom. But shit, at that moment, I really didn't care anymore. The woman had skills!

I finished my food and dropped my plate into the sink of hot water. She smacked my ass as I walked out of the kitchen. I knew that after that playful hit to my rear, I had to see what else Mrs. Santiago had to offer. And boy did I!

One night while Evan spent the night over to his girlfriend's place and Amber worked a night shift at her job, their mom invited me over. She said we had to talk. We talked alright; my dick talked to her pussy as I rammed through her like a nigga straight out of prison.

I must admit Mrs. Santiago had the best pussy I'd ever fucked. Real talk. That seasoned sea of wetness showed me a side of her I never fathomed I'd see a day in my life.

From that night on, we fucked like two rabbits every chance we got. Her husband was always away on business so I wasn't worried about him walkin' in on me breakin' his wife's back out. And hell no, I didn't feel bad about bangin' his wife. Everyone knew he went out of town to cheat while he was on "so called" business trips. If anything, I was helpin' his wife out, dickin' her down while he was away. We had sex in every inch of that house; the stove, kitchen table, Evan's room, Amber's room and I even nutted between the sheets she shared with her husband.

I'm away at college now and I still be gettin' plenty pussy from chicks on the regular, but none compare to Mrs. Santiago. We both understand that it's just sex between us. And now that I'm gone, Evan mentioned to me that a strange man has been entertainin' his mom in his dad's absence. That's cool with me. I never stress over pussy 'cause I can get it anytime I desire. One thing is for sure though: if I'm ever in town and in need of a hot fuck, Mrs. Santiago is just one phone call away!

A Lil' Phone Bone

"Aye baby, what's good?"

Marie sighs. "Nothin'. Just relaxing in this hotel room. What are you doin' babe?"

"I been thinkin' 'bout you all day love."

"Aww!?" she coos through the phone. "You've been on my mind too! How are the kids?"

"Well, they miss their mama, that's for sure. Other than that, they're great."

Marie stands from the bed and enters the mediocre bathroom, that's so small she feels a bit claustrophobic. "Well, that's great. Are they still awake?"

Justin laughs. "Baby, they're never up this late when you're home, so why would they be awake now?"

"Well...you're not really strict when it comes to our kids," she admits.

Justin flips through channels on television. "You have a point, I guess."

"You guess?"

They both chuckle.

"Okay, so maybe I am the nice parent but baby I can't help it. Our little girls remind me so much of you. I can't help but to spoil them."

"Baby, that's so sweet," she smiles.

He laughs. "Yeah, I know. Just like your pussy."

"You're such a freak Justin!"

"Only for you."

"Yeah, you better be only for me."

Marie stands at the huge mirror on the bathroom wall. She carefully examines her body as she licks her lips. Her caramel colored body still looks good enough to eat, if she didn't say so herself. Her tits still sit up well, despite the fact that she's thirty-two and the mother of two children.

"Baby..."

"Yes?" Justin asks, turning off the television that has been boring him to death with insane reality shows he's seen too many times to count.

"What are you doin'?"

"I was flippin' through channels on TV, but nothin' good is on. I'm so tired of all these damn reruns!"

She chuckles as she plays with a lock of her honey brown curls.

"What are you doin' love?" Justin smirks, as his dick springs to life due to the lustful images of his wife on his mind.

"Nothin'. Just lookin' at myself in the mirror."

"You just lookin' at yourself?"

"Yeah."

"Why?"

"I'm just makin' sure I still got it."

"Of course you do!" he laughs. "If you didn't you know I'd have ya ass doin' laps on the treadmill!"

"Justin," she whines into the phone. "I'm serious."

"And so am I," he jokes.

She is silent. His joking can sometimes be rather annoying.

"Sorry babe." His husky voice that was once full of lust has now toned down with remorse for his habit of speaking before thinking.

"Yeah, yeah."

"I just can't be serious with you when it comes to you criticizing your body. It's gorgeous!"

Marie smiles. "Thanks babe."

"You're more than welcome. What are you wearin'?" His playful mood returns.

She giggles. "I'm wearing nothin'."

"Damn."

"What?"

"I wish I could see you now." He gets up from the couch and walks upstairs to their large bedroom.

"Hold on," she says.

Within a couple seconds, Justin receives a picture message from his wife.

"Baby, what's this?"

"Just open it," she laughs into her iPhone.

He does as he is told. A huge grin forms upon his lips as the picture fully loads. "Damn baby. There's no doubt about it. You still got it."

"You probably just sayin' that."

"No, I'm not," he retorts, while still staring at the picture.

"Uh huh."

"Hold on," he informs her.

Justin strips until he is completely naked. He lies down on the bed and stares at the sultry picture of his wife that leaves very little to one's imagination. His heavy erection pulsates through his silk boxer briefs.

He quickly takes a picture of his aroused dick and sends it to Marie.

"Okay, I'm back," he sings into the phone.

"What were you doin'?"

"I had to handle some business babe."

"Like what?"

Marie's phone beeps. She takes it away from her ear and examines it. She has a new picture message from Justin.

"Oh my!" she says, as she opens the message. She places the phone back to her ear. "Justin baby, you are so damn freaky!"

He laughs. "Yeah, I know! Now let's have a lil' bit of phone sex!"

"Phone sex?" His request catches her off guard.

"Yeah. As long as we've been married, we have yet to try it."

"Umm...I don't know." Her voice expresses uncertainty, but deep down inside she wants to give it a try.

"Come on babe. Let's be wild for once and just do it."

"We are wild Justin," she sincerely defends.

"No we aren't. Havin' sex outside doesn't justify you as being wild."

"Actually, it does. Wild animals do it."

"Where are you in your hotel room?" He changes the subject.

"In the bathroom still."

"Get on top of the counter," he demands.

"Why?"

"Just do what I tell you."

His orders excite her deep down below. She

obeys, wondering what he'll command her to do next.

"Okay. I'm on the counter."

"Open your legs."

She giggles.

He repeats himself. "Open your legs."

"Okay," she responds cautiously.

"Now play with that pretty pussy for Big Daddy."

"Big Daddy?"

Marie is a bit taken back by this remark. She has always been shy in the bedroom. She never really allowed herself to let go when she and her husband made love. She usually would just lie there and let him do all the work. He'd never referred to himself as Big Daddy either.

"Come on baby. Play along with me."

"I don't know Justin."

"Come on. I haven't seen you in a month and you'll still be gone for another two weeks."

Marie did know her touring schedule was difficult on her husband and their children. Justin had argued with her about touring for her novel, but writing was her passion and she wanted to reach a larger audience. So, she convinced him that if he really loved her, he'd allow her to pursue her dream.

"Baby, you still there?"

"Yes."

"Play with that pussy for me."

Marie sighs and leans back into the mirror, with her legs up, forming the letter V. She slowly inserts her index finger into her tight vagina. She moans softly into the phone.

"You playin' with that pussy baby?"

"Yes," she manages to whisper.

"Good. Think about Daddy sticking his hot, wet tongue inside of your pussy. Can you picture that babe?"

"Yes...I can picture it."

That was something new to her. It was fresh and exciting. She could actually picture Justin eating her pussy as if it were his last supper. "Mmm..." she moans.

"Can you visualize me inside that treasure chest?"

"Yes baby. It feels so good!"

Justin grabs firmly onto his dick. He jerks it as he pictures himself licking and sucking Marie until her well runs dry. "Imagine me puttin' this big juicy tongue inside of those tight walls." He hears her sigh and moan. "Open that pussy up girl."

Marie doesn't know what's gotten into her. One minute she's fingering herself and the next, she has the bottom of her Spinbrush Pro toothbrush between her legs. It was nowhere as thick and long as Justin's dick, but it did bring her extreme pleasure.

"Ooh baby," she moans, as one hand strokes her nipple.

"Yeah, open that shit up for Daddy girl. You know it feel good!"

He jacks his dick harder. He misses the pleasurable sensations that Marie's pussy sends to his dick every time he slips inside her hole. He misses the way her pussy sucks him up like quicksand.

"Yes Daddy! It feels so good!"

Marie's outbursts of passion arouse Justin even more. She had always been such a timid lover. Could it be that she had finally gotten over her shyness?

"Girl, when I get home, I'ma beat that pussy up!"

The toothbrush inside of her increases its speed, causing her to feel a wave of pleasure. The inner freak that has been hidden for decades finds the light as Marie slips the toothbrush out of her walls far enough to turn the switch to ON, causing vibrations to shoot through her already hot core. "Yes Daddy! I need you to come and beat it up!"

"Uh huh...I'ma make you nut so fuckin' hard girl. Then I'ma nut in that wet pussy. Want me to cream in that pussy?"

"Hell yeah!" she cries, with one hand still grasping the toothbrush and the other now massaging her hardened clit. A feeling that she knows so well begins to take over. It makes her pump the toothbrush harder and rub her stimulated clit faster. "Justin...I'm 'bout to cum!"

"Cum baby. Cum for Daddy. I want you to cum all over that bathroom counter," he says, while stroking his manhood a tad bit faster.

"Oh! Oooh baby I'm cumin'!" she yells as she explodes.

She explodes all over the toothbrush, the counter and floor. Justin continues to talk dirty to his wife as he strokes his dick for a nut. It takes him another five minutes to accomplish this task.

"Damn baby. That was fun, wasn't it?"

He receives no response.

"Baby?"

He hears Marie softly breathe into the phone. He smiles as he falls asleep listening to the soft sounds escape from his wife, who has fallen into a peaceful slumber.

Always and Forever

"What the hell are we doing?" Michele asked her boyfriend of three years as she broke their passionate kiss.

"Babe, we're about to make love," Chad answered, as his strong hands firmly tightened on Michele's delicate breasts.

"Chad, I'm having second thoughts about all of this. I mean…we can't do this."

"Why not babe? You do love me, right?"

"Of course," she said, as she gently rubbed her fingertips over his muscular arms.

"Then why not make love?"

"Because Chad. I have told you my reasons over and over about this. What if we do have sex and I end up pregnant? There is no way we could be parents while tryin' to finish out college. And plus, my parents would kill me!"

Chad sighed deeply as he withdrew his grasp on Michele's breasts. He was tired of having this conversation. If Michele really loved him as much as she claimed, then why not show her affection by taking things to the next level?

"Nothin' bad is gonna happen babe. I promise you that. And your parents will never know unless you tell them."

"Chad are you sure that we should be doing this? What about what the Bible says?"

"God understands. He knows we love each other. Of course, He would expect us to have sex," he reassured her as he leaned over and began nibbling on Michele's neck.

"You damn well know the Bible doesn't tell us anything like that!" Michele remarked, pushing Chad away from her.

"Michele, could you stop making up all of these damn excuses! You and I both know why we came to my granddad's cabin. We came to make love on our anniversary!"

"Yeah but…"

"But what?"

"Look, Chad you don't understand how much I love you. I really want to take our relationship to the next level but I refuse to allow myself to get hurt. What if we result in breaking up after we do this?"

"I refuse to lose you babe. I'd never do anything to hurt you. I love you," he said, caressing her face with his hands.

Before Michele could object again, Chad leaned forward and met his lips with hers. He was determined to show Michele just how much he loved her. He was going to give her his all tonight.

Chad slowly slid his tongue between Michele's lips, seeking the warmth of her mouth. Michele didn't object to Chad's kiss. She too wanted to give Chad her all. There were nights when she'd go to sleep crying because she had turned down Chad's advances many times before.

But tonight, would not be one of those nights. Tonight, would be a night full of passion and love. She would not worry about anything besides loving Chad.

That was why she took him up on his offer of treating her to a romantic night on their anniversary. Michele's mom was on a business trip and thought she'd be home all night. Chad's parents didn't care where he was. A night alone in solace and in Chad's grandfather's cabin seemed perfect.

Chad pushed Michele down onto the bed and climbed on top of her, ensuring not to place his entire body weight onto her. His hands slowly slid up her thigh and found her sensitive pearl, making her moan and squeal out in pleasure. His fingertips gently played with her until one slipped into the warmth of her insides.

She tensed and immediately tightened her grip on his shoulder blades. They had never gone this far before. Of course, they had made out and humped with their clothes on in the past, but all of this was new to Michele. It hurt but it also brought so much pleasure onto her soul.

"Relax baby," Chad whispered into her ear, as his finger rested inside of her tight walls.

Michele softly inhaled and exhaled, attempting to slow down her out of control heartbeat and relax her body.

Chad's soft lips found hers once again, but this time creating a more sensual and passion-filled kiss. His warm tongue wrestled with hers, turning the heat of her body up and raising her heartbeat higher.

He broke the kiss and eased his index finger slowly from Michele's sticky folds. His eyes met with hers and he winked at her as he inserted his wet finger inside of his mouth, sucking every last drop of Michele's essence from his finger.

She licked her lips in awe, now turned on even more.

"Make love to me Chad," she moaned.

"No..."

"What?" she asked, leaning up from the pillow.

"Calm down. I wanna taste you some more first."

Michele wasn't sure if she had heard him correctly. Before she could second guess herself, her dress was lifted up over her head and thrown onto the floor.

Chad pushed Michele back onto the bed and proceeded to kiss her neck. After many make out sessions, he had come to the conclusion that her neck was her spot.

"Mmm...Chad, baby you're driving me insane," she managed to mumble through continuous moans.

"Baby you ain't seen nothin' yet," Chad said, after retiring from her neck and locking his lips onto Michele's left nipple.

Her legs tightly wrapped around his shoulders as tight as they possibly could.

"Aww...Chad...that feels so good," she muttered through her tightly bitten lips.

Chad chose not to verbally respond, but to suck and lick harder, enjoying every second of hearing Michele moan his name. He made sure not to neglect her other nipple, showing it as much love and affection he gave to the other.

"You like that, don't you baby?" he asked, never unlocking the hold his mouth had on Michele's hardened nipple.

"No baby, I love that!"

With that said, Chad gently bit Michele's nipple, causing her to arch her back and moan his name louder as he brought her body to complete ecstasy.

Chad's moist lips slowly released their pressure on Michele's nipple, causing her to want and beg for more. She attempted to pull Chad's mouth back in position, but he had other plans.

He forcefully pulled Michele's arms up to the headboard and slowly brought his head down between her legs. His huge fingers slid down her arms to her exposed nipples and pinched them ever so gently. Chad's tongue wasted no time in forcefully licking Michele's hardened clitoris.

"Ohh...Chad!" escaped from her lips before she had a chance to think.

He let go of her arms and assigned his fingers to another task. His index finger slipped inside of her wet, sticky walls with ease. She was now much more relaxed and wet than before. In a matter of minutes, he was able to insert two more fingers and increase his speed, giving the love of his life the pleasure she desired.

She had never climaxed, let alone fingered herself before. The sensations in her gut warned her that this could possibly be an orgasm preparing to explode.

"Ooh baby...I think I'm about to cum!"

He immediately pulled his fingers out. He

wasn't ready for her to cum just yet. The night was young and they had so much more to experience.

"That was easy," he chuckled, as he moved his mouth to hers and gave her a quick, wet kiss.

"Shut up!" Michele exclaimed, sitting up and playfully giving Chad a push.

Michele wasted no time in unbuckling Chad's belt and unzipping his zipper. She was ready to feel him inside of her. Many females her age had already experienced the countless pleasures sex had to offer. She was considered a late bloomer when compared to those women.

"We've got all night," Chad reassured her with a smile upon his lips.

Michele pulled Chad's body closer and placed wet kisses along his neck. He slowly lifted his shirt up from his muscular body. She then took over by stripping him of his tight-fitting wife-beater.

She admired the view for a few seconds. She had seen him without his shirt on numerous circumstances, but his amazing abs stood out even more tonight.

Her lips found his nipples and weren't the least bit shy of sucking on them like a pair of fresh strawberries. She unfastened the button to his jeans and pushed them down his thighs, continuing to eagerly suck on his tiny, yet perky nipples. Chad put himself to use by assisting her in removing his jeans and tossing them to the floor.

Michele instantly became nervous after looking down to witness the imprint of Chad's penis increase in size through the material of his boxer briefs. It was huge! She could never let him stick that giant thing inside of her tight, not yet, experienced walls.

She made sure that her nervousness didn't show in her facial expressions by slowly gliding her tongue across Chad's firm abs. Her hands maneuvered down his back to his tight and muscular ass, then slid his underwear down from his buttock to his thighs. She felt so much excitement throughout her body when Chad's well-endowed penis made contact with her chest and nipples.

Chad lightly pushed Michele onto the bed and stood up. He managed to slide his underwear off in less than a second as Michele pulled back the covers to the king-sized bed.

Chad found himself thankful for this moment, as his eyes admired Michele's naked body get underneath the covers. After three years of waiting, praying and wishing for this to happen, he couldn't believe it was about to go down.

Michele could not believe it either. She never fathomed she would be in the woods at Chad's grandfather's cabin on their anniversary, preparing to make love. She always imagined waiting until her honeymoon for such a grand event. But deep down in her heart, she knew that she and Chad belonged together. It didn't matter anymore if they waited until marriage or made sweet passionate love at that very moment.

Chad made his way over to his jeans and retrieved a condom from a pocket. He ripped the wrapper with his teeth and placed the condom on his brick-hard erection.

"You sure 'bout this?" he asked Michele.

"Yes," she replied with passion and desire in her eyes.

They had come this far. There would be no turning back now. Lovemaking would go down tonight. There was no doubt about it.

He walked over to her and opened her long, slender honey brown legs. He then buried his head between them and tasted her sweet nectar. Her hot juices oozed from her folds onto Chad's tongue and lips. He removed his head from her sacred temple and tongued her down, allowing her to sample the sweet and wet dessert that teased him between her thighs.

Chad broke their kiss and leaned closer to her, so his penis rested on her clitoris. He rubbed it around a bit, bringing pleasure to them both. Her legs found their way around his lower back and tightly hugged him, forcing his body to come closer.

Chad's hardened penis pulsated as the head broke through Michele's folds. She threw her head back and her fingernails dug into Chad's back as she felt the thickness of his dick opening her pussy up wider and wider.

She deeply grasped and scratched at Chad's back. He paused and stared deeply into her eyes. The love and desire Michele found in his eyes told her this was right and eased the pain she felt between her thighs.

"Want me to stop? Am I hurting you?"

"No, don't stop. I can take it," she answered, reassuring him that everything was alright.

He continued to deepen his journey by inserting at least two inches inside of her. He kissed her nipples and neck as he eased out, allowing the tip of the head to rest at her entrance. He then reentered her, this time inserting another inch. This continued until he had worked all nine inches inside of Michele's hot vagina.

Their bodies were now one. Her nipples were pressed firmly against his solid chest that rested on top of hers. This all felt too good to true. There was no more pain. She only felt pleasure. Michele couldn't believe she had turned Chad down so many times in the past. She had been missing out on so much.

Chad slowly stroked his hips into hers, sending waves of pleasure to them both.

"Mmm...baby," Chad whispered into Michele's ear. "You feel so damn good. Grind your hips baby," he encouraged.

She met his thrusts every time he went deeper inside of her, extending her walls.

"Chad baby...I think this is it! I'm about to cum!"

He began to pump her insides harder. He was determined for her first time to be so good, she'd dream about it every time she closed her eyes at night.

Michele's nails clung to Chad's ass checks, encouraging him to give her all of him. Before she knew it, a wonderful sensation evolved from within her. Chad shot his load into the condom not long after.

"Damn!" he cried, as his fists grasped the headboard.

"So, that's what I've been missing out on for the past three years?"

Chad chuckled as he withdrew his semi-erect penis and kissed her on her lips, giving her a yes.

"Chad put it back in...please," she begged.

She felt empty without him inside of her. She didn't want this moment to ever end.

"What?"

"Just put it back in. Let it rest inside of me."

He obeyed her orders and reclaimed his prize. She was still wet and so tight, but not tight as before. He could have sworn he almost ejaculated again by the way her walls squeezed his penis.

"Damn... I love you so much Michele Waiters," he whispered into her ear.

"I love you too," she said smiling and closing her eyes.

"Chad I love you, always and forever."

In My Dreams Pt.1

I stare at you every day. I tell myself not to look your way, but these eyes have a mind of their own. They can't control themselves whenever you make your grand entrance. You are like a queen on a throne, admired by a flock of peasants.

You have me in a trance. I'm undeniably under your spell. What am I to do? Every time you smile. Every time you laugh. Every time you switch those big juicy thighs I lose what little self-control I have.

I believe you know exactly what you do to me. You intentionally walk the way you do. You intentionally sway your hips from side to side, making my buddy rise between my thighs. You intentionally toss your hair from your shoulders with a single wave of your finger.

I can't believe I am drawn to you like a moth to a flame. Like a bee to a flower. Like my penis to your tight make-a nigga-wanna-scream coochie. Fantasies of you and I cross my mind, day to day, all day long. I want you. My body cries out for you.

Oh, how I long to bend you over on top of a desk in our computer science class. Rip off all your clothes and give you the best sex you will ever have.

I picture myself taking your beautiful black nipples into my warm mouth, shielding them from the cold. You would like that, wouldn't you? I'd do anything and everything you asked me to.

Let me be your love slave. Let me make you cream for hours upon hours. Shower your love all over the bed like rain on a cloudy, stormy night. Do it all over my fingers. All over my tongue. All over my face.

I long to approach you. Tell you how I feel. Maybe describe all the wild and outrageous things we could do together.

But you've got a man. I see the two of you hugged up every day after class. His hands always smack your ass right before you hop into his car and you two ride off with the windows down and the radio blazin'.

Maybe someday we'll cross paths. Maybe someday you'll know how I feel. But until then, I'll keep you in my dreams boo.

In My Dreams Pt.2

I see you Daddy. Yes, baby I see you. You are so shy. It's just so cute to see you stare me down and pretend not to notice me when I look your way.

You're so sexy! I would love to be locked in a room with you, if only for five minutes. I'd love you down baby. I'd love you from those huge, sexy lips to that firm-ass six-pack.

Those muscles! Oh my gosh! Those muscles! Let me rub them, lick them, kiss them. You are all man. I want to be yours.

I've got a man and I do love him, but damn. Damn baby, I know he can't love me like you. I see the desire in your eyes, burning like a flame to a candle. You want this. You want all of this.

This isn't some silly sexual obsession between you and I. Oh no, this is so much more. I see us together in the future baby. You and I, married with four kids and a two-story home in the country. I know I can have a good life with you boo.

Why couldn't things have turned out differently? Why did I have to already have a man and have fallen so madly in love with him?

If not forever, can't I have you for one night? Let me lick you up and down and take you on a roller coaster ride. Let me tease those delicate nipples with my tongue. Baby allow me to swallow that big bulge I see poking out of your jeans whenever you stare me down in our computer science class. Let me suck and lick it vigorously until you explode down my throat. I'll gladly lick up every last drop of you, from the tip of your penis to the contents of sperm dripping from my lips to my breasts.

I'll be waiting for you to make your move Daddy. All of this can be all yours anytime you want. My man can't do it like you. I know because of the fantasies and dreams I have about us becoming one. I don't know when or where you'll finally speak to me but I'll wait until that day.

'Till then, see you in my dreams boo.

Relapse

My four-inch Gucci heels click against the tile floor of the lobby as I gracefully make my way to the elevator. I glance at my watch as I wait for the elevator doors to open. I'm twenty minutes early. Silently, I pat myself on the back. I've been able to arrive to work early for the past two months. I really want my boss to promote me, so I ensure that I am on time every day, appear to be in an ecstatic mood even when I feel like shit, and even ask for extra assignments whenever time permits.

I'm an A&R for one of the most successful record labels in not only the country, but the world. We pull in major bread each year and our list of signed artist continues to multiply. Yeah, we're bankin' in big bucks, but the money-hungry hustla in me craves even more. That's why it's so important that I earn this promotion.

The only thing that stands in my way is Jamie Hudson, a co-worker of mine, that has his greedy eyes set on the job also. I bet the only reason he's even attemptin' to get the position is to get back at me for turning him down so many times. Jamie wants to taste this pussy but there is no way on earth I'd let him, even if I wasn't a lesbian. He is that damn annoying.

Okay, so it isn't just Jamie that I find to be annoying. I believe all men are so fuckin' annoying. They all agitate the shit out of me. I despise the look that appears on their faces when their eyes roam over my full, perky tits as if they had just hit the jack pot. I hate when their dicks jump to life after only witnessing a glance of my fat, but nicely toned ass. Ain't tryna brag but I could crack damn walnuts with my huge ass. My shit has all the niggas, hell women too, constantly eyeing me.

So when the men get all googly-eyed and shit, I twist my hips harder and swing my jet black shoulder-length hair, as if I belong on America's Next Top Model. They can dream all they want. They aren't ever gonna get close to me. This pussy is off limits to all men. Niggas can't even turn me on anymore. My pussy becomes dry as dirt every time I attempt to get my rocks off with some brother that claims he could eat and beat my pussy like I stole somethin'. Please! What the fuck ever!

If you had asked me what I thought of men a year ago, my answer would have been completely different. In fact, I loved dick a year ago. Instantly, I would find myself turned on by the look and texture of it. My mouth would water and almost drool like a dog in heat when I had a big, juicy dick before my eyes. And let me inform you, I never received a single complaint when it came down to my oral skills. A sista was a pro at puttin' her jaws to work. I didn't even need a man to compliment me on how experienced I was at suckin' them up 'til they exploded one of the most intense orgasms of their lives down my throat. I knew my throat muscles drove them crazy every time their heads fell back into the pillow, and whenever their bodies twitched and toes curled while they moaned like a virgin gettin' fucked for the very first time.

Yeah, I was bad. I was an expert at worshippin' the dick like a delicious chocolate desert. I did all that 'til the love of my life broke my heart. After that traumatizing night, I found myself completely turned off by every single individual that had a dick on this earth.

You see, Aaron was my everything. That nigga had my heart, my soul, and my body anytime his trifflin' heart desired. He had seemed so different from all the men I dealt with in my past. He promised me the world and even got down on one knee; something I had dreamed about ever since I was a little girl.

Ever since I lost my virginity to the school's most popular basketball player in high school, my heart had been stomped on time after time; it never failed. Men seemed so sincere after the first few dates. They would wine and dine me, whisper sweet words into my ear and then when a sista let 'em hit the pussy, they decided to flip the script and act brand new. Either they got sprung off the pussy to the point where they'd show up at my job or they'd act as though I never existed by ignoring my calls.

But when Aaron came into my life I thought my bad streak with men had finally come to an end. He was a very successful investment banker. Every sista that came into contact with him wanted his dick either down their throats or rammin' the fuck outta their loose-ass pussies. The man was that fine!

I almost didn't give him a chance 'cause he happened to be twelve years my senior. I had no interest in a man who was forty-two years of age. But Aaron had swag and the heart of a guy in his twenties.

There wasn't even a speck of gray hair on his body.

What had blinded me from realizin' the dog he actually was, had been the fact that he told me he didn't mind waiting until our wedding night to have sex. A man tellin' me he didn't even need a sample of my goodies before tyin' the knot really blew my mind. All the men from my past wanted a hit of the pussy after just one glance into my captivating eyes.

Aaron remained true to his promise. There were many nights when I almost ripped all his clothes off and rode his dick until the sun came up. We managed to sustain from sex until the night he proposed. That night I told him to throw that commitment out the window. That night he tore my pussy up like it was a piece of gold. He blew my mind to the point that I'd allow him to nut inside of me and have his babies with absolutely no regrets. The dick was fuckin' fabulous!

I admit he had a sista sprung. When he lost his job due to the failing economy, I allowed him to move in with me. Aaron didn't have to pay a single bill. All he had to do was dick me down every night. He ensured me that he was in the process of finding a job. One month of unemployment transpired into six months and eventually an entire year. The nigga had it good. Aaron didn't have to cook a meal; all he ever had to worry about was devouring the full course meal that remained hot and ready between my thighs.

All my girls told me I was a damn fool but I didn't care. All that shit entered one ear and quickly exited the other. The dick was too good to ever let it go. I was down for the ride, until I came home one night after a long day of workin' overtime. I almost had a heart attack when I walked in on Aaron fuckin' some bitch's throat while another one ate the bitch's nasty pussy. I flipped out ten times worse than Janet Jackson did in *Why Did I Get Married Too?*. I have no idea how I managed to beat both of those sluts, all while releasing my anger on Aaron with my favorite pair of red stiletto heels. Hell yeah, I left bruises over his "what used to be" precious face. But those bruises didn't compare to the ones he engraved deep within my fragile heart.

That was it for me. I was done with men and all of their bullshit. That same night I called my brother over and had him dispose of the expensive white suede couch Aaron and his hos left contaminated nut over. After that was taken care of, my brother found Aaron and beat his ass so brutally he had to spend two weeks in the hospital. It served him right. I had been damaged for life. The one man I thought could be trusted let me down by playin' me like I didn't mean a damn thing to him.

Soon after, my experience with women began. Men couldn't do it for me anymore so I had to get off somehow. Creamin' all over a vibrator wasn't as intense as being brought over the edge by an actual person.

My first experience with a woman was quite awkward. Havin' someone else's boobs rub up against me felt weird and made me extremely uncomfortable. I met the woman on an online dating website and she was absolutely gorgeous. I believe she was mixed with Black and Latino. Her long, curly brown hair and dark brown eyes were enticing enough to seduce any man or woman.

I don't recall her name but the experience is as vivid in my mind as though it occurred yesterday. We met at a Holiday Inn not more than ten miles from my apartment complex. I most definitely wasn't gonna invite some stranger into my home. People are crazy nowadays. Shit, you even gotta be careful if you stop to assist someone on the side of the road with car trouble. Loonies will chop you up in a heartbeat!

I was so nervous when we met inside the hotel lobby. Once inside the suite she had already booked, she seductively danced for me while stripping every piece of clothing from her thick body. Now, I've never really been attracted to women, but this girl had my coochie twitchin' and soakin' wet. After the entirety of her clothes had fallen to the floor, she walked over to me and whispered into my ear, "Relax, I don't bite…unless you want me to." With that said, she licked my earlobe and pushed me back onto the bed. Before I knew it, I was completely naked with her head buried between my legs.

I went home with a huge smile on my face. My first lesbian experience turned out to be quite a blast, but the fact still remained that my pussy still wanted to be banged up by a thick and heavy rod. Lickin' and suckin' at my core was all good and dandy, but shit, I really got off on being punished with somethin' stiff between my legs.

A plethora of more same-sex experiences followed until I met Toni. Toni was the definition of a real stud. She wore baggy jeans, fresh Timbs, Polo t-shirts and name brand hats. She could pass for a man to an old lady without her heavily medicated glasses any day. I guess that's why she worked out so perfectly for me.

I met Toni at a club called Pride. It was my first

time at a gay club, so once again I was as nervous as I had been when I met the gorgeous woman from online. For half the night, I sat at the bar sippin' on alcohol as I watched everyone hump and grind on the dance floor. I turned down every chick, man, and transsexual that attempted to have a dance with me. Yes, I did say transsexuals. They were all over the place and I must admit that they had me feelin' a little insecure because some of 'em looked better than I did in a dress. Ain't that an ego killer!

Anyway, the way Toni approached me had more swag than half the guys I've ever dated put together. After only one conversation, I was backin' my fat ass up on her as if she had a dick. Later that night I ended up at Toni's place and boy did she show me the mad skills she possessed in the bedroom! She rocked my boat so damn fiercely that I found myself hollerin' for her to never stop. The next day I could hardly walk 'cause of how open Toni's nine-inch strap-on had my pussy. She worked that shit as if she had actually been born with it.

The opening of the elevator doors causes my thoughts of Toni's spectacular sex game to vanish. I step onto the elevator and acknowledge Anna, a woman who works on the third floor, and press the button that will take me to the fourth floor.

As the elevator door begins to close, a black suede shoe steps onto the elevator, preventing it from closing. Thick, yet well-manicured fingers push the doors back. I can't help but roll my eyes to the ceiling when I discover who is stalling my "on time" streak when I could've easily been to the second floor by now.

It's muthafuckin' Jamie Hudson; the one and

only human being that irks my nerves like they never have been irked before. Ugh! I do not wanna be breathin' the same air as him!

He casually walks onto the elevator. He says hi to Anna and then proceeds to wink over at me before flashin' his set of pearly white teeth. I roll my eyes once again.

"Hey Lisa," he chuckles, while eyein' me up and down like he's ready to open my legs and go at my clit with his wet tongue.

"Hey," I mumble.

"Someone havin' a bad morning?" he asks, as though he's really concerned.

I mumble, "Fuck you."

"I wish you would," he adds seductively.

I gasp and stare at him hard. The funny thing is that I pretend to be angry but my pussy actually is overwhelmed with excitement right now. It finally hits me; the reason why I can't stand Jamie's ass.

When I stare into his eyes, he reminds me of my ex. There's something about him that appeals to me the same way Aaron had. I want to shake my head 'cause this whole time I've been placing all of my anger for my ex on him. That isn't fair to him, but it still doesn't change the fact that I don't want another piece of a dick a day in my life.

The elevator door opens. Anna smiles and genuinely tells us to have a good day as she exits. As the doors close, I silently curse to myself. I had absolutely no desire to be on the elevator alone with Jamie.

I close my eyes and perform the breathing exercises my therapist taught me to use whenever I allowed my anger for men to overwhelm me. I slowly count to three as my body inhales and exhales the anxiety. The sudden halt of the elevator taking me to my destination causes my eyes to instantly open.

My eyes become fixed on Jamie, who is standing by the elevator control panel. Any bit of anxiety I had managed to rid my body of has returned.

"What happened?" I ask in frustration. This dumb elevator cannot cause me to be late for work. That damn promotion will be mine!

He begins to slowly approach me. It feels as if I'm about to hyperventilate. "What are you doing?" I ask as he backs me up into a corner until he's so close that the sexy scent of his cologne teases my nostrils. My pussy begins to talk to me. She informs me that I've been holdin' out for entirely too long. She wants a piece of dick and she wants it now!

"What did I ever do you to make you hate me so much?" his deep voice whispers softly into my ear. *'Cause you remind me of my ex*, is what I almost responded, but instead I took the easy way out.

"Move Jamie. I have a ton of work to do in my office." I shove him out of the way and attempt to reach the elevator panel. My attempt doesn't go as planned. Jamie grasps me by my arm and pushes me back onto the wall.

My thighs are now fightin' with my mind as they desire to wrap around Jamie's thighs and allow my little pussy to get beat down the way its been craving. "Jamie," I plead. I wanted my cry of help to sound forceful and assertive, but it actually was full of lust and pleasure.

"You ain't goin' nowhere 'til you answer my

question," Jamie demands while licking my neck.

I am completely paralyzed. I want to curse him out and punch him in the face. I want to stuff my four-inch designer heels up his ass for being so damn aggressive with me. But I ain't gonna lie, I also wanna ride the hell out of his huge dick. The thick imprint that my eyes wander across every time Jamie's solid body stands before me, confirms that HUGE detail.

"Answer my question girl." My pussy is on fire now! It's beggin' me to give up the goodies. My body soon falls victim to Jamie also as he lifts my legs from the floor in one swift motion. My heels fall to the floor while Jamie forces my thighs around his waist.

My pussy now screams as his huge dick teases it by throbbin' against it through our clothes. What is this man doin' to me? I've never craved a piece of dick so bad in all my life. It's usually men that are continually lustin' after me. Funny how quickly the tables can turn.

Before I can even blink my eyes, Jamie unzips the zipper to my pants. "You gonna answer me girl." I squeal out in pure delight as his thick index finger roams inside of my soakin' wet walls. He pulls his finger out, examines it and then says, "Hmm...so I guess you really don't hate me." He smirks before placing his finger inside of his mouth. As he slurps away my juice, he closes his eyes and moans as if he's savoring the taste like a Nestlé Drumstick.

His fingers enter into my hot cave once again. I stare deeply into his eyes as he fiercely finger fucks me. All kind of thoughts race through my mind. I can't believe this is actually transpiring. The look in Jamie's eyes informs me that he's been sexually attracted to me for quite a while now.

He places me down to my feet, long enough to quickly strip out of his clothing. I do the same. It seems like we're in a race to see who can get out of their clothes the quickest. He wins. I forget all about the bra and panties I still have on once my eyes witness how big his penis actually is. I swear my eyes almost pop out of their sockets. I mean, I knew Jamie was packin', but I didn't know he was packin' like this!

His dick is so big and beautiful. It reminds me of a delicious king-sized Snicker's bar and boy do I want to let it melt in my mouth! He grins at my fascination. I can assume that he's grown accustomed to it. I'm sure some women freak the hell out after seeing all that Jamie has stored underneath his boxers. I'm pretty sure they make up some excuse like they're on their period and rush out the door, fearful that Jamie will rip their delicate pussies apart. Hmph! There isn't an ounce of fear inside of me. I want to see how much of his juicy dick I can take before I cry out in both pleasure and pain.

"You like what you see shawty?" he questions, with so much lust in his eyes.

I nod. Words cannot escape from my lips. The thoughts of getting off this elevator are now long gone and now the only thing on my mind is getting a taste of the piece of mouthwatering chocolate standing before me.

"I like what I see too girl." He licks his lips and his dick jumps at me, as if it's callin' out to me to come and ride it.

I silently tell myself that everyone slips up every now and then. Hell, drug addicts nearly always have a relapse. This was nothin' different. My goal is to get enough dick so my pussy will calm down and then I'll be on my merry way to gettin' my pussy licked and fucked by Toni's tongue and dildo. *Yes, this is just a one-time thing*, I coach myself. My mind agrees with this wholeheartedly but my pussy screams otherwise. It informs me that I'm a damn fool if I think for one minute that I'm done with dick after this. It tells me I cannot run from dick any longer. I lightly pat it through my black silk thong, lettin' it know that I am the one in charge of what and who enters my sugar-sweet walls.

Jamie seductively approaches me with desire in his eyes and excitement in his erect penis. He pulls me by the strap of my bra so hard that my bra pops off. "Oops!" he smiles. This man definitely gets pussy on the regular. Jamie wastes no time in showing me that I am in fact correct about his bedroom skills. He leans down to gobble up a mouthful of my soft C-cup breasts. I moan as his wet tongue flicks and draws circles on my hardened black diamond. He shows both of my breasts love and affection, not allowing either a chance to feel neglected.

As he does this, I lightly pinch his nipples. I know a lot of men pretend to be too hard and rugged to get off on havin' their nipples sucked. I let 'em talk all the shit they want, but when my lips are tightly locked on one of their nipples while my hand jacks off their dick, I swear I have 'em moanin' and askin' me what it is that I'm doin' to them.

Jamie allows me to have my fun with his now hardened nipples until he's ready to taste the juice that drips from my pussy. "Get on your back," he instructs as he points to the floor. I waste no time following orders. My body shivers as it comes in contact with the cold tile floor. I'm sure so many people have left all kinds of germs and dog shit from their shoes on the floor, but at this moment all of that is irreverent. I wanna see what this man can do.

My eyes lock onto his as he retrieves his clothing from the floor and places them underneath my back, shielding my naked body from the cold floor. His lips find mine. Our mouths explore one another in a passion-filled kiss that gets my pussy even wetter. While his tongue darts inside my mouth, his hands pull my panties down and toss them to the side.

I moan through our kiss as his fingers enter the sticky, hot walls between my thighs. My walls wrap around his fingers with ease. His fingers move slowly at first, then increase their tempo as they sink into my fountain of love. Right now I am speechless. Maybe it's 'cause I'm about to be pounded by this fine-ass man and I haven't had a real dick inside me in a hot minute.

His tongue leaves my mouth. It licks down my breasts and toned stomach until it reaches my shaven pussy. A wide smile forms on his lips. He has found his pot of gold and will now treasure it with great satisfaction.

"Oooh shit…damn boy!" I manage to say, while my pussy receives the much-needed attention it's been fiening for. I watch in amazement as Jamie's tongue licks at my core with such ease. It's almost as if he belongs there. His mouth sucks gently on my clit, while his fingers bring my walls so much delight. His eyes look up to find me starin' intensely at him. I can't describe the expression on his face in full detail, but there was no denyin' the passion in his eyes. He is like a kid at Christmas that has stayed up all night just to open presents underneath the tree.

Jamie licks my clit with his thick pink tongue, then kisses my lips sweetly, all while never ending the rapid pace his fingers play inside my box. I had locked my goodies up for so long that now I knew there was no way I'd hide them ever again.

His mouth then begins to suck on my neck. This all feels too good to be true. Toni did a fantastic job of makin' my pussy nut every time we fucked...but this, oh my gosh! This man has me 'bout to call out a bunch of swears I never make a part of my everyday vocabulary. It takes me no time at all to release my juices all over those talented fingers.

Jamie takes his fingers from my overflowing vagina and smears my juices over both my nipples. He then proceeds to suck the substance away like a mad man. This man is a true freak...and I love every minute of it!

I lick my lips as Jamie begins to stroke his swollen member. The large tip rests comfortably on my clit, teasin' it. Just as he's about to take a deep dive into my sea, I feel the elevator begin to move upward. Jamie and I immediately begin to search for our clothes and put them back on as soon as we possibly can. As the doors open, we are greeted by a ton of people that have impatiently been waiting for the elevator.

I am thankful we both managed to get dressed before anyone of our co-workers caught a glimpse of nudity. We receive all types of glares as we exit the elevator, but I am not concerned about any of them. I find myself giggling like a schoolgirl when I see Jamie grab my bra and panties, casually placing them inside his pockets.

I briskly walk to my office. Jamie follows closely behind. He knows very well what the deal is. I close the door behind him and we go right back to where we left off. That man proceeds to put me in positions I didn't even know existed. We proceed to fuck and suck in every single inch of that room.

Jamie's wet tongue performin' circles on my clit immediately bring me out of my daydream. Seems like every day I take a glimpse back over how Jamie and I hooked up in such an awkward, but enticing way.

It's been a year since Jamie and I discovered the joy we could physically bring one another. Surprisingly, he has brought me that and so much more. I dropped Toni as soon as I made it home that night. There was no way I was living another day of my life without a piece of stiff dick.

As far as the promotion at work goes, neither of us got it. Anna ended up receiving it instead. Call me a hater, but that heifer had to have been fuckin' our boss...but it's all good. Jamie and I started our own indie label and we're makin' more money than we ever could have imagined.

Oh...I almost forgot to inform you that I am engaged also. Yep! Jamie and I will be married in a couple months and I will be able to receive a thorough dick-down every single day I desire. It's funny how things can change. One minute I was bumpin' coochie with women, the next I'm a woman addicted to the thrill of dick between my legs. Well...not just any ol' dick; only Jamie's. And now that I think about it, I never did get my bra and panties back from Jamie. Oh well!

Devotion

My devotion to you proves how real love can actually be. It feels like I've been searching for someone as special and unique as you my entire life. I've patiently waited and now that I have you, there's no way I will ever lose you.

My devotion towards you; my soul mate, is why I took the remainder of the day off from work. I picked up a few groceries, so I can cook for you. Catering to you is something I could never grow weary of.

Tonight, I'll open the door for you as you enter our home. I'll take your coat, sit you down on the sofa, and ensure that you're comfortable. Your toes will become prisoner to my strong hands as I massage away every inch of tension that comes from a long, hard day of labor.

Once you're completely relaxed, I'll carry you to the kitchen and sit you down at the table. You will smile when you realize that tonight is all about you. I will proceed in feeding you the home cooked meal I spent all afternoon preparing for you.

With your stomach good and full, our lips will meet for a simple, yet passionate kiss. You'll be up in my strong muscular arms once again. To the bedroom we go, my love!

I will carry you over to the bed as a trail of fresh

roses lead the way. Candles will be lit around our king-sized bed, where we do all the things that lovers do.

The scenery's gonna simply take your breath away. I've never expressed my romantic side until I fell in love with you; my queen.

My lips will begin to roam your neck. I know this will get you hot and bothered. You love it when I make those sucking noises on that sensitive spot.

Within a matter of minutes your clothes will fall to the floor, piece by piece, until you're completely naked. I'll sit there and stare at you as you lie upon our bed.

You've always been such a beautiful woman. My manhood will surely, like always, instantly harden while staring at your beautiful nakedness. After giving birth to three kids and enduring ten years of marriage, your body still looks as tight and sexy as it did the first time we made love.

I love you and I thank God for you every single morning, evening and night. You are the most precious gift any man could ask for.

I'll leave you lying there as I go downstairs to retrieve an item I forgot. Before I exit, you will be blindfolded to ensure that my surprise remains a complete mystery.

I'll place the can of whipped cream I retrieved from the refrigerator down as I softly kiss your lips. There's no denying the fact that my dick will protrude through my boxer briefs because you never fail at getting me hot and bothered. I thankfully know that Viagra will never be needed during our love sessions.

"I love you baby," will escape from my lips.

You don't have to utter a single word. I'm aware

of how much you love me and that is why I do the many things I do for you.

The cold can of whipped cream will be thoroughly shaken in my hand and I'll cover you with it from your lips to your toes. I'll begin to kiss your lips first, then work my way down to licking the white cream from your neck. You'll squirm and moan my name as I lick and suck a wet trail on your delicate skin.

My mouth will then find your toes. I'll slowly devour each toe, one by one, until every bit of whipped cream has been sucked away. I love the power my mouth has over your body.

Your moaning will escape from your lips louder and louder as my mouth invades your breasts. I will prove my love for you as I travel down from your succulent breasts to your thick, but beautifully toned thighs.

My finger's gonna enter the tight, wet walls between your legs, while my tongue continues to explore your inner thighs. I'll pull my finger out and suck away all of your juices.

You'll taste so sweet, as you always have. I can't deny that I'm addicted to your sweet, sweet syrup. I've craved placing my head between your thighs for hours. I love it when you cum all over me.

I'll decide to let the whipped cream linger on your skin a bit longer. Your sweet essence is hypnotizing. My tongue loves to enter and flick at your folds.

I will lick and slurp at your core until you moan my name louder. I'll continue going until you arch your back and grab the head board. My tongue will continue licking until you cum. I want you to cum all over my face, and hands. Smother my face with your love.

After you cum, my desire for you will remain. I'll keep going until you've cum five or six times. I'll then clean you and allow you to rest as I make my way downstairs to clean the kitchen.

I'll return as soon as I finish. I'll undress completely and lie down with you. I'll give you permission to remove the blindfold before you fall asleep in my arms.

I will hold you tightly in my arms. You are my love, my joy, my world: my everything. I'll treasure the ground you walk on until the day I die. I'll devote my all to you until I take my very last breath on this earth.

The Pussy Monsta

I tried my hardest to withhold my anger as my ruby red fingernails tapped away at the dinner table. I had just gotten my nails done earlier that afternoon, but at the moment I didn't give a damn. There was so much frustration built up inside of me and I couldn't unleash it in public, so my poor nails had to endure the wrath of my anger.

The buzzing of my cell phone that sat comfortably on my lap, startled me so much that I almost knocked over the glass of red wine I'd been sippin' on for the past ten minutes. I retrieved my cell, only to toss it on the table and send the caller to voicemail. It was my girl Mona. I already knew what the deal was. She was most likely only calling me to see if I had been stood up again. We spoke on the phone last night and she told me not to get my hopes up about tonight because she just knew things would not go as planned, as always.

"Tameka I'm tellin' you that nigga don't give a damn 'bout you," Mona told me, while I rolled my eyes 'cause Lord knew I didn't wanna hear it. "He only wanna get ya goodies then leave like he always do.

Girl, I'm tellin' you don't fall for that shit. Don't be a fool in love. Ain't no dick that good to the point where you give a nigga yo all and get nothin' back in return."

"Mona," I said, cuttin' the seriously annoyin' lecture off. "Please, shut the hell up." Mona and I were the type of best friends that made it necessary to always keep it real with each other. Tellin' her to shut the hell up, simply meant that I kindly wanted her to shut her trap and change the subject. "Whatever Larry and I do is our business. Do I tell you how to live your life?"

I could hear her suck her teeth. "Fine…but don't ya ass dare call me when he leaves you waitin' for him…again."

"Larry is doin' his best to change Mona. He really is," I defended.

"Okay…whatever. Just leave me out of it from now on," Mona told me before hangin' up.

As I sat alone in that jazz club, I pondered over what Mona had said. I knew she was just trying to be a good friend, but I had been too blinded by love to interpret her words of advice. She knew exactly what I was enduring. She was right; I was nothin' but a damn fool in love. A damn fool in love who sat alone for almost two damn hours waitin' for the so-called love of my life to walk through the door.

It's not like I was dressed up like any other woman that night. I had dressed to impress. My makeup was completely flawless. My sister, who's the best stylist miles around, cut my hair into a stunning bob with honey brown highlights throughout my jet-black hair. Gold hooped earrings that sparkled, even in the somewhat dim lighting, were upon my ears. A sexy slim red dress covered my toned body, along with matching shoes that had five inches on the soles. Yes, ya girl knows how to work some heels!

So, as you can see I was looking good enough to eat, if I don't say so myself. I can't count the number of guys that approached me that night. So many men wanted to get between these thighs and see what a sista was really workin' with. Whether they were there with their girlfriends or sportin' a wedding band that they figured I was too dumb to notice, all eyes were definitely on me.

Being admired by so many men wasn't the issue that I couldn't grasp my fingers around. The problem was the fact that I was waiting all alone on a man that promised me that night he'd prove himself to me. Larry ensured me earlier that evening that he had big plans for us. He said we'd discuss the details over dinner while we enjoyed the music played by local artists.

My thoughts of Larry vanished as the audience applauded a couple who had just wrapped up a spoken word performance. I honestly hadn't heard a damn thing they had said since my mind had been elsewhere, but I clapped as though I heard every single word that escaped through their lips. The only reason I knew they were husband and wife was because the guy mentioned it when they approached the stage.

I wanted to kick myself for not paying a lick of attention to my surroundings. I loved open mic nights at the Rooftop Lounge. They occurred once a month so I made sure I attended them as frequently as I could. Throughout the several months I spent attending those special nights, I realized that I appreciated the words the artists expressed a lot more than the shit I would hear on the radio. I hardly even turned on the freakin' radio anymore. All I ever heard was some nigga talkin' 'bout how he wanted a bitch to suck his dick or let 'em fuck. What happened to the real fuckin' music? Where were the sweet, sweet love songs that our parents listened to, that probably helped created us? Sure, some artists tried to bring the good music back on the scene, but they were easily overlooked by shit that people assumed would be more radio friendly.

"Excuse me, Miss. Are you ready to order?" my waitress asked, as she approached me for the third time that night.

I hesitated at first. I had sent her away twice already, without ordering a single item from the menu but wine. I loved the food they served and it was quite unusual for me to sit so long and not have ordered one or two meals by now. Something inside of me encouraged me to just say enough was fuckin' enough. Too much of my night had been wasted, waitin' for a man who clearly had no intention of showing. I handed her my menu and told her to just order me whatever was her favorite dish. She smiled and answered, "Sure! I know just what will make your night!"

As the waitress walked away, I couldn't help but wonder why she said she'd make my night. Was it that damn obvious that I was upset from being stood up? That definitely was not a good look. At that moment, I made up my mind that I would not allow a man to ruin the remainder of my night. I was turning thirty-five in a few weeks and I promised myself that another year of my life would not be wasted with men who didn't give a fuck about me. It was time for a change.

I was finally able to observe my surroundings and as I actually paid attention to it all, I wanted to kick myself again. This time it was 'cause I brushed off a ton of sexy-ass dudes, all because I had been so stuck on Larry's ass. "What the fuck is wrong with you girl?" I mumbled aloud to myself. Had Larry's dick been that good? Had he put it down on me so good that I had become blind to the countless other men in the sea? That had to be the case 'cause he damn sure didn't have me sprung by the way he treated me. That nigga was unreliable, but his dick was so damn reliable in bringin' me pleasure each and every time he entered my pussy.

The agitating voice coming from the stage demanded my attention by startling me and everyone else up in that joint. I honestly wanted to cover up my ears 'cause it was killin' me to have to sit there and listen.

"You know I love you girlllllll," the guy onstage who thought he had a voice like Maxwell, sang through the microphone.

"We sure as hell don't love you," I said, without meaning to say it aloud.

The people seated at the table next to me overheard my thoughts and began to laugh. These weren't just any old chuckles. They were die hard laughing like I was a fuckin' comedian or somethin'. I found that to be hilarious, so I laughed right along with them. It didn't take long for people all over the club to start laughin'. They must've been laughin' at homeboy as he attempted to hit another high note that damn sure wasn't fit for his vocal range.

At first it seemed like he would continue trying to win the crowd over with his non-singing ass. But as we all kept laughin' our asses off with tears in our eyes, he pulled a punk move. Homeboy dropped the mic and ran offstage, wailing like a damn child. That only made the laughter multiply, causin' us to sound like an audience seated at the Apollo Theatre. And I didn't feel a tiny ounce of pity for the dude 'cause his ass had to have known he sounded a hot mess!

We all clapped, while still tryin' to control our laughter as Samuel Devine walked onstage. Samuel was the club owner and at sixty-eight years old he could easily pass for thirty-eight. The man had some amazin' genes.

Tonight, he wore a sharp black suit with a bold red tie. It looked absolutely stunning on him. If I had been in my sixties I'd definitely be tryin' to climb that tree.

There were plenty women who I had seen firsthand not givin' a damn about Samuel's age. These chicks were as young as eighteen. And from what I hear, Samuel sure as hell didn't give a damn 'bout their age either. Word on the street was he slang dick around like it was made of gold. He got pussy on the regular, not only because he had money, but also because he still possessed mad sex appeal.

If ya ask me, fuckin' and suckin' a man in his sixties when you ain't even twenty is rather disgusting. I can understand if there wasn't such a gap between the ages, but for a man to be over fifty years older than you? I think not. Samuel was fine, but his ass wasn't that damn fine. Shit, I'd rather live in the Playboy mansion and fuck Hugh Hefner. At least in that case I'd be livin' like a queen and catered to.

Sometimes I could only shake my head at females in society today. They didn't know shit about makin' a man wait for the goodies. Things were gettin' so bad to where they couldn't even wait until the first date to let a nigga smash. All that shit made no sense to me.

As Samuel continued to entertain his crowd of drunk and loud guests, I got up and went to the restroom. I had to pee like hell. I couldn't hold my shit any longer and I knew Larry would be a no-show, so no one would miss my exit.

It felt like I had been on the toilet for at least three minutes. I was startin' to grow a bit impatient waitin' for my bladder to relieve itself. I most definitely blamed that shit on the alcohol.

A sigh of relief escaped from my lips as I stood from the toilet seat and dumped the tissue I placed around the lid into the toilet. I didn't play that shit. Ever since I was a child, my mama told me to never sit my ass on a public toilet seat without puttin' some tissue down. Doin' that was damn near close to lettin' a nigga stick his dick up in you raw. It opened yourself up for nasty-ass germs and possible infections.

I nodded my head to acknowledge a woman who dried her hands and exited the restroom. My hands pumped the soap dispenser at least four times to make sure I had a good amount of soap to rid myself of the germs my hands had picked up.

My eyes rolled as I overheard the audience clap. Another act was goin' up onstage and I was the least bit thrilled about it. Whoever was about to go up, had to really show their skills 'cause homeboy who'd just exited the stage, needed to be slapped for such a horrific performance. I couldn't understand how people who couldn't sing thought they could blow like Whitney Houston or Joe. Someone in their life needed to tell them they couldn't sing a lick and needed to throw the towel in.

I was wipin' my hands when I heard somethin' so sweet, so damn irresistible that I dropped the paper towel to the floor and rushed out of the restroom without thinkin' twice about the nasty germs my hands would pick up by touchin' the door handle. I was that mesmerized.

Steppin' out of the restroom, my eyes witnessed somethin' more beautiful than what my ears had heard. Sittin' up on the stage was a man so deliciously fine that I literally coulda smacked my own mama!

Walkin' over to my table, I eyed all the women in the spot. All of their eyes were upon that sexy-ass piece of meat onstage. The men seemed to be entertained also. Some of them were a bit too entertained if you ask me. I shook my head 'cause they were suspects for the DL lifestyle I had heard extremely way too much about.

I damn near tripped as I sat down. Homeboy hit a high note that caused my pussy to leak, lettin' me know a flood was on the verge of exploding at any given moment. I was a sucka for a man who could sing his ass off. It made my pussy hot and ready for a man to sing in my ear as he bumped and grinded inside of my soakin' wet pussy.

My eyes closely examined the figure that summoned my pussy to react. That beautiful voice had a bangin' body to go right along with it. He wore a baby blue cap with a white t-shirt that was covered by a striped blue, black and white cotton vest. Baggy blue jeans covered his legs, along with big Timberland boots.

My hands begin to travel down my legs and underneath my dress before I could understand what the hell was goin' on. It took every ounce of strength inside of me to remove the hold my hands had on my thighs and place them onto the table. I didn't want anyone to think I was the type of freak that got down in front of crowds of people. I mean, I've always been adventurous when it came down to sexual encounters, but allowing just any ol' body to see me fondle my pussy was not about to go down. Not that night or ever.

Okay girl, it ain't like you never heard a man that could sing his ass off before, I silently coached myself as I closed my eyes for a little pep talk.

True, I had heard many men with voices that could only be sent from heaven. But there was somethin' different about this brother. I just couldn't put my finger on what it was.

He closed his eyes and belted out a note that caused everyone in that joint to go bananas. I couldn't stop starin' at his sexy ass. I was under a trance I had no desire to ever rid myself of. I even continued to stare him down when he opened his eyes and his gaze met up with mine.

Our eyes just stared at one another. He continued to seduce me with his voice as his eyes told me he could do even more damage to my body behind closed doors. I'm not the average chick to just give up the pussy to any smooth nigga that comes my way, but from that moment on I knew that homie could get the goodies if he wanted it. He had my pussy on fire just from lookin' at me and using that sexy-ass voice of his. I was curious to see the other skills he possessed.

I must've been so caught up in all the freaky things me and loverboy could do that I missed his exit offstage. When I came back to reality, I cursed myself. I had allowed my fantasies to take over my mind so much that I didn't even see him take a bow or maybe even wink at me. That's how powerful that man's stare had been.

Everyone else who performed that night didn't mean shit to me. I had my head in the clouds and there was no fuckin' way I wanted to come down! A part of me was hopeful that I'd catch a glimpse of that gorgeous man before the club closed and it was time to go home. Hell, I was even hopeful that he'd approach me at my table, take my hand, then lead me to the bathroom where we'd go at it until out bodies exploded.

After the final act performed, Samuel returned to the stage. And don't ask me who the final act was and what they did because I don't have even the slightest clue. They could've been pullin' rabbits out of a hat for all I cared. That was the least thing on my horny-ass mind.

Anyway, Samuel thanked us for coming and told us to drive safely, which really meant, "Get the fuck out," in a nice way. I retrieved my purse from the table, took one last swallow of alcohol and then made my way among the crowd to exit the club.

I was a bit disappointed that my fantasy didn't come to be reality, but I was still glad I had gone out that night. I didn't get his name but ooowee, I had made up a name for him. He had those delicious lookin' pussy eatin' lips, so I decided I'd call him The Pussy Monsta. Those lips looked like they could torture a mean pussy until it nutted all over the damn place!

I yarned as I made it to my car. I was a bit tired but I knew as soon as I got home my thoughts of The Pussy Monsta would wake me the hell up. Oh yes, I had my imagination runnin' wild at all of the things I could with that man! *If only I could've spoken to him,* I thought as I began to step into my ride.

"Excuse me!" I heard in the distance from a male voice.

I turned around and almost fainted when I saw that sexy piece of chocolate approachin' me. What a damn coincidence.

"Sorry to alarm you," he apologized, when he made it over to my car.

"No problem at all," I smiled.

It most definitely had not been a problem! He had alarmed my pussy in a good way and from the way things were lookin' I couldn't push the SNOOZE button even if I wanted to.

"I just saw you back at the club as I was singin' and somethin' 'bout you caught my eye," he told me, displayin' the cutest set of dimples I had ever seen.

"And you did a great job by the way," I responded. "That voice of yours is somethin' else!"

He lifted his eyebrow and gave me a flirtatious look that made me wanna jump into his muscular arms at that very moment.

"Thank you. I'm glad you enjoyed my performance."

I opened my mouth to add another comment, but I instantly became sidetracked as a breeze of cold wind blew my dress up, exposin' my smooth-shaven vagina. I was in shock at first. The wind actually felt kinda good on my clit. It wasn't until he smiled at the glorious view before him that I pulled my skirt down. *Damn, I should've worn fuckin' panties*, I thought. However, the lustful look in his eyes made me reconsider that thought. It didn't take a genius to realize my admirer enjoyed the view, and if he enjoyed it, it was all good with me.

"Damn shawty, you look like you got that good-good," a man that looked like he belonged on the street beggin' for change, said as he stood a couple feet away from us, lickin' his crusty-ass lips.

"Yo, what the fuck did you say?" The Pussy Monsta questioned, with a cold stare that turned me on even more.

"Man I ain't said shit to yo ass," the rude-ass fucker said, like he had the nerve to be gettin' irritated and shit.

"Muthafucka do it look like I give a shit 'bout if you was talkin' to me or not?" The Pussy Monsta said, as he stepped to that nasty piece of shit. And I can't lie y'all, the angrier that man got, the more turned on my pussy got.

"Yo, who the fuck you think you talkin' to?"

"I'm talkin' to yo bitch ass," my warrior stated. "Yo, you got a lot of nerve talkin' to this lady like that. Where the fuck yo manners at?"

"I ain't got no manners for no hos," the bum said, while frownin' his ugly face up at me and then he stared at me from head to toe. "This chick came out here on a cold-ass night with no fuckin' panties on under that dress. Who the fuck does some shit like that? Nobody I know. That bitch is a ho and I advise ya not to get serious wit her 'cause I doubt if her damn legs can stay closed."

The series of events that happened next, happened so damn fast that I can't recall them all to y'all if I tried. The Pussy Monsta punched that nigga so damn hard that I swore I saw one of his teeth fly out of his filthy mouth to the pavement! After that he gave that fucka one fierce-ass blow after another until he was laid out on the pavement.

If I hadn't been so turned on by watchin' the whole thing I would've laughed 'cause that rude mutha got what was comin' to him. But seein' the way The Pussy Monsta handled that dude made my body react. I could feel myself leakin' as the warm nut from my pussy ran down my cold legs. This nigga was the truth.

The Pussy Monsta shook his head at the sorry-ass nigga he had just knocked out. I'm pretty sure he could see little birds flyin' around his head as he tried to come to terms about what had just gone down.

"Come on ma," his sexy ass said to me in a soft, concerned tone. "Let's get out the cold."

At that moment, I didn't really care where he took me. As long as he would put his big strong arms around the small of my waist and kiss me with those full lips, I knew my night would go well.

I took his hand and began to walk away from my car, until I decided I had one more thing to accomplish. I briskly walked to that filthy shit talker and kicked him with every ounce of strength in me. I sent one kick to his large belly and another to his nuts, which I'm sure weren't bigger than your average size marbles.

The intensity of my heels comin' in contact with his balls must have been pretty serious 'cause his lame-

ass woke up out of his daze, moanin' and hollerin'. I
kicked him one more time between his legs before The
Pussy Monsta took me by the hand and ushered me
away from him. He must have noticed the fiery in my
eyes every time my heel made contact with the bum's
body.

"You got some built-up anger in there?" he
asked me through laughter.

I laughed right along with him. "No...not at all.
He was just really rude and I think his ass deserved it."

"I agree. No one should talk to lady as beautiful
as you like that."

I blushed. I didn't know if it was because he had
such a way with words or because I was beyond horny
at that point, but a sista was cheesin' hard.

He led me over to the entrance of the club. I
stopped dead in my tracks as he began to walk up the
steps.

"What's wrong?" he asked.

"The club's closed."

"Don't worry 'bout that," he smiled. "I got
connections."

Without any further hesitations, I followed him
back inside of the vacant club. The place was empty,
which wasn't a surprise. However, I was surprised to
see the mess of empty glasses on the tables and trash on
the floor completely gone. I found that to be quite
impressive. Samuel got his shit done in a timely
fashion.

"There you are John," I heard a voice say
cheerfully from across the room.

It was Samuel. He approached us with a big grin
on his face.

"John, I been lookin' all over for you."

Hmm, I thought. So The Pussy Monsta's actual name was John. I placed that thought in the back of my head for future reference. I would have hated to accidentally call him The Pussy Monsta to his face. Just that thought alone, made me smile.

John noticed this, causin' him to smile at me. Samuel watched the way our eyes flirted with one another in awe.

"So who's this beautiful young lady?" Samuel asked John.

"Oh...this is, um." John stumbled over his words. "I'm sorry. How rude of me not to even ask for you name."

"It's no problem at all," I smiled. "I'm Tameka."

"Well it's a pleasure to officially meet you Tameka," John replied, grabbin' my hand and bringin' it to his lips for a sweet kiss.

I blushed. Couldn't help it. That man was bringin' out the teenager in me. It felt like I was sixteen all over again with a big crush that gave my stomach butterflies.

"And you're John, right?"

"Yes, that's me."

We laughed, then both shyly averted over eyes away from each other.

Samuel burst out into laughter watchin' the way we behaved. "Aren't you gonna introduce me?" he asked.

"Oh yeah! My bad," John responded. "Tameka, this is Samuel Devine, my father. And Dad, this is my lovely friend, Tameka."

His Dad? Had I heard him correctly? The local

celebrity Samuel Devine was his father?

I took a sec to observe both of them. I coulda slapped myself in the head for not noticing the strong resemblance from the start. Blame it on my pussy. All she cared about at that moment was gettin' ate out like a desert.

"Nice to meet you, young lady," Samuel told me.

He shook my hand with friendly intentions, but the look in his eyes told me he digged the way I looked. I kinda felt uncomfortable 'cause my mind was only on his son. But at the same time, I found myself flattered.

"Pleasure to meet you also," I replied.

I think John picked up on the vibe his father was givin' me 'cause the next thing he said was, "Dad could you give us a little privacy?"

Without any hesitation, Samuel replied, "Sure, sure." He then reached into his pocket and dug out a set of keys. He took one from the key chain and handed it to John. "Lock the place up for me."

"Will do," John answered, lookin' over at me with a smile.

"Nice to meet you again, Tameka," Samuel informed me, before walkin' out of the club, leavin' John and I alone with our thoughts.

"So Tameka, tell me a little about yourself," John stated, as he ushered me to a table in front of the stage, then pulled a chair out for me.

"Well," I began, after he sat down directly in front of me. "I'm originally from the south, but I moved out here to get away from the boring and quiet life."

"I don't think the south's boring," he admitted. "I find it to be extremely relaxing actually."

I chuckled. "Well, try livin' there for twenty-one years and then we can have this convo again."

He laughed and shook his head. We had a chemistry I can't describe. The more I talked, the more he was feelin' me. I could easily see this by the way he licked his lips and flashed flirtatious smiles my way.

Time quickly began to pass and our conversation deepened. He told me he had lived in New York all of his life and he wished he could have been brought up in a more simplistic lifestyle like I had. John was ready to branch out and leave the Big Apple while I on the other hand, was enjoying the hell out of it.

As we continued talkin', I also learned that John and his father had reconnected only a few years ago. John was raised single-handedly by his mother while Samuel was busy chasin' ass and not concerned with raisin' a child. He told me Samuel finally came to his senses and begged him and his mother for forgiveness. It took a few months and a lot of prayer before John could allow his heart to heart to forgive, but now that his father was in his life, they were inseparable.

After spendin' time with his son, Samuel realized John had an amazing voice and played the guitar beautifully. He told him he should perform one night at his club and here John was. It had only been his first night performing and he already received a standing ovation and plenty of wet pussies in the audience.

"So what do you plan on doin' with that voice?" I asked seductively. "Are there any plans to become a professional singer? With that voice, you could become a household name."

He shook his head immediately. "Naw, when people make it big and become famous, they tend to forget where they came from. I ain't 'bout to turn into one of those cats, feel me?"

"Yeah I feel you Pussy Mons-"

Once again, I wanted to knock myself out! How could I have allowed that nickname to slip? *His name is John, Tameka,* I told myself silently. *John! Not The Pussy Monsta!*

"What did you just say?" he asked, as one eyebrow rose in curiosity.

"Um...nothin'," I replied, without makin' eye contact. I had fucked up big time and there was nothin' I could do or say to cover that shit up.

"Naw...go 'head and tell me what you said shawty. Be real with a nigga."

The way he talked so calmly to me, put my body at ease. That voice of his, right along with that New York accent was just enough to get me up out of my dress.

I took a deep breath before I allowed myself to respond. "Okay, seein' you up on that stage did somethin' crazy to my pussy." As the word "pussy" rolled off of my tongue, John adjusted himself in his seat. I already knew what that meant. I had gotten his dick hard without even tryin'. I continued to talk, addin' more and more of a seductive tone to my voice. I wanted to see just how hot and bothered I could get him.

"I mean, I literally rushed out of the bathroom to see where that amazin' voice was comin' from. When I saw it was you, I had to rush over to my table and take a seat, 'cause my pussy was cursin' me out for just one taste of you."

He laughed, while takin' a brief tug at his erection. The look in his eyes told me everything I said was exactly what his dick wanted to hear.

"That's what's up ma. So, how did I get the name Pussy Mons."

"It's Pussy Monsta", I corrected him.

We laughed in unison.

"Okay…how did the name Pussy Monsta come about?" he asked.

"Ever since I was old enough to talk I had been in love with Sesame Street. I loved Elmo, Big Bird, but most of all I loved Cookie Monster. I thought the way he gobbled up cookies was funny as hell. And seein' you up on that stage singin' made me start to fantasize about your lips. Looks like you can eat a pussy up. I pictured you eatin' my shit with the same passion Cookie Monster has for his chocolate chip cookies."

"Uh huh," he said, strokin' his goatee with his fingers. "Interesting."

"I hope my little twisted version of a kiddy show doesn't make you think any less of me," I admitted, now a bit embarrassed.

"No, not at all," he laughed. "It's actually kinda cute. Turned me on a little too."

"Is that so?" Now I was the one who had to adjust myself. Funny how the tables turn.

"It is."

"Glad I could give your night a bit of excitement."

"Oh, you've done quite more than that sexy," he said, as his eyes roamed down to his lap.

My pussy began to drip like a ceiling leak on a

wet and rainy night.

"So you think I can eat pussy pretty good?"

His question came to me as a complete surprise. He put me on the spot, but I was never known for backin' down.

"Yeah, you look like you could turn me into a fien."

He stood up from the table and approached me. His protrudin' erection called out to me as I stared at it like I hadn't had a good meal in weeks.

"Wanna see just how much of a fien I can turn ya sexy ass into?"

A devilish bad boy smirk appeared to his lips. *This is it Tameka*, my pussy informed me. *This man wants to eat, so let his ass eat!*

I batted my eyes while sayin', "Yeah let's see if you know how to put that mouth to good use."

John held out his hand and I placed mine inside it as I stood to my feet. I grabbed my purse and started to head for the door.

"Where you goin'?" he asked.

"To my car. You can follow me to my place."

He grabbed hold of my curvy hips and said, "Naw baby. We ain't gotta do all that." He then whispered in my ear, sending a delightful chill down my spine. "We can stay right here."

"Here?" I asked, to make sure there wasn't a buildup of wax in my ears.

"You heard me baby girl," he stated, as he took me by my hand to the stage.

"Here?" I found myself asking for a second time.

"Yes," he laughed. "Nobody's here. It's just you and me."

I nervously walked up the stairs, following his lead. I was a freak, always have been, but he was talkin' 'bout fuckin' on the stage of his father's club! I mean, anybody could've walked back inside because they left their purse or somethin' of value. They could've walked right into a show that would put porn stars to shame.

"Don't cha worry ma. Big Daddy got you," he said, as he pulled me in for an embrace and whispered into my ear.

This man had game. How could I go from actin' like a timid virgin to a nasty freak ready to ride John's dick like a pony? He was that fuckin' good. And he didn't even have to try hard like niggas I'd been with in the past. Spittin' game came effortlessly for him. And he had me right where he wanted.

I melted into his arms as we began to slowly sway around the stage. No music. Just our hearts pounding and private parts thumpin'.

Nothin' could've prepared me for what he did next. Absolutely nothin'! He placed his lips at least an inch away from my ear and then began to softly sing. That shit right there had a sista ready to say skip all the damn foreplay! I was ready for the dick right then and there!

As we danced, I listened to the words that came from that angelic voice. I wasn't familiar with the words but it was beautiful. The song was about a guy who watched a woman from afar and from the moment his eyes met with hers he knew she was the one he wanted to spend the rest of his life with.

That man literally had me gone! I didn't come back to reality until he stopped singing and ended our seductive dance. He stared me in the eyes so passionately it scared me for a second. It was almost as if he wanted more from me than just a dip inside my pussy. Call me crazy, but I coulda sworn his eyes were tellin' me that.

I think he sensed me overanalyzing the situation. Next thing I knew I had his tongue in my mouth as his hands roamed up and down my body. I accepted his kiss greedily, while moanin' as our tongues played with one another.

We stood there makin' out and rubbin' all over each other for at least five minutes. I didn't mind one bit. I enjoyed every second of his lips being pressed against mine.

John's hands found my clit without the slightest bit of trouble. His meaty index finger played around with the juice that had oozed out of my extremely wet insides. He then removed his hand from underneath my dress and swirled his tongue around his finger. I coulda nutted right there as I witnessed John savor my scrumptious honey.

"I can already tell you got that good-good ma," he said after makin' sure the remainder of my juice had been licked away from his finger.

"Oh, for real?" I grinned.

"Hell yeah," he confirmed with pride.

John grabbed ahold of my thighs, then lifted my body up into the air as his head went underneath my dress. I closed my thighs as tightly around his neck as I could, without chokin' him, then held onto the curtain above us for support.

A squeal escaped from my mouth when John's tongue licked my pussy from the bottom all the way to my clit. He allowed his tongue to hit my clit repeatedly with as much force as his tongue could allow. As my moans of passion became louder and louder, John worked that magical tongue of his fiercer and fiercer.

"Johhhnnn...fuck," was all I could say between deep breaths.

"Mmmhm," he moaned, while suckin' hard on my clit.

"Eat that pussy baby," I begged.

He released the pressure his mouth had on my clit then plunged his tongue into my pussy. He darted in that shit up, down, side to side and even in a circular motion.

"Yo shit...taste...so...damn good ma," John told me, while his tongue ate me out like a fat man during Thanksgiving dinner.

I wanted to thank him, but was too caught up with the pleasure he was givin' me. I began to rotate my hips back and forth. He moved his head along with my rhythm until I started to feel a nut on the rise.

"That's right John. That shit got me 'bout to nut!"

John instantly removed his tongue from my center, took me from his shoulders, then flipped my body, causin' my dress to fall down to my breasts as my pussy was an inch away from his face.

"I'ma show you just how much of a Pussy Monsta I can be," he said, before smackin' my ass and divin' back into my pool.

I can't explain all the thoughts that were runnin' through my head at that point. But one that stood out the most was that I hit the jackpot with this man.

"Shit!" I wailed out, while he went to town on

bringing my body complete ecstasy.

Once again, I was gone! But not so gone to the point that I'd forgotten how much I wanted his dick. It's amazin' how the craziest things can get accomplished when you're horny as hell. Even though I was upside down, I didn't have the slightest bit of trouble undoing John's belt and slidin' his jeans down to his knees.

The imprint of his dick stood out proudly through his boxers. My mouth instantly watered, causing a small amount of drool to escape from my mouth and hit the floor. I massaged his dick in one hand and played with his heavy set of balls in the other. John was definitely turnin' out to be my kind of man. He was handsome, polite, full of swag, could sing his ass off, and was packin' like a fuckin' horse!

"Go 'head and suck...that...dick ma," he encouraged, with his tongue still deep inside my pussy.

Shittttt! He didn't have to tell me twice. I whipped that sucka out through the opening of his boxers and began to twirl my tongue around the head. He leaked a lot of precum, but I didn't mind 'cause it tasted so sweet. He definitely ate a healthy diet.

I would have loved to have been a fly on the wall at that moment. I bet it would've been a magnificent slight to witness myself takin' John's huge dick down my throat as he munched on my pussy upside down.

My eyes observed John's dick once more before I prepared my mouth for labor. It wasn't just big. It was also thick. Thick and juicy. Rubbin' my fingers up and down its length and protrudin' veins excited me.

In other words, his dick was beautiful. However,

it was the biggest I'd ever seen in person. Larry's dick was about six inches and the biggest I'd ever had was about eight. John's dick stood out tremendously from all the others. He had to be at least ten or eleven inches max.

I was nervous, but also curious. I was up for the challenge. *How hard could it be?* I asked myself. Ten inches isn't that big, right?

Wrong! Dead wrong! It was quite a struggle to stick that shit in my mouth, let alone down my throat. I always thought I was a damn good headgiver, but suckin' on John's dick made a sista think twice about that. I found myself chokin' and coughin', strugglin' to fit that sucka down my throat. And it didn't take long for me to feel the side effects from being upside down too long.

John must've done the "69" standing up a lot 'cause he knew exactly when the time came to put me down. He took his time in lowering me down onto the floor while never ending the position we were in. He resumed to eating my pussy, but stopped when I started gaggin' on his dick.

"It's cool ma," he stated. "Most chicks have trouble suckin' my dick, so don't sweat it."

I frowned. "But I really do wanna suck it…without chokin'."

His face lit up as he looked over his shoulder at me. "I'll coach you through it, okay?"

I nodded my head.

"Open up beautiful."

I obeyed and followed each step he gave me. Turns out I just needed to open wide, relax my throat muscles, and focus on breathing as I sucked. After five or ten minutes passed, I was able to swallow almost all of it.

Pleased with his well-taught lesson, John began to use that talented instrument he called his tongue once again.

"Open that throat up," he demanded, as he began to fuck my throat, slow at first, then buildin' up to a rapid rhythm.

I managed to keep up, chokin' only a few times. The incredible sensations from his tongue and thrill from swallowin' his dick began to get the best of me. Before long I felt a nut preparing to surface. I warned John of my upcoming climax. He licked his tongue faster, nibbled on my clit and rapidly fingered my walls.

"Johnnn!" I cried through the most intense orgasm of my life.

I released all over John's lips and goatee and left a huge puddle on the floor. He pulled my tits out from my dress and busted a thick nut soon after, all over them. I rubbed it in, pinched a nipple, then tasted his cream.

We shared a sweet, yet fully enjoyable kiss, then cleaned up and headed outside to my car. As I got into my car, I couldn't help but feel saddened I might not see John again.

"What's wrong sexy?" he asked, leanin' into my car.

"I just, don't want this night to end," I admitted.

"And who says it has to?" he asked with a mischievous grin.

To top that wonderful night off, he followed me back to my crib and gave my pussy the best beat down in history! And afterward he ate my pussy out for over an hour, showin' me why he indeed did fit the title of The Pussy Monsta.

The best part of it all is that he eats my pussy every single day of the week, rain or shine. John fell in love with my pussy so much that I'm now rockin' an engagement ring. I couldn't be happier...and neither could my pussy.

Mirror, Mirror

Mirror, mirror on the wall, who's the downright freakiest female of them all? Who's the best when it comes to swallowin' a big ol' juicy dick entirely down my throat? Who's the chick that's so fuckin' bad my name belongs in the Guinness Book of Records for the world's most outstanding dick worshipper? Hell, do you have to even think twice? It's me of course!

Ain't no chick in plain sight that can hop on a dick in the blink of an eye and ride it backward, while milkin' a nigga's sweet nut with my walls, like I can. Never been one to toot my own horn, but toot toot! I'm the shit.

How do I know I'm the shit, you ask? The answer's quite simple. It's all in my technique. You see, I closely observe everything that goes down when I'm doin' the nasty. Every move and every squirm is checked and counted for through one of my many mirrors.

There are mirrors all along the wall of my bathroom, mirrors in my living room, dining room, and even on the ceiling of my main bedroom and guest rooms. It's fuckin' mirrors galore!

Ever since I sucked and had my first taste of dick, I desired to perfect my craft. I wanted to be the damn near best when it came down to pleasin' a man.

So when I got my own place, mirrors became my best friends. I used them to show me every detail of my body as it moved.

There are so many benefits to fuckin' and suckin' before, not just one, but many mirrors. I remember bein' fucked like there would be no tomorrow by this dude I met awhile back. We started on the stairs that lead to my bedroom, then eventually fucked our way to my bathroom. He sat me up on the counter with his firm hands and began to bang my pussy up! It was quite refreshing because there's a mirror aligned on the wall opposite of my sink mirror. As he fucked me, he got off on the many faces I made in the opposite mirror and I did the same through the other.

There's nothin' like fuckin' in front of a mirror. Watchin' a nigga choke you while his ass strokes and pounds away at ya insides can make you cream instantly. Don't believe me? Just pull out ya mirrors and find out for yourself. Try it one time and you'll find out why my mirror proudly proclaims I'm the freakiest of them all!

Never Judge a Book by Its Cover

Lookin' back over your childhood, can you remember a kid with huge glasses and buckteeth that was so puny other kids would toss him around like he was a football at recess? Remember that nerdy dude that everyone bullied and copied his homework when the teacher wasn't looking? Or was he so much of an outcast you don't even recall seeing such an individual? Either way, I sadly fit that description as a child.

I was skinny as a toothpick and was picked on constantly because of it. Teachers loved me, while my peers despised me. I did have a small group of friends throughout my middle and high school years. Marcus and Tom were just as nerdy as me. We all were the best of friends until the time for college approached. I decided on a college in Atlanta, Georgia that had an amazing computer science program, while Marcus moved to LA and Tom relocated to Florida.

My parents weren't too keen on me moving so far away from Texas, but I felt it was extremely necessary to do so. I had nothing but bad memories in Texas. I was never really happy because of my status in society. All the guys in my graduation class had already had sex with tons of girls, while I hadn't even had the pleasure of seeing an actual pussy in person.

I had seen plenty of porn though. When I say plenty, I mean plenty. I had become a lover of porn. Didn't matter if it was full of Black pussy, Asian, Latino or White. Pussy was pussy to someone who never had it before. How could I discriminate or be picky?

My addiction to porn had become so bad, I began to collect my porn DVDs in empty containers used to store blank DVDs and CDs. To be completely honest, I believe my collection grew to about five or six containers. That's about 500 to 600 DVDs of raw, uncut hot sex. And there's no shame in my game. I was horny. Horny and lonely. Females never looked at me. When I'd pop in a flick, I'd jack my penis thinking about one of the gorgeous babes at school opening their legs and allowing me to sex them until they screamed my name.

Tom and Marcus were quite impressed with my stash of porn. In fact, we all used to trade the latest DVDs we'd burned from our laptops and have a ball jacking off in the privacy of our rooms.

Well, I didn't have much privacy. One night as I closed my eyes and softly moaned the name of a classmate, my mom decided to burst into my room. It shocked the hell out of me. I was so surprised that all I could do was lie there as my dick ejaculated a thick nut right before her holy eyes! She grabbed ahold of her chest, like she was about to suffer from a serious heart attack.

As she tried to summon the right words to scold me, I threw my comforter over my erection. The damage had already been done though. I bet my mom thought she had walked into a nightmare. I'm sure she never imagined she'd witness her son experiencing an orgasm so strong it coated my chest, dick, balls, the comforter and headboard. I never fathomed in a million years that she'd find out how much of a heavy shooter my dick could be.

"I, I don't believe this Curtis!" mom cried, as she stormed out of my room.

"Damn it!" I mumbled getting up, closing my door, then cleaning up the mess I had made with tissue.

After I ensured every trace of my nut was removed and the moaning coming from my television had ceased, I threw on a t-shirt and shorts. Words cannot describe the embarrassment I felt as I went to find my mother. My friends wouldn't have been able to believe what had just transpired. Having my mother walk in on a routine masturbation session was unfreaking believable!

I found my mother in the kitchen washing dishes. She used that chore to clear her mind when things became too stressful. She said it was something soothing in dipping her hands in the hot water.

"Mom I-"

"I don't want to hear it, Curtis," she said, while throwing her hands up in the air, sending water to the floor.

"You should have knocked."

She then dried her hands on a nearby dish towel and turned her body toward me. I don't think I'd ever seen her look so pissed before.

"I should have knocked?"

I didn't answer. Seeing my mom so upset scared

me quite a bit.

"I should have knocked?" She repeated before laughing out loud.

"Yes, Mom. Look, I'm sorry you had to see that but come on! I'm a senior in high school. Don't you expect me to touch myself and watch porn?"

"Curtis I don't want to hear this." She turned her back to me and resumed washing dishes.

"Let's be logical Mom. You didn't expect me to masturbate? I'm human. I do have hormones."

"Curtis!" mom yelled, turning her head quickly toward me.

The look in her eyes told me to just leave it alone. I returned to my room and finished up my homework.

Later that night, my mom informed my dad about what she had discovered after entering my room uninvited. My dad laughed in her face and told her she was in the wrong for not knocking before stepping inside. That only pissed her off more.

My mom entered my room again, without the slightest warning. Thank God I had decided to wait on masturbating until I hit the shower! Mom most likely would have really had a heart attack then.

She didn't say a word to me as her eyes scanned around my room. Mom rushed over to my closet and began searching through it. When she didn't find what she was in search of, she pulled out the drawers to my dresser, then began to look underneath my bed.

"Mom, what are you doing?" I nervously asked, not wanting her to run across my secret stash I kept beneath the bed.

She ignored my distractions. I was the one about

to have a heart attack when she pulled out my extensive library of porn. Mom shook her head, looked at me with a disappointed stare, then picked up three DVD containers. She walked out of my room with them, only to return to retrieve the remaining two.

I'm aware of how sad this sounds, but it felt like my mother had taken away a piece of me. That collection of porn had become a part of me. Every day, sometimes three to four times a day, I allowed my mind to escape to an erotic world full of fat pussy just begging to be fucked. What was I to do without having a single DVD? Sure I could have easily downloaded some more, but there was no telling if my mom would search and confiscate those also. I almost cried when I thought about it…almost cried.

And I could've cried tears of joy when my dad returned my stash the following night. He told me he understood completely about how horny I was. He also informed me that he had a talk with mom and told her she should've been thrilled I was entertaining myself with porn instead of having sex with any and everything walking with a vagina. Mom didn't like it, but she saw his point.

The only thing my dad was concerned about was the large collection I possessed. I told him I just found it to be interesting. We laughed and he told me some woman would be lucky to have me because of my experienced eyes.

Those words stuck with me as I made the transition to college. He said I'd make a woman blush in the bedroom, but I couldn't for the life of me figure out why I was still a virgin. I was eager to see what all the fuss was about. I wanted to find out why men moaned when they stuck their cocks inside of a hot pussy. I wanted to make a woman scream my name so loud anyone ten feet away could hear it.

But waiting all those years to lose my virginity turned out to be a valuable lesson. Good things come to those who wait, for patience is a virtue.

That big moment occurred at a time in my life when I figured I'd die without ever taking a plunge between a woman's legs. It's a little extreme, I know. But I was a late bloomer and my situation was becoming even more stressful when I discovered Marcus and Tim had both lost their virginities. Tim even lost his in a threesome. Talk about a blow to my ego!

It was on a cold winter's night that I explored the always pleasurable fruit that only women can possess. I was a junior, ready to finally graduate from college and take on grad school before conquering the world. My class schedule had been loaded down with courses and I spent hours studying every day, so a part-time job was completely out of the question.

However, I did work on computers for my fellow classmates for a small and reasonable fee, depending on how much labor the repair required. I had quite a few customers starting out. As time progressed and more people became satisfied, word got around that I was the go-to guy for any PC related issue. Before I knew it I had acquired computers all over my room. Luckily I didn't have a roommate, due to his sudden realization that college wasn't for him. I ended up using his vacant bed as a resting spot for many computers.

With the workload I had, on top of repairing

computers, all I wanted to do was relax my body with a hot shower, then fall fast asleep in my twin-sized bed. Once I got into the shower, all I could do was sigh. The heat from the water felt so amazing.

No matter how relaxed my body got, the solid muscle that hung between my legs didn't want to join the program. My hands almost became prisoner to temptation, but I decided against it since all I really wanted at that moment was to sleep. My dick could wait.

It's weird how things occur when you least expect them to. As I walked from the restroom with only a towel on, there on my bed sat Mia Farrow, a popular cheerleader whose breasts never failed in making my mouth water.

"Hi, Curtis," she smiled.

"Hey, h…hey Mia."

"I'm sorry for just dropping in but my laptop been actin' up and I need it fixed tonight. Your door was unlocked so I figured I'd just wait for you. I know this is last minute but whatever you charge, I'll pay. Could you do this for me?"

"Um…yeah. Sure," I stammered.

"Great!" she exclaimed.

She stood from my bed, took off her jacket, then bent over to unzip the pink laptop bag positioned on my floor. I immediately became hard as a brick staring at the blue thong she wore.

When she turned her head toward me, the first thing she noticed was my dick that poked against the towel. She appeared shocked at first, but after allowing it to soak in her head, a smile appeared to her lips.

"Oh my," was all she said.

Embarrassed, I used both hands to cover my erection. My towel instantly fell from around my waist. Mia's eyes grew wide and that sexy smile of hers got even bigger. I become such a wreck when I get nervous. That became evident when I attempted to gather the parts of the towel that had come down. Things didn't work out in my favor. The entire towel dropped to the floor, exposing my super hard erection.

"Dammmmnnnn!" Mia exclaimed. "Curtis, I had no idea you was packin' like that. You put so many dudes on this campus to shame!"

I grinned as I quickly retrieved my towel and placed it back into position around my waist.

"I'm so sorry about that. It was an accident. I promise it was Mia." I apologized wholeheartedly.

"No need to apologize," she smirked, with a sly grin. "No need at all."

I rushed over to my dresser and began to retrieve a pair of boxers and shorts to cover my body.

"You don't have to do all that," Mia told me in the most sexual tone I've ever heard in my life.

"Huh?" I questioned, not believing what I was hearing.

"You don't have to put those on. This is your room. No need to do all that to make me feel comfortable. If you wanna walk around naked, then by all means do so."

I hesitated a bit before responding. A female had never hit on me before and it sure did sound like Mia was at that moment. I liked it, but it made me nervous as hell. What was I supposed to say? What was I supposed to do?

"It's okay Mia," I confirmed. "I don't mind

covering up."

Mia's upbeat and highly erotic tone was replaced with a look of irritation. I couldn't help but feel stupid for my remark.

"So let's see what's wrong with your computer." I added, trying to lighten up the mood.

"Sure, sure. Why not? That is the reason why I came in the first place, right?" she added dryly.

"Um...yeah."

I had just ruined the perfect opportunity for me to finally feel the insides of a vagina. Even if I hadn't gotten to third base, at least I could've licked her pussy or done something that would update my empty sex résumé.

We both sat on the bed, with an awkward distance between us, as I looked over her computer. It took me a good thirty minutes to find the issue and reboot the computer with no problem. Just when I was about to pack it up and send Mia on her way, because I felt horrible about turning down such a hot chick, she asked me to figure out why her computer would never connect to the school's Wi-Fi.

That took no time at all to fix. I pulled up Internet Explorer to test it out and it worked perfectly.

"What site do you wanna test the connection with?" I asked, while yarning. I was beyond tired.

"Just look in my bookmarks and choose a site from there," she told me, while strolling through her touchscreen phone.

I clicked on her bookmarks menu and had to blink my eyes several times, then focus on the screen to make sure I was reading the websites that were listed correctly. There was nothing but porn, porn and more porn. There had to have been at least one hundred sites displayed before my eyes and all I could do was sit there stunned.

"Oh...my bad. I was texting someone," Mia stated, after noticing I had yet to click on a site.

"Try that one," she suggested, while pointing to a site that was named, "Samantha's First Taste of Big Dick".

I sat there for a moment, contemplating whether or not I should have listened to her. Sure, I did love porn. In fact, I loved porn more than the average man, but I've never had the pleasure of watching a flick with a chick before. It was nerve wrecking.

"Chill out," Mia said, realizing how uneasy I had become. "We just testin' the internet out Curtis."

With that said, she moved my hand from the mouse and clicked on the video she had her eyes set on. It loaded up in two seconds flat and before I knew it, I was watching a black woman with large breasts finger herself.

The woman was stretched out on a black couch that was nowhere close to being lavish. It didn't matter because the moaning and squirming from her body easily distracted the viewer from the simple surroundings.

About a minute into the video, a tall brown skin guy entered the room. He was dressed in a red Polo shirt with blue jeans. However, those clothes soon came off after the woman seducing herself begged for him to fuck her with no mercy.

The man smiled, approached the woman with nothing but his boxers on and began to suck hard on her nipples. He swirled his tongue around each one, sending the chick over the edge while she continued to finger herself. As she moaned, my penis began to harden and grow right before my eyes...and Mia's.

Out of my peripheral vision, I observed as she licked her lips while staring at the now fully hardened flesh between my legs. I was still nervous as hell but the porn was making the situation a thousand times easier to cope with.

Mia and I sat in silence for five minutes or so. We didn't utter a single word until the guy in the flick placed his dick inside the chick's throat and began to pound in and out her mouth. She gagged as tears fell from her eyes. They had to have been tears of joy because even a blind man could see how happy sucking dick made her.

As the guy began to work her throat faster and faster, I began to imagine myself in his shoes, invading the wet mouth of a woman I'd never met before. I even got so caught up in the moment that my penis began to jump and pulsate. It was almost like my dick was begging to be sucked and rammed down a woman's throat.

Mia began to laugh after observing the muscle between my legs cry out for attention. My bad nerves returned and I used my hands to cover the imprint through the towel.

"Awe...don't be embarrassed." Mia continued laughing, but sounded quite serious. "I'm laughin' 'cause I never in a million years pictured you to have such a big dick!"

I knew what she meant. All my life men in the locker room and even my own friends had been envious of the abundant blessing I was holding. I didn't understand what the big deal was. I had heard somewhere that size didn't matter. It was all in the way a man used his tool. But from the way Mia was eyeing my package, I knew then for sure that I had something ladies would enjoy.

"Not to say I thought you were small or anything," she said, defending her case. "You're just so tall and skinny that that piece of meat shocked me."

I remained silent. I really didn't know what to say.

"It actually makes my mouth water, Curtis," Mia added.

That was all she had to say for my dick to jump once again. She squealed in excitement. She got so excited I thought she would have an orgasm just from observing my penis.

"That woman in this porn don't know shit 'bout suckin' dick baby. Want me to show you how it's supposed to be done?"

No words had to be said because my dick did all the talking. He yelled out, "Open up that throat!" while jumping at her again.

"I'll take that as a yes," she responded, removing the comfortable position my hands had on my dick, pulling the towel from around my waist and then swallowing my entire shaft down her throat.

I had to lie back on the bed. This was a sensation I had never experienced before. It was completely different from jacking off with my hands. It was ten times better!

I moaned and smiled like a kid in a candy store. The lock she had on me was magnificent. What was even more magnificent was the smile she gave me as her lips and throat worked like they wanted to be the highlight of my life thirty years later.

"Oh my God," was all I could mumble.

A strong and powerful orgasm was on the rise. My mouth wanted to tell Mia to move out the way because this volcano was preparing to erupt. But my body was on vacation. It wouldn't allow me to say or do anything at all to ruin the moment.

Mia figured out that I was about to cum by the way my breathing increased. She removed her mouth just in time as I squirted loads upon loads of nut in the air. A bit of it even hit her face.

"Wow. You almost lasted five minutes," Mia said, wiping the nut from her cheek.

She stood from the bed. As she began to pack her laptop and walk toward the door, I silently cursed myself. I had gotten so close to getting a taste of pussy and my eager dick was about to ruin it all.

No, this will not transpire, I told myself. *Not tonight, anyway.* I sprung up from the bed, pulled Mia by the arm and then locked her lips onto mine. It was my very first kiss, but I worked my tongue inside of her mouth as if I knew exactly what I was doing. I backed Mia up against the door, with my naked body pressed against hers. My excited dick poked her chest, ready and eager to finish our playdate. I massaged her already hardened nipples through her t-shirt. Her body felt so good pressed up to mine. It reminded me of a romantic film, except this time I wasn't forced to observe from a TV screen. I was now actually casted in the movie.

And it wasn't just any movie. The performance I gave needed to be nominated for big awards. I deserved an Oscar for how fast I got her out of her clothes. An Academy Award needed to be next because of how well and precise I sucked on her round breasts. And a Grammy should've been handed to me for how well I made Mia sing as I used my mouth between her thighs.

That's correct! For the first time in my life I ate pussy, loving every single moment of it. I was positioned on my knees with Mia's body lifted from the floor into my arms. My head was buried at her core, licking and biting, just as I had seen so many times in porn.

I smiled extremely hard when Mia moaned, "Damn, Curtis! You must do this a lot baby."

I deserved ten awards for that comment alone. I was a virgin eating a chick out like I had been doing it forever. Talk about talented!

My tongue darted in and out of Mia until she nutted all over my tongue and had to beg me to stop. She tasted so divine and a part of me feared I'd never get the opportunity again, so I could not help myself.

She led me over to the bed, then laid down on her back with her legs spread open wide. My dick was leaking tons of precum because of how turned on she had me. Her pussy looked beautiful as it summoned my mouth silently. I ate her out for several more hours until she told me to fuck her with no mercy, just as the chick from the porno had.

"You have any condoms?" I asked her without having to think too hard. I wasn't so horny that I couldn't use my brain to think. Babies weren't on the schedule for me until several years down the road.

"Yeah, hold on a sec."

She ran over to her pants, pulled out her wallet, unsnapped it, then pulled out a condom from a compartment. My hands held my dick firmly as she walked back over to me. Mia winked playfully at me, tore the condom wrapper with her teeth, then rolled it on my dick with her mouth.

You ready for this? I asked myself silently.

The time had finally come. I had patiently waited long enough.

Mia got on her back, then opened her legs wide, exposing a trimmed and well-kept pussy. Her hands rubbed my back up and down while I positioned the head of my penis at her opening. I tapped it on her clit several times before opening her lips and entering inside.

Let's just say it was heaven on earth, or something almost identical to it. The tightness of her vagina gripped me hard, suffocating my dick in a groundbreaking chokehold.

With each minute, each second, Mia pulled me deeper and deeper until I filled her up completely. When I tell you I filled her up, I filled her up! I worked her so good I swear she was screaming out several languages.

As we fulfilled our sexual desires, we attracted a horny audience. My suitemates next door hollered out chants and words of encouragement for me to tear her pussy up. All the excitement next door excited my dick even more, making me pound Mia's vagina like a dog in heat. The sound of her juices and my pelvis smacking against her body made it all even more worthwhile.

We had sex for about two hours until our bodies

couldn't take it anymore. After resting for about ten minutes, Mia asked if I had a ruler. I had no clue why she wanted one but I informed her that one could be found in the top drawer of my desk. She found it, then used it to measure the length of my soft dick.

"Hmm…ten inches," she smirked.

I had always wondered about the exact size of my dick, but never went as far to measure it myself. I figured it had to have been around eight inches, so my estimation was a bit off.

"Let's see how big you can get on hard," she added, before placing my rock inside her warm mouth.

I was able to grow to thirteen freaking inches! Mia informed me of how surprised she had been to take all of me inside both her throat and pussy. It fascinated her so much she told all her girlfriends about me. Before I knew it I had females coming by my room at all times of the day to see what all the talk was about. And I showed them with pleasure.

So, the moral to the story ladies, is that old saying "big things come in small packages" wasn't just created out of thin air. It's true. Never judge a book by its cover because you never know what you could be missing.

Wife Swap

I never, in all the days of my life, imagined I'd get an erection while hearing my wife moan and scream, "Oooh yes! Dig deep in my guts Daddy!" from the pleasure of another man's dick, divin' deep into her core. I also never thought I'd be bangin' the back out of my co-worker's wife while my co-worker fucked my wife. And not to mention, all of this shit happened right before my eyes without me feelin' not even a tad bit jealous. It all actually turned me on.

This didn't just happen out of the blue. We didn't all just decide one evening after dinner that we were curious to see how good sex would be with different partners. Things gradually escalated to the way they are now.

Kim and I once had a marriage that had a solid foundation to it. We used to tell each other any and everything. Communication was one of our strongest traits.

But as the years passed, things changed for the worst. I began to see less and less of Kim because of long hours at work. We had sex once a week at that point, but that decreased to at least once a month. I know we were both sexually frustrated since we used to fuck every damn night in the early stages of our union. But it's true when people say things can surprisingly change in the blink of an eye.

The woman who used to be so appealing to my eyes had become boring and dull. I know being a stay at home mom is hard work, but damn! I still expected her to try and keep her looks up. I still loved her regardless of how much she let herself go, but sometimes love isn't enough. Kim had lost her sex appeal and it turned me off so much I struggled to get a hard-on every time we did "the chore" of having sex.

Now I'm the type of man who loves sex. Jackin' off in the shower doesn't even compare to how good it feels to be inside a nice and wet pussy. And since things were far from perfect at home, my sexual frustrations began to hinder my performance at work.

I've always been a hard worker at the Pepsi factory, so when I began to slack off with my enthusiasm, Max, a close co-worker of mine, sat with me at lunch and took the initiative to ask if everything was alright.

"Yeah man," I confirmed to him. "I'll be okay."

"Don't look like you'll be okay," he added with much concern in his facial expression and tone of voice.

I sighed. "To be quite frank, Kim and I haven't been intimate in awhile."

He looked relieved, then laughed, "Is that all you worried about?"

"What you mean, is that all?" I didn't find shit funny. "I take my sex life serious man."

"I understand. I understand," he responded, chillin' out with the annoyin' laughter. "Try and spice the shit up a bit man," he advised. "Try role play...or using toys or somethin'."

"Already tried that shit."

"What?" he asked me like somebody told him the world was 'bout to end.

"Yeah...nothing's worked. I love Kim with everything in me, but the shit in the bedroom ain't workin' no more. I don't wanna end my marriage over somethin' like this."

Max saw the frustration in my eyes. I could tell he didn't know what to say but suddenly a bright idea popped into his head, causin' his eyes to get big.

"You ever tried to bring other people into the bedroom?"

"What?"

"Other people in ya bedroom," he repeated.

"Naw, naw. I heard you the first time. I just can't believe you asked me some crazy shit like that," I admitted. "Only a fool would do some shit like that. I'm tryna save my marriage, not end it."

He shook his head. "Man you can't believe everything you read in those magazines and see on TV. It doesn't ruin all marriages. People just have to walk into it with the right mindset. You gotta keep in mind that it's only for entertainment and when it's over, you'll be back to the regular routine of one on one."

"And how the hell do you know so much about this shit?"

He paused, then responded with no sign of embarrassment in his voice. "'Cause my wife and I are swingers."

"Wait, what did you just say?"

He repeated himself and I still couldn't believe that shit. Max didn't look like the type of guy who did shit like that, not to say I know how people who do that should look. Just sayin' that when I saw Max and his wife, Amanda, together, they always looked so happy. They were always so playful. He'd smack her ass, then she'd giggle and kiss him. Or she'd rub his dick in public then they'd go rush off to a restroom. It was shit like that that made me believe they honored that one on one shit...but damn, was I wrong.

Max told me to think about tryin' it with him and Amanda one night. I instantly dismissed that idea. I've always been a freak, but never ventured out to do anything that freaky. He later told me he understood how I felt and he had been the same way when his wife first introduced the idea to him. But ever since they gave it a try, they'd been as happy as newlyweds.

I thought the fuckin' idea was crazy as fuck. But a month later, I ended up blurted the idea out after a night of terrible and dull sex with Kim. Of course, she flipped out. She even started hittin' me with a pillow.

Uttering that comment ruined the remainder of our boring sex life. She hardly even wanted to look at me. I understood that it hurt her feelings, but I had needs and so did she. I knew very well that she wasn't into our sex life, just as I wasn't.

Kim didn't begin to entertain the idea of inviting other partners into our bedroom until she saw Max and Amanda in the flesh at a company picnic one Saturday evening. I saw how much she envied those two love birds. She wanted our spark back. And so did I.

Later that night while in bed, she asked me if I really thought the idea would help out our marriage. I said yes, not only because I was horny, but also because I honestly did believe it would bring some life back to our relationship.

Kim nodded her head and told me to set it all

up. She was willing to give it a try, for our marriage. So the next day I told Max the news. He told me he'd get back to me with the details on where and when it'd all go down later that week. I agreed and that was that.

I waited. I waited. And waited. And waited for what turned out to be a full week before Max told me anything. I thought about asking him what was takin' so long to set it all up, but didn't wanna seem like a nag, so I waited it out.

Max told me the following Friday would be perfect for dinner at his place, followed by what would go down as the beginning of a new chapter in my love life.

I was excited as hell to see what all the positive talk about a Wife Swap would be like. I hadn't even heard of the term Wife Swap until Max broke it all down for me. The first encounter was planned to include Max and his gorgeous wife having sex in front of me and Kim. The idea was for Kim and I to get so aroused that we would soon after begin to fuck also.

The second encounter would be a bit different. Max would fuck my wife and I would fuck his. There was both a positive and a negative to the situation. The positive was that I'd always thought Amanda was a fly woman. I wanted to know just how erotic sex with her could be. If her sex game was anything like her looks, it'd be off the damn chain!

But the negative side of the ordeal was that Kim was my wife and even though she bored me, I loved that woman to fuckin' death. When we said our wedding vows, I meant every single word. So to even participate in the Wife Swap would have gone against everything we promised all those years ago.

I allowed myself to ponder on those thoughts for a while but soon came to my senses. I needed some good sex and was about to fuck my friend's wife...right in front of him. How fuckin' hot was that?

That Friday rolled around before we knew it. Kim and I arrived at Max's two-bedroom apartment in no time at all. His place was about an hour away from home, but we made it there in about thirty-five minutes.

"We apologize for the place being so small," Max told us after welcoming us inside.

"Oh, no need for that bud," I reassured him.

Sometimes I wished Kim and I still lived in an apartment. It killed me to have to dig into my pocket every time something broke and needed fixin' immediately. Those days when all I had to do was call somebody and they'd come and fix the issue in a jiffy, were long behind me. But then again, it was nice to have the privilege of calling my home my own.

"It's good to see you guys!" Amanda said cheerfully, as she joined the three of us in the living room.

Kim and I stood from the couch to greet her. As I embraced her, I felt her hands brush against my ass then gather up enough meat to pinch it. My body jerked unexpectedly. Amanda laughed but Kim looked at me as though I embarrassed her. But I wasn't worried about her disapproval at that moment. I was anxious for things to get poppin'.

However, things didn't start out the way I anticipated. Amanda cooked a bomb-ass dinner that put Kim's cooking to shame. Not tryna talk bad 'bout my baby, but she can't cook for shit.

We ate until we couldn't eat no more, then returned to the living room. Amanda suggested that she sit next to me while Max sat next to Kim. We all agreed. But before sittin' down Kim gave me an uneasy look. I used my eyes and a lovin' smile to assure her that we were doin' the right thing.

"So, what's your favorite position?" Amanda boldly asked me, after not even a minute of sittin' down.

"Ummm..." I mumbled, unprepared.

"Amanda, what did I tell you about usin' ya head before speaking?" Max questioned with bass in his voice. It was the most bass I've ever heard out of him to be honest.

"I'm sorry, Daddy," she replied quickly.

Maybe it was just me, but the way Amanda responded to Max sounded too seductive for regular conversation. Then again, maybe I was just horny and everything her fine ass said was seductive. I don't know. But the way she said it made my dick brick up immediately.

"Let's see what's on TV," Max suggested.

"Yeah," I agreed. "Ain't the game on?"

"It sure is."

Max got from the couch, turned off the lights, then turned the television on to football. As all of this was going on, Amanda began to massage my swollen dick through my slacks. And boy did she stroke my shit just right.

As time began to slip away, Kim and Max made small convo about what was going on in the game. That's another reason why I fell in love with her. Who doesn't love a woman who loves to watch football with her man? Too bad I was too occupied to pay attention.

Amanda's tongue found my ear and she startin' nibblin' on it, then lickin' and blowin' in it. It made me squirm a little and when she unzipped my pants and cupped my nuts in her hands, all I could do was moan.

Kim immediately stood up and used the light from the television to confirm what we were doin'. She shook her head, then gave me a look that made me wanna disappear. She looked so hurt, so betrayed. It was as if she didn't expect me to go through with our plans; like she thought it'd be all talk and no action.

"Excuse me," Kim said to Max, before turning her nose up at Amanda and me, then rushing off down the hall to the restroom.

"Damn. I'm so sorry y'all," I said sincerely. "I really thought she could handle this."

"Don't you worry 'bout a thing," Amanda said softly.

She squeezed my dick one good time, then kissed my cheek. She rose from the couch and walked to the bathroom. Once she approached the door, she knocked gently.

No answer.

She knocked once more.

Still no answer.

Next time she knocked harder, almost to the point of banging.

"I don't wanna talk to you Simon," Kim spat through the closed door.

"It's not Simon. It's me…Amanda."

Kim allowed her brain to process what she'd just heard, then responded, "What do you want?"

"I just wanna talk."

"We have nothin' to talk about."

"Look...I know this whole situation is new for you. I just wanna talk about it. We're not gonna make you do somethin' you really don't wanna do Kim. I promise you that. Now please just open the door. It'll be me and you...talkin' one on one."

And just like magic, the door cracked open. Amanda turned her head towards us, and even through the darkness I could see a big smile on her face. She entered the bathroom, then shut the door behind her.

Meanwhile, I zipped my pants back up. It only felt right while being alone in Max's presence.

"Don't stress over it," Max said nonchalantly. "My Amanda is very persuasive. She'll get your wife out of there in no time."

I nodded my head, believing every word he said. A woman as fine as Amanda could talk her way into gettin' anything and everything she desired. But I began to doubt that thought when it had been twenty minutes since Amanda entered the bathroom with Kim.

"I'ma go see what's takin' so long," I told Max, standing up and walkin' down the hall.

"Alright," he replied, now with his eyes glued to the TV screen.

When I approached the door, I raised my hand to knock but the sound of somethin' fallin' over stopped me. I knew Kim could have a temper when people tested her. I was prayin' she hadn't knocked Amanda's lights out.

"Yo Max! Get over here!" I yelled, then opened the door to see somethin' that made my jaw drop and dick harden to its full potential.

Right in front of me was my wife butt-ass naked. She was bent over the toilet seat while Amanda, who was still clothed, ate her pussy out from the back. Kim moaned and breathed heavily as Amanda smacked her ass and moved her head back and forth. It made me begin to believe Kim secretly had a few lesbian fantasies in her closet 'cause she hadn't moaned like that for me in a hot minute.

"What's wrong?" Max asked, after rushing over to me. "Ohhhh," was all he said when he saw what was goin' down in the bathroom.

The shit seemed surreal. My wife, who in the past used to frown her face up at girl-on-girl action was actually gettin' her pussy licked by Amanda. I never thought I'd see the day. Never!

"I told you Amanda was an excellent persuader, didn't I?" Max added, nudging me in the shoulder.

All I could do was nod and then turn my attention back to the live action that was happening right before me. Before I knew what I was doing, my hand was between my legs, massaging the already awaken beast. With no shame at all, Max pulled down his pants and stepped out of them while revealing the fact that he wasn't wearing any boxers. He then began to beat his thick erection as his mouth watered at the sight of his wife eatin' out mine.

"What you waitin' for?" he asked, without looking away from the ladies.

"Huh?"

"Ya pants...how you gonna get ya dick sucked with them still on?"

Yeah...Max definitely had plenty of experience with shit like this. He wasn't ashamed of it either.

Gettin' nude in front of a man used to be uncomfortable for me, but after that night I had no trouble at all strippin' with a dude around. After that night, I can truly say I was sexually liberated.

I stripped down so only the top half of my body was covered, then began to stroke my dick just as Max did. We stood there jackin' until Kim soaked up the toilet seat and Amanda's face with her nut.

Amanda looked at me and smiled when she saw my massive dick in my hands. She wiped the cum off of her face then sucked every drop of it from her hand.

"Your wife's delicious," she told me.

"Can I taste it?" Max asked, lookin' over at me, then to my Kim who was recovering.

I nodded. Amanda walked toward me on all fours. She smiled mischievously before wettin' her lips. Kim moaned loudly as Amanda swallowed half of my dick. Hearing Kim moan like that made my dick begin to pulsate like hell, as Amanda wet my dick up to perfection. When she finished suckin' my dick, I could've sworn I had just dipped my dick inside of a pussy 'cause of how fuckin' wet it was.

And just when I thought things couldn't get any hotter, they did. Our sexual escapades continued in the bedroom where I fucked Amanda so good she had to bite down on my shoulder blades and Kim rode Max's dick so well he started moanin' louder than she did. It was like a damn playground in their bedroom.

The final act of the night occurred with Max positioned on his back while Amanda mounted onto his dick. I came in behind Amanda and pushed my Big Willy into her tight asshole. Max and I fucked her until she begged us to stop. I almost nutted when Max pulled out and there was an exceeding amount of nut from Amanda's pussy drippin' from his dick. She had no issues when it came down to lickin' and slurpin' it all down her throat, either.

While Amanda sucked Max to an orgasm, I titty-fucked Kim, slidin' my dick back and forth between her D-cups. There was a side of my wife I never thought I would see as she inserted a finger into my ass, makin' the experience feel even more enjoyable. I busted all over her tits and chin. Kim surprised me even more when she used her hands to rub all my nut around on her body. I busted again just watchin' that shit...and I didn't even have to touch my dick.

Kim and I thanked Max and Amanda repeatedly when it was all over. We had so much fun that we didn't wanna leave. Max promised me that we'd do it again soon. For the second time around, I suggested we have fun at my place. More rooms, more fun, right?

Later that night, Kim and I made love in our bedroom. And it wasn't that boring shit I was used to. It was exciting, sexy and unforgettable. She fell asleep in my arms afterward, with my dick still warm and secure inside of her pussy. That had to have been the best night of my life. Not only did I save my marriage, but I also lived a little. I broke my boundaries and discovered how much fun you can discover if you take a chance. Kim and I even branched out and found more couples at the park, at the movies, and even people who've visited our church. I know that's fucked up...but it is what the fuck it is. Don't judge me until you try it. Hey, speakin' of tryin' it, what are you and your wife doin' tonight?

Until the End of Time

She lies alone in an empty bed. The only sounds in the room are a clock on the wall that ticks entirely too loud and a flat screen television positioned directly in front of the bed. These distractions mean nothing to her, for her mind is focused more important matters.

She's been married to her high school sweetheart for twelve years. Over a decade has passed and she never has been able to give birth to a child, despite numerous attempts and thousands of dollars being spent to doctors who gave them hope.

Her eyes scan the room and fall upon a portrait placed on the mahogany nightstand. It's a photo she took a few years back with the love of her life. They look so happy…so joyful. Even to this day, he lights up her world. He still kisses her like he did back in high school and faithfully informs her of how much he loves her every single day.

So why would a woman who has a man so loving and so caring feel so heartbroken and sad? Why would her heart be full of sorrow when she has a love that women pray for every day of their lives?

The answers to those tear-jerking questions invade her mind constantly, never allowing an ounce of hope to surface. No matter how much she attempts to throw the truth out the window, it still finds its way back into her home; into her heart.

It all began a year and a half ago. She usually would regularly get breasts exams, even though cancer wasn't an illness that ran in her family. But one day she convinced herself they weren't necessary any longer. After several years of exams that came back negative, she saw no need in getting tested.

Sadly, after almost two years of not being tested, a glance in the mirror made her do a double take. A small lump on her breast almost made her jump out of her skin. And after an immediate visit to the doctor with her husband by her side, it was confirmed. Breast cancer had become a part of her.

As each day passed, she wished she could go back in time and undo her careless behavior. Doctors informed her that if the cancer had been caught sooner, things would've looked much more hopeful for her survival. If only she hadn't skipped those exams. If only she had paid attention to her intuition.

After over a year of receiving chemotherapy and numerous radiotherapy treatments, she knows her time is almost over. This didn't have to be told to her by a doctor. Her husband isn't responsible for informing her this information either. No one has to tell her, for she can feel the end is near as each minute slowly passes her by.

The mirrors around the house that used to be allies are now enemies. They provide very little comfort in helping her believe everything will be alright. The mere sight of herself makes tears fall from her eyes. The long light brown hair that once flowed down to her butt has all vanished, only leaving her head completely bald. The firm, athletic shape she once had pride in achieving has diminished to a frail, sickly frame. Every time her eyes meet up with the image staring back at her in the mirror, she has to tell herself over and over again that it is in fact herself, not a stranger.

He enters the room with a plate of breakfast in his hands and a warm, genuine smile upon his face. This brightens up her already depressing morning. Being able to see his face every day makes coping with cancer so much more bearable.

He is her everything. And she is his. It explains why she's so heartbroken over having no choice but to leave him. It brings pain to her soul to know she's leaving him without a single child to keep him company. All he'll have are the pictures, videos made, and memories of the life they shared over the years. It's plenty to cherish, but it isn't enough.

"Good morning gorgeous," he says cheerfully, gently placing the breakfast tray before her.

This brings a smile to her lips. "Good morning, baby."

The man's perfect in her eyes. Any man who could watch his wife as her body became weaker and weaker had to be a heaven-sent gift.

"How'd you sleep?" he asks, placing a kiss on her forehead.

She inhales the delicious scents that surround the room. She'll miss his cooking. The way he throws down in the kitchen could give top chiefs some tough competition.

"I slept okay. Nothin' spectacular," she jokes.

"Well...this food you're about to eat will be spectacular! Now eat up."

"You're right about that," she agrees. "As always."

"That's right! You know I put my foot into that food girl." He kisses her cheek then prepares to exit the room.

"Baby, wait," she pleads.

He stops in his tracks and doesn't have to look in her eyes to know she has something deep on her chest. He knows her like a book.

"What's wrong?" he asks cautiously, turning around to face his wife.

"I...I need to talk to you about somethin'."

"About what?" Now he definitely knows something isn't quite right.

"Come have a seat next to me," she tells him, patting a space on the bed.

As he approaches her, he takes her weak frame into consideration. He doesn't want to have this conversation, out of fear she'll say something he'd rather not hear. But he sits upon the bed and gently strokes her cheek, waiting for the dreadful news.

"You know I love you, right?"

"Of course," he smiles. "I love you too, baby."

"And my time spent with you over the years has been wonderful. I'm so thankful God gave you to me and me to you 'cause I-"

"Babe," he cuts her speech short. "What are you tryin' to say?" He'd rather she get to the point instead of prolonging the conversation.

She sighs, then places his hands into hers. This is

the hardest thing she's ever had to say, but it must be said. The weakness of her body silently informs her the time remaining is unknown. Another day. A couple hours. Maybe even thirty minutes.

"I'll just get to the point," she declares, looking away from him.

"Okay?"

She takes another sigh before summoning up the strength to tell her husband the awful news. "My time here is limited babe."

"We already talked about this." He stands to his feet and walks over to an open window. "We know there isn't much time left, but I don't wanna talk about it. I just wanna enjoy the time you have left with me.

"But you don't understand," she protests.

"I do, so let's just drop it."

She takes a moment to process her thoughts. She almost allows the conversation to end, but what's on her mind has to surface.

"No...I can't drop it."

"Baby, please I can't-"

"I'm dying. I don't know if I'll live to see tomorrow, or if there's enough life inside of me to be here in the next hour babe.

He slowly turns to face her. The look in her eyes confirms this tragic truth. He wants to punch the walls, throw his phone, or yell until he releases some frustration. It isn't fair. They belong together. Always have. And now she might not even live to see another hour?

"Look...we both know you're sick," he says, as though it doesn't stay on his mind every single second of the day. "But things will get better baby, I promise."

"Don't make promises you can't keep."

"But I can. You're going to get better," he tells her, while sitting back onto the bed.

She places her index finger to his lips. She's heard enough. He can't seem to accept the fact that time is being wasted while he's stuck in denial.

"No, baby. There's nothin' you or anybody else can promise me. Nothin'. My time here is almost over…and I'm not scared of dying. I'm only scared of losing you."

The tears begin to fall down from his face as reality sets in. She wipes away his tears, only to release tears herself. It doesn't take long for them to both begin releasing tears in each other's arms.

He allows his tough exterior to break down inch by inch with each tear. She comforts him. As they hold each other, no words are spoken. Nothing has to be said, for the dead silence seems so loud that it speaks for itself.

They lie comfortably in each other's arms for hours. Now that denial no longer hides the truth, he doesn't want to spend another moment away from her. Everything else in the world has become irreverent. Work, errands, and hobbies that makeup everyday life don't mean a thing to him. She's his number one concern.

Out of nowhere she whispers, "I want you to make love to me."

He opens his eyes. Doesn't say a word.

"I want you to make love to my body…one final time."

He nods, without having to think twice about the situation. As their eyes connect they know this might very well be the final time their bodies become one.

He positions her flat on her back, as delicately as possible, then removes the black panties from her waist. Sorrow consumes him like the aftermath of a great depression. This could very well be his final time touching, cherishing, and tasting that flesh between her thighs.

He decides not to waste anymore time worrying about how much longer he'll have her near. He allows these thoughts to exit and his tongue to enter her already moist vagina.

She sighs softly, closing her eyes. He has always been so talented with the task of bringing her body pleasure. He was her first, and now he'll be her last.

Gentle strokes glide against her folds, while his thick middle finger works magic of its own inside of her. He removes his finger, consumes every ounce of juice upon it into his mouth, then parts her folds with both hands, dipping his tongue into the fire that burns below.

Within a few minutes her body begins to tense up, signaling to him that it's almost time for a release. He puts an end to the pleasure of his tongue and prepares her for the satisfactory pleasure of his dick. It sits at her opening, pulsating, ready to enter its home, one final time.

He plunges in and out of her, all while never becoming too rough on her body. She rides him slowly and contracts the muscles of her vagina as tightly as her body will allow. As they let their bodies feed off of one another, they intensely stare one another down like never before.

By the time it's over they've had several orgasms and their bodies are both drenched in sweat. He lies flat on his back and pulls her body near until she lies on top of him. His fingers stroke her skin as they catch their breath. Before long, he's fast asleep.

That was one thing she always had been able to pride herself on. There was something about the power of her vagina that would always knock him out after a night of passion. That was the plan all along. She can't bare for him to see her take her last breath. That would be entirely too much to take.

She closes her eyes, well aware that this will be the final time she closes them. Her lips lightly kiss his chest, knowing they'll never kiss his soft skin again. She then takes one deep breath before her body gives out and her soul informs her that there will be no more pain.

Even though she departs from this earth prematurely, she was awarded the gift of true love for over a decade. This true love will continue to thrive and prosper in her absence, for a true love as strong as theirs can survive until the end of time.

Devotion Pt. 2

Love is more than just a four-letter word. It can heal a troubled heart, bring a cure to the pain of loneliness, and even cause one to lose their sanity.

Love is more than just a word one calls out in the moment of an intense orgasm. It's more than lust. More than infatuation. It keeps the cold warm at night. It serves as a reason to wake up every morning and get through the day. No matter how tiring and enduring a day in the big bad world can be, coming home to love every night makes it all worthwhile.

Some people can search this earth a million times for that one true love. They can travel to Egypt, book a trip to the Islands, and even sail the seas. However, even if they search high and low for the thing that their hearts desire to fill that void left empty in their souls, the search can still become a wasted effort. For love isn't something you can just wish upon a star for and it'll magically appear before your eyes. It comes when you least expect it. It appears when you begin to believe love will never become a part of you. It appears and takes you for an exhilarating ride full of unexpected twists and turns.

I know so much about this sweet four-letter word because it hit me in the face when I wasn't looking for it. Love came in the darkest hours of my life and turned everything I dreaded into everything I cherish. I found love when I began to believe I'd die without it. I found love...in you.

And this love, this sacred union we've been so blessed to have found, shall forever be cherished deep within my heart and soul. Many men have stepped on this poor heart of mine, such a long time ago. I decided I would lock it up and throw away the key. But you...you gave me a reason to love again. You showed this fragile soul of mine that everything I could ever need lies in you. So this heart of mine, it belongs to you. You can have the key and hold onto it until you take your final breath.

No other man can make me smile as brightly as you do. No other man gets me as excited as I do whenever we speak. No other man makes my blood rush and heart pace a mile a minute when we make sweet love underneath the covers. No other man has ever made me feel as special and unique as you do whenever you look into my eyes and whisper those special three words to me.

Some people will never run across a love like this, so forever will I grip it tightly, never intending on letting go. I see my future in you. You build me up when it feels my world has come crashing down. Because of this, I will forever be devoted to you. Without you, there's no me. As long as this heart of mine continues to thump inside my chest, my love shall always remain devoted to you.

Body II Body

I want that sweet pussy on my lips.

I reread the unexpected text message once more to make sure I'd read what I thought I had. I definitely wasn't dreaming.

Quit playin' and cum over!

I glanced over at my husband to ensure he was still sound asleep. Last thing I needed was for him to see me texting another man at three in the morning when I should've been laying up underneath him.

Don't you want this tongue inside that pussy?

I needed him to stop texting. He wasn't giving me any time to think and he knew exactly what he was doing. My pussy could never turn down a licking...especially if it was something that could put me into a deep slumber afterward. What woman in her right mind could turn shit like that down?

STOP! I texted back. I was two seconds away from throwing on some clothes and jumping inside my car.

He immediately responded. *We both know he ain't lickin' that kitty the way it should be licked.*

A deep sigh escaped from my lips. Why the fuck did he have to be right? My husband hadn't pleased me down below in weeks. And the last time he did, it was absolutely nothing to brag about. Even a virgin who'd never been touched before would've been disappointed.

His head game was terrible but his fucking was a damn abomination. I swear it felt like as soon as we'd get started, it'd be over. Bobby had never been a minute man. But as he entered his thirties things changed drastically. Maybe it was the long hours at work. Maybe it was the couple extra pounds he'd gained that he couldn't drop no matter how hard he tried. It could've been a number of things.

But whatever it was, I couldn't just sit around and deal with it. I was too horny for that. I was in my prime; a grown-ass woman whose sex drive was through the roof.

I informed my secret lover I'd be over soon, then slowly eased out of bed. Bobby would've cursed my ass out if he knew what I was about to do. Better yet, he would've choked the shit out of me. I think it was that thrill that excited me.

I tiptoed into the bathroom and stared at myself in the mirror. Even without makeup, my skin was smooth and blemish free. Bobby loved when I wore makeup. He was in love with perfection. He didn't want to see my pores or an occasional pimple upon my face. But my new lover, on the other hand, hated my face with makeup. He believed my true beauty shined when there wasn't a drop of it upon my face.

I washed my face, made sure my kitty was fresh and was in my car in no time. I didn't even bother changing out of my robe. What was the point? My clothes would come right off anyway.

On the short drive, all I could think about was how good I was gonna be fucked. I hadn't seen my lover in almost two weeks. My pussy was well overdue for some good lovin'.

Things were getting so heated between my lover and I that I had to pretend to be into my husband whenever we'd have sex. There was no point in getting all excited and shit when I'd have to finish the job once he fell asleep. Lord knew how frustrating that could be!

I didn't want to deny him sex just because he lost his mojo. So I just let him think he was still the man and got my rocks off elsewhere. What he didn't know wouldn't hurt him, right? That's what I tried to tell myself. But something inside of me kept telling me I was in the wrong. Those thoughts didn't last for long though. When I'd get horny, all I could think about was the new piece of dick I was riding on the regular.

"'Bout fuckin' time," my anxious lover said to me, once I'd made it to my destination.

"It didn't even take me thirty minutes," I remarked as I stepped inside.

"Still was too long. My dick been fienin' for you," he said, as he tugged at his dick through his pajamas.

I smiled, then untied my robe and allowed it to drop to the floor, exposing my fully nude body. His dick sprang to life as he walked toward me.

"You know Daddy gonna fuck the shit outta you, right?"

"That's what I want," I replied, ready to feel him deep inside of me.

I didn't have to utter another word. He fucked me right there on the floor. We gave it to each other like wild animals. He left bite marks on my neck. I left scratches on his back, something I never could do while with my husband. He would always complain about how I was too rough. But with my side piece I could freely allow my inner freak to come out and play.

Almost an hour later we made it upstairs to the bedroom. My body rested on top of his with my fingers toying with his chest hair. His fingers ran through my short curls, relaxing me so much that I didn't want to ever leave.

"Why are you still with him?" he asked out of the blue.

"What?" I asked, staring up at him. I thought we had finally laid this convo to rest.

"Why the fuck are you still with him? He doesn't please you like I do. You love me and I love you."

"I never told you I love you," I immediately told him.

"You don't have to say it. I see it in your eyes whenever I'm inside you."

I became silent. Truth be told, I did love him but those words could never escape from my lips. I loved my husband also and when I said my vows that I'd be there for him through sickness and health, I meant every word. I couldn't be faithful anymore, but I would never leave him.

"Tell me you love me," he whispered into my ear, then nibbled at my earlobe.

I sighed, then replied, "I can't do that."

I could feel the relaxed mood instantly change. I had no idea what was going through his mind. All I could hope for was that he wouldn't make a big deal out of it. The only man I needed to be saying those three words to was my husband.

"I don't understand," he said, as he released me from the tight embrace. "I know you love me. I see it in your eyes every time we make love. You can't deny that shit."

I still had no words to utter. How do you tell a man who loves you that you can't say it back because you honor your vows, but you're out cheating anyway? What a mess!

"Just say it," he continued. "Say it and I'll never ask you to say it again."

No lie, I was tempted to say what he wanted just so I'd never have to say it again. But there was also a possibility that things could change drastically if I allowed those words to escape from my lips. What if he'd want me to leave my husband? What if he wanted us to build a life and family of our own since the feeling was mutual?

"I can't baby...I just can't," I told him, hopeful that this would be the final time we addressed it.

After a moment of silence, he said, "Cool." Then he rolled over onto his stomach with his head turned away.

I let out a deep sigh of frustration. It was my own fault. If I had remained true to my faithful husband I wouldn't even be in such a predicament. If I had simply turned down the flirts and the way this man made my heart flutter, things wouldn't have spiraled into a mess.

My thoughts continued to race for what felt like hours. My lover was in a deep sleep but all I could think about was how I was hurting him.

I looked over at his chocolate, muscular back. I craved to run my manicured fingertips across it. My lips wanted to make contact with his smooth skin, then show him how much I loved him by making love to

him. But what good would that do? I did that every
time we got together. And if I didn't utter the words
from my lips, it wouldn't be enough to satisfy him.

He rolled over onto his back. I watched as his
chest moved up and down in a steady motion. I wished
I could place my head on his chest and listen his heart
beat as I also drifted off into a deep slumber. But the
clock on the nightstand informed me I had no time for
sleep. I had already overstayed my welcome and
needed to be heading home within the next hour or so,
before my husband awoke.

I found it strange that even though all of my
sexual frustrations had been fulfilled downstairs, I still
had the urge to climb on top of him and ride him until I
felt his dick squirt deep inside me. Time was limited
and I knew I'd be taking a risk if I started up another
round of hot sex. But at that moment I didn't care
anymore. I would be concerned with the consequences
later.

In a swift motion, I pulled the covers back, then
positioned my face so it was directly in front of his soft
dick. I admired its beauty, even on soft, before taking it
inside of my wet mouth.

Softly, I sucked nice and slow. He stirred in his
sleep as his dick began to harden and lengthen inside
my mouth. As it grew I massaged his balls in one hand
and rubbed his surfboard abs with the other. He
moaned, waking up more and more with each slurp
upon his dick.

"Babe," was all he said.

He didn't have to say another word. I knew he
was loving the feeling I was bringing forth to his body.
Every time I gave him head he'd have to control his nut

so he could last longer.

We moaned together as I sucked harder and got his dick wetter. My hand moved down to my dripping wet pussy and inserted a finger inside. His hand roamed to my right nipple and pinched and teased it between his fingers. I removed my fingers from my soaked pussy and brought them to his face. He lifted his head and sucked away at my wet fingers.

Watching that man suck my juices turned me the fuck on. I moved my head faster, while sticking a finger into his tight ass. He flinched at first, then relaxed and allowed me to work my way inside.

That was another thing I loved so much about my lover. I'd always had a desire to try new and exciting things between the sheets and he had no problem with it. My husband on the other hand would never go for me sticking a finger up his ass. He didn't give a fuck if it was the male G-spot. He wasn't going for any of that shit.

"Fuck," my lover moaned, opening up his legs and bending his knees so I had more space to play inside of him. "Damn girl. What you doing to me?"

I allowed my mouth to do the talking as I removed his dick from my throat and my fingers from his ass. He didn't know what the fuck hit him when my tongue licked his tight hole. He shivered, which caused me to giggle silently.

I honestly don't know why I did it. I'd never had the urge to put my tongue back there before, but something told me to do it and judging from my lover's reaction, he loved it! That encouraged me to continue the exploration.

"Oh my God!" he cried out, when I parted his

cheeks with my hands and stuck my tongue inside his opening.

I darted my tongue in and out, making him lose his mind. As my tongue swirled inside of him, my right hand began to jack his hard dick. Precum moistened my hand as I pumped his dick like I was trying to milk every ounce of nut out of him.

"Oh shitttttttt!" he yelled, as he exploded a load all over my hand and hair.

I removed my tongue and proceeded to suck up all the nut that continued to pour out of his dick. He held onto my head as he squirmed and moaned.

"How was that?" I asked with a huge grin, after I'd slurped up every bit of his nut.

"Fuckin' awesome!" he laughed.

I brought my lips to his and shoved my tongue inside his mouth. His huge hands cupped my ass cheeks while my body pressed up against his. My tits began to harden from the pressure of the body-to-body contact. His tongue played with mine, turning my body heat up another notch.

I felt his dick rise up against my ass, which gave me the right away to slip it inside of my impatient pussy. I was so fucking wet so there was no struggle getting his extraordinary length completely in.

"Ride yo dick," he whispered in a husky tone.

I began to rock my hips back and forth slowly.

I asked, "Oh, it's mine?"

"Fuck yeah, it is," he replied instantly. "You already know this."

"Yeah, I know it's mine," I said, working my hips to a quicker pace.

He smacked my ass, then said, "Tell me this

pussy's mine."

I fell silent. Why'd he have to be so difficult? Yes, it was his but I had to be careful with words like that. He couldn't be putting ownership on me when my husband came first.

"I said tell me it's mine," he demanded, smacking my ass much harder this time.

I moaned, but still refused to say what he needed to hear. Instead, I rode him even faster. My fingers clutched onto the headboard, causing it to rock with great force every time my hips moved.

My head tilted toward the ceiling as my eyes rolled to the back of my head. I was about to cum so hard. I could tell it was gonna be even more explosive than before.

But just when I felt myself about to release loads of passion onto his dick, he pushed me off of him. I was confused at first, but knew what was going on as soon as he put me in doggy-style and applied pressure to my back to get a good arch. He wasn't gonna let me cum until I said what he wanted to hear. Tricky bastard!

He slid back inside of me with one solid thrust. I moaned and tried to move. But he pulled my hair with one hand and held onto my waist with the other. I wasn't going anywhere. I was his prisoner until he was finished doing what he pleased with me.

"Say you love me baby," he said softly.

When I didn't respond, he pulled out until only the tip of his dick remained inside me, then rammed himself back in, until his balls rested against my skin. He repeated himself, with unmistakable agitation in his voice.

"Baby, go easy," I pleaded, with hope he'd show

a tad bit of mercy.

"Nawwww, fuck that," he told me. "You gonna take this dick exactly how I give it to you."

He began to fuck me harder than he ever had before. I was hollering louder each time he pushed inside of me. I wasn't used to such rough play but it kind of turned me on to feel him taking control of me.

I felt myself about to bust again so I did my best to conceal it. I wasn't trying to get my shit interrupted. But he knew my body so damn well that even though I reframed from twitching or moving, he was well aware of what was going on.

He pulled out of me, leaving me more pissed than earlier. I took my orgasms seriously. If I couldn't nut, I'd walk away angry as fuck.

My lover placed me on my back, opened my legs and pushed himself back into my ruthlessly-teased pussy. She wanted that nut just as much as I did.

Once again, there was no mercy given. He rocked me so fierce that a nut was on the rise not even a minute later. I prayed to God that the man would allow me to release. I needed to release! Goddddd, I needed that nut!

I know this sounds terrible, but God must've answered my prayers because I was able to achieve exactly what I craved. My nails dug into his flesh as my teeth bit into his neck like a thirsty vampire. He hollered from the pain but didn't stop the hurting he was putting on my pussy.

"Shittttt!" I called out. "Shit, shit, shitttt!"

He moaned loudly in my ear as my juices began splashing out onto his dick and our bodies, adding a sticky mess to our already sweaty flesh. No one had ever fucked me so hard and I was sure no one would ever compare.

By the time I'd finished releasing my load, it appeared that he was just getting started. One thing I loved about my love was that he could literally go for hours without busting. It was such a relief since I couldn't get an all-nighter at home, but that night I was exhausted and wanted him to hurry so it could end.

He wasn't anywhere near finished though. My pussy continued to bust for the next hour and a half. There was no doubt in my mind that I'd have to soak in the tub when I made it home.

"Tell me you love me baby," he whispered, between kisses to my lips.

"I can't," I mumbled, through my dry-ass throat.

"Say it," he ordered, then lowered his head to lightly bite on my left nipple.

"Nooo," I cried.

He bit a little harder, causing tears to escape from my eyes. He maneuvered his hand down to my clit and squeezed.

I came instantly with a never-ending flow of cream that trickled from my fountain. He came right along with me with an explosion harder than my own.

"Fuck baby!" he said into my ear.

"I love you! I loveeeee you sooooo much baby!" I exclaimed without thinking.

We laid there for a while, his body on top on mine and my legs wrapped tightly around his waist. Body to body; in a sinful disaster that had become so deep it was too late too ever let go. Our sweat and the sticky evidence of what had gone down had dried completely. My rapid heartbeat was now beating quietly. But my thoughts had yet to subside.

"Stop thinking so much," he eventually told me.

"Who says I'm thinking about anything?"

He released his dick from the captivity of my pussy, rolled over onto his back and said, "I know you, remember?"

"I can't help but to think about-"

"Shhh," he interrupted me. "Don't say another word. You need to go home and be with your husband, babe. I'll be here whenever you need me."

"Are you still going to the annual picnic next Saturday?" I asked, hoping he hadn't changed his mind.

"Yeah, I'll see you there."

I smiled lightly. We'd probably end up excusing ourselves and go fuck in the restroom. It was dirty as fuck because he was my husband's co-worker and over the years they'd become very good friends. It was never my intention for a full-blown affair to transpire though.

I looked into his eyes, kissed his lips then left, even though it killed me inside. On the drive home, all I could think about was how fucked up my situation had gotten. I did love him and I had no idea what would happen. But I knew something had to change. I couldn't continue to have my cake and eat it too, right?

Beast

"Hold up! Hold up nigga!" a broad I was bangin' started hollering loud in my ear.

"What?" I was annoyed as fuck already 'cause every time I pushed in deeper, she started whining.

"I can't do this shit."

"What?" I pulled out just enough to look at her. "What the fuck you mean you can't do this? That ain't what you said earlier."

"I know what the fuck I said, but this shit ain't fuckin' working. You are too fuckin' big," she complained.

"That ain't what you said ten minutes ago when you was jackin' this dick," I told her, trying to keep my cool.

"Ugh! Just get off of me. I'll jack ya dick so you can get ya nut."

That offer didn't sound appealing to me at all. I had brought her sloppy ass over to fuck. And fuckin' was what I wanted. When I was done she could take her triffin' ass on home.

"Man, just chill," I told her, pushing myself as deep as I could go into her loose pussy.

"Ouchhhh! Stop! I can't take it."

"Relax. It won't hurt after a few more minutes," I tried reassuring her.

I went very slow, tryin' not to hurt her too bad, but tryna to feel some type of pleasure also.

"Please just stop," she whined, with her ugly-ass face screwed up.

"Yo, I'm goin' slow. So chill."

"No! I will not chill nigga. Get off me!"

I kept goin', ignorin' her ass. Pretty soon I knew she'd feel good. You can't expect a big-ass dick to go inside you and not feel any pain. I was surprised she even felt anything at all since her pussy had no fuckin' walls.

"Help!" she screamed at the top of her lungs. "Help me! This nigga rapin' me! Help! Rape! Rapeeee!"

I put my hand over her mouth and did my best not to punch her ass in the face. She didn't want the dick anymore, so I was done with her ass. I put her out, butt-ass naked, then tossed her clothes and slammed the door. She could get dressed in the street for all I cared. One thing I didn't take lightly was that rape shit. I had already been to jail earlier that month for some bullshit charges. I wasn't 'bout to take my black ass back 'cause of that ugly-ass trick.

The only reason I fucked with her like that was because she'd had all my homeboys already. Most women can't handle my dick so I figured if she could take all of those dicks up in her pussy, she should've been loose enough to take mine. Guess I was dead-ass wrong.

I looked down at my soft dick. "Sorry Beast. I tried to get you some play. Bitches be trippin' yo."

I know all y'all wondering who the fuck Beast is. Beast is a name this chick called my dick after I fucked her brains out. She was my first, but she told me I fucked like I'd been fuckin' for years. She was even more surprised by the size of my dick. I've been nothin' but bones with very little body fat my entire life. She would always joke that all the meat on my body was dangling between my legs. So, I kept the name. I kinda liked it. Plus, it described my stick to perfection.

After makin' sure the water temperature was just right, I hopped in the shower and jacked my dick thinkin' 'bout fuckin' the shit outta Halle Berry and Stacy Dash at the same damn time. I had a thing for older women who looked young as hell.

When I got out the shower, I put on lotion from head to toe. I knew a lot of thugs who would never be caught dead putting lotion all over. But I wasn't 'bout to walk around looking ashy as fuck. I'm a hood nigga. Always will be. But bet on yo life you'll never catch me slippin' with my appearance.

"Yo," I said, answering my ringin' phone and lookin' in my closet for somethin' fresh to put on.

"Hey baby. What's up?"

I looked at my phone and cursed aloud. It was my own fault for answering without checkin' to see who it was.

"Why the fuck you callin' me, girl?"

"'Cause I miss you...and I miss yo big fat dick Daddy."

"Well, it sure as fuck don't miss yo ass."

"Why it gotta be like that?"

The bitch was trippin'. We dated for about a month until her seven-year-old son called me one day and asked why I was fuckin' his mom. And those were his exact words. What kind of shit is that? I didn't even know she had a kid. Turned out she was married with four kids…and was only twenty-two.

If I had known the truth from the beginning I probably still would've fucked her. She wasn't my wife. But I knew fo' sho I wouldn't have dated her knowing she had so much baggage.

"'Cause you made it like that," I huffed into the phone. "Shouldn't have lied in the first place."

"Come on now. Would you have still been interested in me if I had been honest?"

"Hell no," I confessed quickly. "But I still would've fucked you."

"I want more than that. I want you all to myself."

I sucked my teeth. "Bitch you need to be worried 'bout that crazy-ass husband of yours that be tellin' yo kids you a ho."

"I ain't worried 'bout his sorry ass. If he could slay this pussy right, he wouldn't have to worry 'bout all that." She paused then said, "So 'bout you and me. When we gon make this shit official?"

"Bitch, bye."

I hung up on her ass then tossed my iPhone on the bed. I made a mental note to block her ass when I got a chance. The last thing I needed was another woman stalking me. Been there, done that.

After picking out my attire for the day, I decided to stop by my boy Leroy's crib. I hadn't seen him in a minute since I had started my new job. He on the other hand wasn't working at the moment. After getting laid off two years prior, he didn't feel the need to work anymore, especially since he had a fine-ass woman to take care of him.

I didn't understand how he did it. Personally, I

have and always had too much pride to ever let a woman or anybody else for that matter take care of me. I had been my own man since I left my mom's place at age sixteen. And it would forever be that way until I died.

"Jacob!" Leroy's wife greeted me at their front door. "I didn't know you was comin' over."

"Hey Tiara," I said with a smile. She was lying like fuck. I was pretty sure Leroy had told her I was coming over. He had straight up OCD and he hated when the place looked a mess. Tiara probably had been cleaning the house up until my arrival.

"It's so good to see you. I missed you boo."

Here we go again, I told myself.

"Why don't you ever call?"

"You ain't my homeboy, that's why. You my homie's wife. That shit ain't cool."

"Fuck that," she said with a grin, as she stepped way too close for comfort. "I'm tryna get a piece of this dick."

She grabbed a handful of my meat then gave me the most seductive face I'd seen from a woman in a very long time. She started movin' her hands up and down, makin' my shit hard though my jeans.

"Tiara, what the fuck you sayin' to that man? Let him inside," Leroy yelled from the living room.

She rolled her eyes then gave me a wink. She stepped aside and allowed me to walk inside, but made sure to tap my ass as I walked by.

"What the-" I said, turnin' around to find her smiling her ass off.

She winked again and whispered, "You got my number, so use it."

I did have her number, but only 'cause *she* put it in my phone herself.

I shook my head then headed to the living room to holler at my boy. Bitches were trippin' hard that day. Wanted the dick so damn bad but couldn't even handle my shit. What the fuck?

"Yo!" Leroy yelled out, gettin' up from the couch and dappin' me up.

"What's up my nig?" I asked.

"Nothin' much. Just chillin' yo."

He was always chillin'. The nigga needed a job that didn't consist of sittin' on his ass all day watchin' SpongeBob. That's right. Muthafuckin' SpongeBob Squarepants!

"Tiara, what the fuck happened to the outfit you had on earlier?" Leroy asked, as she came struttin' into the living room with two glasses of gin and juice. "Why the fuck are you wearing a damn robe with yo tits all out?"

"Calm down. I was about to shower, but then Jacob rang the doorbell."

"Shower my ass. Put those glasses down then get the fuck to showerin'."

Tiara disappeared into the bedroom with an undeniable look of disgust plastered on her face. She knew she was dead wrong for that shit. Just like the time she tried to fuck me 'bout two years ago.

I didn't know Leroy wasn't home that day when I showed up to his crib uninvited. Tiara opened the door, shocked to see me, but also clearly excited. She told me Leroy had gone to the unemployment office, but I could wait on him until he got back. I accepted the invitation only because she mentioned he'd be returning soon.

Little did I know, she had other plans up her sleeve. As soon as I was in the house, she jumped on me and shoved her tongue in my mouth. Immediately, I pushed her trifflin' ass to the floor and headed for the door.

"Wait!" she called out after me.

"What?"

"I'm sorry Jacob. I don't know what came over me," she said, as she walked toward me. "I just been so frustrated for months. Since Leroy lost his job he hasn't touched me. He barely even talks to me."

She was on the verge of tears and I was feeling sorry as hell for her. Tiara was a sexy chick. She deserved good sex on the regular just like the next chick.

"Damn, I didn't know that."

"Yeah," she continued. "I really didn't mean to do that. My body is just goin' crazy right now."

"It's cool. I'll keep this between us. Just don't try no silly shit like that again, alright."

She nodded her head, then gave me a tight hug. We had never hugged before so it felt awkward, especially after the shit that had just gone down.

When I tried to end our weird embrace, Tiara reached between my legs and squeezed my dick. I looked down at her, ready to curse her ass out. She was actually smiling. Probably because of the size of my dick. Even though it wasn't on hard, it was still pretty impressive.

"Hold up now," I told her, not wanting things to get out of hand. "What the fuck you doin'?"

"'Bout to suck this big stick," she laughed, then

pushed me to the door, got down on her knees and quickly pulled my lengthening dick from the zipper of my jeans.

Okay, I know this shit is gonna sound fucked up. And I don't blame y'all for thinkin' I ain't shit. But as soon as Tiara's tongue flicked over the head of my dick, I was gone. I have never in my life turned down an opportunity to receive some head and I wasn't about to start that day either.

I closed my eyes as she worked her magic. At that moment, she wasn't one of my closest friend's wife. She was just some broad licking my stick.

"Mmmhmm," I moaned. "Suck that shit girl."

My fingers interlocked into her weave, massagin' the braids that held her extensions in place. I wanted to see just how much of my dick she could take, so I fucked her throat without a bit of compassion. She gagged and cried but kept on wettin' my dick up.

I was impressed once almost all of the twelve and a half inches were stuffed down her throat. I wanted to make this a regular thing. That's until I looked down at her lust-driven eyes and realized what we were doin'. It was wrong. Dead-ass fuckin' wrong. Some good friend I was.

I decided it was time to jet. But then I heard a car door outside shut, I started to panic and sweat like a lil' bitch.

I tried to push the bitch off of me, but she just kept on suckin' on my shit. The closer I heard footsteps approach the door, the harder she sucked. And when I heard keys jigglin' outside the door, I busted a hard, thick-ass nut down Tiara's throat.

Now, I knew we both should've gotten caught

and had our asses beat. I know I was wrong and I bet Leroy would've fired shots at both me and Tiara if he had caught even a glimpse of what we had been up to. Thank God he didn't.

I was able to put my dick away and Tiara sprinted upstairs to the bedroom so fast I could've sworn she'd been a running back in a past life. Leroy entered that house not knowing a damn thing and I'd take that shit to my grave.

"That woman is somethin' else," Leroy said to me, bringing me back to the present.

"Yeah, she really is," I agreed without hesitation.

"I just know she cheatin' on me." He shook his head. "And when I find out…it's her ass."

I had absolutely nothin' to add to that comment.

"And whoever the muthafucka she fuckin is, gettin' it too."

Quickly, I changed the subject. I was pretty sure Tiara got her side dick on the regular and I was glad we had never taken things that far. I couldn't do that to my boy, and I loved my life too much to put it in jeopardy.

Leroy and I chilled for a few hours, talked, smoked, you know, shit niggas do when they chill together. Then I had to bounce. I had promised my mom I'd stop by her crib for Sunday dinner so I damn sure couldn't miss that shit.

Before I could even get out of the driveway, my hands were rubbin' across my dick. I was long overdue for a nut. But not just any nut. A nut from a fuckin' a tight-ass pussy was what I needed. Seemed like that wasn't possible though, since no one could handle my dick. So jackin' had become my one and only option for bustin' a nut.

I had tried one of those fake pussies that claim they feel just like the real thing, but that shit wasn't worth it. I remember being cautious as fuck when it was delivered to my door. I was nervous of anyone seeing me with it, even though it was packed away in a brown box.

Stickin' my dick inside of it felt great at first, but when I tried to push all of my dick inside I had a change of heart. I wanted to be able to push every inch inside, but no toy or woman was able to fulfill that desire.

So, there I was at the fuckin' red light jackin' my dick. I had no shame. This had become a hobby of mine recently. My love for havin' sex in public was the root of it.

I massaged my stick in my hands while driving and as soon as I would approach a red light, I jacked rapidly. I accidentally ended up blowin' the horn at the car in front of me when my hard dick hit the sterling wheel. Whoever it was gave me the middle finger. That was the least thing on my mind though. If they had a problem with me they could come suck my big fat balls while I busted this nut on their face.

I imagined it to be a woman in the car ahead of me that saw me jackin' in her rearview mirror and decided to pull over and let me have my way with her. I jacked quicker as thoughts raced about fuckin' her throat, then slippin' inside of her pussy. I was about to bust a nice-ass nut, but the sound of sirens prevented it from happening.

I looked around me to find a police car to the right of me. The female officer signaled me to pull over as the light turned green.

"Fuck!" I yelled, hittin' the sterling wheel.

That was the last thing I needed. I had had enough trouble with the police in my past.

"Are you doing what I think you were doing, sir?" the attractive officer asked me, once she made it to my car window.

Even through her uniform, I could imagine how nice her body looked naked. Her skin complexion was just right too. I was a dark man loved who loved himself some sexy-ass redbones!

"I'm not sure what you mean, officer," I lied as best as I could.

Her eyes roamed down to my lap and widened.

"Oh my God!" she cried out, then looked around to see if anyone had overheard her.

I looked down and could've shot myself. I'd done a terrible job of stuffin' my dick back into my jeans. The head was inside but she could clearly see I had a monster down there.

"What the fuck," she whispered, staring down at it hard. "It's sooo big." She quickly realized what she was doing, then said, "I'm going to need you to step out of the car sir."

"Really? I really have to get going somewhere."

"NOW!" she ordered.

I fixed my jeans to the best of my ability, then got out of my car as quickly as I could.

She just stood there for a moment, watchin' me. I ain't gon lie. A nigga was nervous as fuck!

"Turn around."

I obeyed. She then began to pat me down. Her hands started at my back and moved down to my thighs.

"I don't see why you need to do this," I said, once I thought she was done.

"Shut up!" she yelled, forcin' my body onto my car then pressin' her body against me and grabbin' at my dick. She began to rub me right then and there, in public. Cars were driving by, but I'm sure no one suspected I was actually getting molested instead of being searched.

"Mmmm," she moaned, once my dick was brick hard.

I wasn't complainin' at that point. I would let her sexy ass molest me all night if she wanted.

Next thing I knew, I was handcuffed and put in the backseat of her police car.

"You takin' me to jail lady?"

"Didn't I tell you to shut up?" she asked, staring me down in the rearview mirror.

I wasn't scared of goin' to jail. I had been there long enough to know what to expect. But I wasn't 'bout that life anymore. I wanted to go back to school, make my mama proud. The hood would forever be a part of me, but bettering myself was my main focus.

We rode for about five minutes until we reached an abandoned building. Now I ain't no fuckin' dummy. And I wasn't up for some shit I'd seen in plenty of horror movies. If that bitch wanted to murder me, she had another thing comin' to her.

When she opened the backseat door, I was prepared to kick the shit outta her pussy then run for the hills. But those violent thoughts subsided when she began to undress right in front of me. I couldn't see her face, but I was sure she had to have been smilin' 'cause of the way my dick began the throb. I immediately pulled it out and started jackin'.

Now I had been lucky to have seen and done a lot of freaky things in my past, but this was beginning to become the best yet. All those threesomes and freaky women weren't shit compared to this. I mean, who could say they actually experienced what I was doing at that moment? Not many!

Once she had stripped away every piece of clothing, including her black bra and panties, she climbed into the car and ordered me to lie on my back. I did so in a heartbeat as she shut the door.

"That dick is beautiful," she said, lookin' down at the piece of meat in my hand. "I want it."

"Then take it," I smiled.

She gave me a look that said she didn't appreciate my cocky attitude, then took my dick into her hands and inserted it inch by inch down her throat.

It felt like her throat had no end and my dick could go deeper and deeper until every inch was buried inside her mouth. And that's exactly what happened. It amazed me how good she was. Sure, I'd had awesome dome before, but this woman didn't even have to prepare her throat for my dick. She just took it, which lead me to believe she had absolutely no gag reflexes at all.

I could only take 'bout five minutes of her excellent deep throatin' before I was 'bout to nut. I warned her, but she wouldn't stop. She didn't stop until she had sucked up every drop of my nut.

Wiping my cream from her lips, she smiled to herself. Looked like she had plans to really put that pussy on me. That was cool with me. She released me from the handcuffs and tossed them into the passenger seat.

I was already out of breath before we had even started fuckin'. She didn't care. She wanted a piece of Beast. And he rose again, despite how exhausted I had become from the nut.

Beast slipped inside of her wet pussy with little trouble at all. I wasn't the least bit surprised by this. Any bitch could get it inside. The trouble began when I tried to push in all of it. I didn't want to screw the opportunity up so I allowed her to do all the work.

I pulled her micro braids down from the updo style she was rockin'. She looked gorgeous with her titties bouncin' up and down, while her tight pussy walls pulled me deeper and deeper inside of her. She looked like a goddess and I wanted to fuck the shit out of her; give her something she'd never forget.

"Fuck me nigga," she whispered, as though she could hear exactly what I was thinkin'."

Shittt! She didn't have to tell me twice. I sat up so I could suck her tits. She moaned in my ear and grinded back and forth.

That was enough foreplay for me. I pushed her body between the two front seats, then fucked her just how I had imagined.

"Fuck, yesss! Fuck this good pussy!" she cried.

"This some bomb-ass pussy, bitch."

She turned her head back and stared at me.

"Watch it, nigga," she warned. "Don't forget who the fuck you fuckin'. I ain't one of these hood bitches you used to fuckin'."

"My bad," I apologized quickly.

A couple of seconds later we were back to fuckin'. I pulled her head back by her micros, then kissed her lips as my dick pumped in and out of her. She kissed me back and used one of her hands to grab onto my ass and push me in deeper.

"I want all of it," she moaned, when I gave her mouth air to breathe.

"You sure 'bout that?"

She sucked her teeth. "Just do it."

And I did just that. I pushed every last inch of Beast into her pussy. She yelped so much I thought she was cryin'.

"You want me to stop?" The shit felt amazin', but I didn't want to fuck her pussy up so bad that she'd take me to jail afterward.

"Did I say stop? Keep fuckin' me," she ordered. "I can take it."

The tiredness I felt earlier was long gone. I followed her orders and a few minutes later she started throwin' her ass back, meetin' up with my thrusts. I smacked her ass, she bit my arm. I pinched her nipples, she played with my sac. All of this continued until I could feel myself about to bust.

"I'm cummin'!" she yelled.

We both came in unison. It was out of this world amazin'! It was by far the best nut of my life and the shortest amount of time I'd ever came while inside of a pussy. That woman just had some unbelievable shit between her legs.

"That was...too good," I told her, as I pulled my dick out and fell back into the backseat.

She smiled. "You know I ain't done with you, right?"

"Oh word? I'm down," I told her.

"Then get over here and eat this pussy."

She sat down on the armrest and opened her legs as far as they would go. I wasted absolutely no time in stickin' my long tongue out and eatin' her pussy like it was a fancy dessert at a restaurant. It tasted so good that after she came all over my face I didn't stop until she came again.

After cummin' so much I figured she would've had enough. But she wanted some more of Beast. And I had no problem givin' her what she wanted. Who knew when I'd be able to find someone to take all of me again. I decided it was wise of me to fuck as long as she could hang.

We fucked one more time inside the car that night before takin' things to the roof of the car. I fucked that pussy so good she could barely get back into the car. And I couldn't help but smile when I saw all the cum we'd left on the roof. It was hot as fuck.

On the way back to my car, there was silence. It was as if nothin' had ever happened. I didn't mind, but I at least thought I deserved a thank you or somethin'.

"Okay, get out," she said, once we reached my car.

"Damn, that's it?"

"Yeah. You knew what this was."

"You know what, you right. I don't know why I'm trippin'. Thanks for a good fuck."

I reached for the door handle, but she stopped me by pullin' at my shirt. Her lips met up with mine for a wet kiss with her tongue dartin' in my mouth. I kissed her back, knowin' this would be the first and final time I had her body.

When it was over, she directed her attention to the sterling wheel, which was my cue to get the fuck out. Once inside my car, I made a mental note to call my mom when I made it back to my crib and apologize for missin' dinner. But it had been well worth it.

"Well, my friend," I said, pattin' Beast through my jeans. "We finally did it. We finally did it."

The Art of Sucking Dick

There's nothing and I do mean nothing more thrilling than having a nice thick dick fill your mouth so good you can barely breathe. Nothing can ever outdo the pleasure one feels when all that hard work of head bobbing and deep-throating is rewarded with a nice heavy, delicious load splashing down your throat. Yummy!

Uh huh! You don't have to say it. I already know some of y'all looking at a sista with ya heads shaking and eyes rolling. Some of y'all don't understand how I can be so nasty and have no shame. The saddest part about it is most of y'all are closeted freaks who can't comprehend how liberating it is to be in tune with your own sexuality. You women piss me off. Embrace your inner freak honey!

I love sucking dick and I am not the least bit ashamed of it. Big dicks. Little dicks. Thick dicks. Pencil dicks. Doesn't matter. As long as it's a dick pumping down my throat, I'm good. Color doesn't bother me either. Black. White. Indian. Asian. Whatever! Just let me suck it until you bust!

Now I haven't always been such an open freak.

Growing up I tended to be quite shy. My mother was a
single mother who had sex for money to put food on
our table. I'd overhear her crying out in the middle of
the night as some dude pounded away at her pussy.
And those weren't cries of ecstasy either. They were
cries of pain, anger and embarrassment.

As a teenager, I began to see just how fucked up
the world could be. Men are always looked upon as
"the man" for how many bitches they can fuck. And
females are called sluts and hos when we wanna get
our rocks off. Some believe that men should still be
working a nine-to-five while women should stay home
and nurse babies. That's a whole bunch of shit and I
ain't down for it.

My momma was put down by countless men.
She had no power in her relationships. And after seeing
that shit happen so many times, I decided things would
definitely not go that route for this sista over here.
That's right. I have a successful job, my own money,
house, and car. I don't need a man for shit.
Okay…wait…maybe just for the dick!

Now don't get me wrong. I don't suck dick just
for the pleasure of it. But also for the power I feel when
I do it. When my mouth is closed tight, with saliva
coating the dick up, I feel like I rule whoever I'm
pleasing. It's almost like I'm making the man prisoner
to me, like my mom was made prisoner those nights I'd
hear her hollering in pain. I guess you could say I
flipped the script. You probably think it makes no sense
and I should seek professional help. Been there already
and by the end of that therapy session I had his ass on
the desk as I sucked him to a nut. What? He wanted to
see just how good I was…so I had no problem showing

him.

There's no helping this habit. I know I have a problem that's gotten out of control. But fuck it...as long as I'm happy doing it, that's all that matters.

As for now, I am young, wild and free and currently waiting on my dick of the night to show up at my door. It's been quite a while since I last hit up Kevin. Now that I think about it, I really do miss the way his dick tastes. I can tell he eats a nice, healthy diet just by the taste of his creamy dressing. It tastes so good I could use it every night to wet up my salad.

Maybe tonight I'll have him handcuff me to the bed, then put his thighs around my head and fuck my throat without any mercy. Yes, that sounds perfect! Oooh, and then he can bust his tasty, dressing down my throat...or wherever he pleases. Kevin's fine as fuck and I've never had an issue with him coating any part of my body. Tiny dicks and unattractive men are a different story. I even tie my hair up when my escapade of the night involves an unattractive man. I pay too much for my weave to have just any man fuck it up.

Oh, there's my doorbell. Time to get down with the get down. But before I go, ladies remember a man loves a chick that can suck a dick with expertise. And if you don't know what the fuck you doing or how to get that sweet juice to come oozing out his dick within five minutes, hit me up! Maybe I can do a live demonstration. Toodles!

A Love Worth Waiting For

His balls were big and heavy; just the way I like them! His dick was as thick as a cucumber; perfect for slurping. His eyes were the most beautiful hue of green I'd ever seen on a black man. This man was a fuckin' ten out of ten and I fell prisoner to his charm. Only issue was that I obviously wasn't his type.

I've known Ontario since middle school. And I've never believed in love at first sight but I fell in love the instant I looked into his eyes. We were just kids then so his body wasn't anything as spectacular as it is now. But even in the sixth grade, Ontario's body would've given grown ass men a bit of jealousy.

So up until my Junior year of college, I secretly hoped Ontario and I could someday become an official item. I wanted the kind of relationship I saw on television all the time. I wanted a man, not a boy, to love me as I am. Trust and commitment came right along with that. Ontario and I had been best friends for so long that I didn't see why we couldn't just jump right into a relationship. It made perfect sense to me. Hell, I had already seen him naked. He never had any insecurities about dropping his drawers in front of me before taking a shower. The way his dick would hang and swing, hitting his thighs as he walked, would make me crave giving it some tender love and affection. I even attempted to suck it one night.

Ontario and I were chillin' over my house one Saturday night, after studying for a brutal final exam in a Trigonometry course I should've never gone through the trouble of enrolling in. When all the school work had been completed, we decided to watch *Tie Me Up, Tie Me Down*, my all-time favorite Antonio Banderas movie. It was my choice to watch it. Ontario had never seen it and even though it was entirely in Spanish, I figured he wouldn't mind the steamy sex scene that I watched often when I was all alone in my bedroom.

"Your Dad won't mind us watchin' this?" he asked me, while starin' hard at the DVD cover as I waited for the popcorn to finish popping.

I laughed. "No, he knows I'ma undercover freak. We watchin' it in my room anyway."

"Cool," he responded, as we both laughed in unison.

We spent so much time talking and laughing that I carelessly let the popcorn burn. I threw the ruined bag away and popped another, this time succeeding. I then lead the way to my bedroom, started the movie and turned off the lights.

After ten minutes of the film had passed us by, I glanced over at Ontario and burst in laughter. Even through the darkness, I could sense his confusion.

"Don't worry, you'll understand it as the movie progresses," I reassured him.

"Um…okay, but you know I failed Spanish. So this shit won't be easy," he confessed, with much doubt.

"Chill out. I got you. If you still don't understand, I'll translate the shit for you."

"Aight," he replied, with a sexy-ass grin as we resumed watching the movie.

Throughout the film, I stole a couple more stares his way and realized how into the movie he was. His excitement really grew during the sex scene, literally. His dick got so hard it started throbbing through his shorts. Witnessing that shit made a sista horny as shit. My mouth watered. My tits got hard. My pussy ached. I told myself to make a move. What did I have to lose? I had already seen him naked. I was only taking the next step by actually touching his dick.

I slowly reached over and grasped it in my hand. It was even thicker than I remembered. My mouth couldn't wait to engulf that big lollipop!

But before I could even take his shorts off, Ontario jumped up from the bed. He rushed over to the door and flicked on the lights. His eyes told me how speechless he was. But this wasn't a good type of speechless. It was more of a disgusted kind of shock.

"What the fuck Olivia?" he lashed out.

"I...I, I'm sorry."

"You're sorry?" he asked, as though he didn't believe me. "Why would you even do somethin' like that? We're best friends."

"I said I'm sorry Ontario. Isn't that enough?" As soon as I asked that question, I realized just how stupid it sounded. Of course it wasn't enough. We hadn't even kissed and I just decided to grab a handful of his dick because I was horny. I could see how it didn't make any sense.

"Hell no. It's not enough!"

"Lower your voice," I warned, standing from the bed and walking over to him. "Do you really wanna wake up my dad when he has to get up early for work tomorrow?"

That calmed him down just a tad bit. He and I both were aware of my dad's insanity. Waking him up was a guaranteed curse out and possibly a beat down, depending on how generous he felt.

I took Ontario by the hand and led him back to my bed, then patted an empty space beside me. He was cautious to sit next to me at first, but he did it anyway with a long, exaggerated sigh.

"Look," I slowly begun. "We've been really good friends for a long time. I just felt-"

"You just felt what?" he questioned, standing up.

"Let me finish," I pleaded.

"So, finish already man," he responded, with his voice raised.

"Watch your tone," I warned for a final time. I hated having to repeat myself.

"Sorry," he told me sincerely, as he resumed the position he previously had on the bed.

I took a minute or two before I resumed speaking. I had to really gather my thoughts because I wanted to say exactly what was on my mind.

"Okay, so I've known you for years and over time I've developed these feelings for you." I took another long pause before just coming out with the truth. The truth shall set you free, right? "Okay, who the hell am I kidding here? I love you Ontario. I've loved you since the first day I laid eyes on you. I don't see how you could overlook something so intense. Everyone can see the love I feel for you. My parents, my friends, your friends; they've all told me how bright my eyes sparkle whenever you walk into a room. I've never felt this way about anybody before. Not ever."

"Why didn't you tell me this before?" he asked, with a puzzled expression.

"How could I tell you something like that? We're best friends. I didn't want to scare you away if I told you."

He chuckled and shook his head as he replied, "Well, do you honestly think grabbing my dick would be any better Olivia?"

I shrugged my shoulders. "I didn't think before I did it. Well, I did think but I wasn't thinking clearly."

"Oh, that's obvious," he stated flatly.

I turned my head back to the television screen. I was uncertain of how I would get myself out of what I'd done. I figured I had already fucked up the friendship and there would never be any going back to how things were before. If only I'd used my head instead of giving in to my hormones. But what did he expect to happen when he'd walk around showcasing his dick?

"So you not gonna say anything?" he asked, after about five minutes had passed.

I sighed. "I don't really know what to say Ontario. I just poured my heart out and you haven't said much."

"Well, here's the truth Olivia," he began.

I took a deep breath, but even that couldn't prepare me enough. If he told me the friendship was over, I'd never be able to forgive myself.

"I love you too."

"You what?" I immediately asked, not completely sure if I had heard him correctly.

He laughed. "I love you too girl. You know I'd do anything for you. You my ace...my homie for life."

My excitement quickly diminished. I had just been shot down and thrown into the dreaded "friend zone". I was beyond embarrassed and what I desired at that moment was for Ontario to go home so I could cry myself to sleep.

"I've known you love me for years now," he confessed coolly.

"You have?"

"Yeah. I can see it whenever I tell you I'm going on a date with a chick. That jealousy in your eyes is obvious."

I had no idea he could see how upset I became when he'd be with other women. I really became upset whenever he'd inform me he'd had a night of great sex. But I figured I had my poker face down to a tee. I suddenly began to wonder what else he knew.

"Don't be embarrassed," he said, as he covered his hand over mine. "I think it's cute."

He thought it was cute? What the fuck? That was so not what I wanted to hear.

"It makes me uncomfortable when I see you with guys also." I almost spoke, but bit my tongue because I had no idea what would follow. "Those guys I see you with don't deserve you. You're a good girl Olivia. You deserve someone who'll treat you like a queen."

"I'm touched," I told him, touching my chest. "I really am."

"Is that all you have to say?" he asked, as worry lines appeared on his forehead.

"No, that's not all I have to say," I replied, with my voice a tad bit shaky. "What happens next? Does this change the course of our friendship? Will I still see you after tonight?"

"Girl, cut that shit out. You should know my black ass ain't going anywhere."

"You promise?" I asked, as an attempt to ensure he meant every word he'd just said.

"Hell yeah I promise," he replied, pulling me in for an embrace.

I smiled and placed my hand on his back. If things would never transpire to a relationship, I could live with that knowing that he'd always remain in my life.

"I care about you too much to ever walk away from you," Ontario added, before placing a kiss upon my forehead.

I looked up at him and smiled. He stared back at me with an intense stare. It was a look I'd never seen on his face before. It kind of scared me at first. If I didn't know any better, I would say it was pure lust staring back at me. But I quickly dismissed that notion. From the way he reacted when I grabbed his dick, there was no way in hell he was interested in taking things to that level.

I was speechless when his kisses continued. He kissed my cheek, my nose and then my lips. I was shocked, but damn sure wasn't about to pull away. I had literally dreamed of the day when our lips would meet and I could experience how his big, juicy lips felt against mine.

The kiss lingered for a few seconds until he pulled back. I could see regret and fear in his eyes. I had no regrets so I showed him just how much I wanted it when I wrapped my hand around his neck and brought my lips to his.

I feared he'd resist and stop things before they went too far but he did just the opposite. Ontario's tongue parted my lips and I was more than happy to accept it. His fingertips ran up and down my spine as my hand traveled across his stomach. Even though his shirt I could feel each muscle that formed his six-pack abs.

I couldn't believe what was actually happening. One minute my bra was on the floor and his mouth was sucking on my tits like crazy. The next I was on my back, legs spread with his big-ass dick buried in my pussy.

It didn't even take as long as I thought it would to get him inside of me. Maybe it was because I was so wet. Or maybe it had something to do with how much I loved him and was comfortable letting him enter me. Whatever it was, I was eternally grateful 'cause his dick wasn't anything to take lightly.

"Am I hurting you?" he asked, once my pussy had engulfed all of his manhood in a tight chokehold.

I shook my head then kissed him. I wanted it. Needed it. I had so many years of pent up sexual frustration. Every single time I'd had sex in the past, I pretended the man fucking me was Ontario. When I lost my virginity, I visualized it was him roaming inside me, not the nerd from my twelfth-grade science class who practically begged to be my first.

"It doesn't hurt at all," I admitted, using my

hands to explode his back.

He looked surprised. "Really?"

I laughed then nodded. He felt amazing inside of me. He filled me up more than any man ever had. I had no doubts that sex with him would do more than take my breath away.

I began to move my hips around in circles. I made sure to squeeze my pussy muscles as tightly as I could to show him what he'd been missing all those years. Looking into his eyes, I could sense how badly he craved to tear my pussy up.

"Damn," he moaned. "Yo shit so fuckin' tight girl."

"And yo dick so fuckin' big," I whispered.

We laughed but our smiles quickly vanished when we locked eyes with one another and finally gave our bodies what we had been patiently waiting for.

My hands wrapped around his neck, while he clutched the pillows and began to bounce in and out of me. The bed shook and squeaked loudly. I didn't mind though. If my dad overhead it, oh fucking well. I wasn't stopping for anything in the world.

"Mmmm, fuck me," I pleaded, as I pulled his head toward me.

"This what you want?" he asked, as his body began increasing in speed. "This what you want baby?"

"Yessss!" I hollered. "I want it. I want it! Fuck me!"

And he fulfilled that request better than I imagined. Ontario intertwined his fingers into mine, then pinned my arms above my head. He brought sweet, sweaty kisses to my lips as his dick moved around in slow circles. I closed my eyes and bit my bottom lip, trying prevent myself from crying out too loud.

"Open your eyes," he commanded, while his body became still.

I opened them and began to jump to conclusions. Had he stopped because he felt it all was a mistake? Was he going to put his clothes on and leave me with a wet and neglected pussy?

I believe he sensed all the fears crossing my mind. Which would explain why he suddenly began to pump into me with hard strokes. He wanted my eyes on him but I had no more control over that. My eyes rolled to the back of my head as orgasm after orgasm rolled through me hard, like thunder.

"Ontariooooooo!"

"Mmmmhmmm, you love this dick?"

"Yes, don't stop!" I cried.

The next voice I heard was from the other side of the door. It was my father.

"Olivia! What the fuck you doin' in there?"

Ontario continued to pump and I continued to holler his name.

"I know you ain't brought no nigga up in my house Olivia!" my dad screamed, as he began to beat on the door.

I was surprised I could hear him over my loud cries. My dad continued to call out threats and what he would do when I opened the door, but I ignored him. He wasn't about to fuck up my groove.

"Damn baby. I'm 'bout to nut," Ontario moaned, as he quickly pulled out of me.

I grabbed his soaking wet dick and placed it between my breasts. He began to fuck my tits while staring into my eyes. The eye contact we maintained was incredible. But that nut he pumped out onto my chin and mouth was even more incredible.

"That was fuckin' amazing," he said, catching his breath.

"I knew it would be," I replied, as I wiped his nut from my lips then sucked it from my fingers.

He smiled and kissed me softly. I never wanted that night to end. But I didn't want my dad to break down the door and we had class in the morning, so I snuck him out my bedroom window and told him I'd see him in a few hours.

As I tried to fall asleep that night I wondered what would happen next. Even if we never had sex again I would've been happy to just have had the opportunity to feel the weight of his dick. Fortunately for me, we did have the pleasure of making love again. Again, and again, and again. And eventually things transitioned to the next level and we became an official item.

We've now almost wrapped up our final semester of college. Marriage is soon to be in the works. And now that I think about it, it's crazy how we probably would still be just friends if I hadn't made a move that night and grabbed his dick. Everything happens for a reason. My wait to be his girl had taken me almost ten years. But the lengthy wait turned out to be well worth it all in the end.

The Consultation

"I really want my breasts larger," I stated, as I used both hands to lift my small breasts. "I don't think I can live with them being this small anymore."

"I see," Dr. Michael said, standing up from his desk, then walking over to me. "Stand up for a second," he informed me.

I stood up and removed my hands from my breasts, allowing them to hang freely. I even surprised myself with my boldness. Usually, I never was comfortable with the idea of allowing a man to observe my breasts. The night I lost my virginity, I kept my breasts covered the entire time because I was so fearful of them being seen.

But with Dr. Michael, I found myself to be completely comfortable. There was no doubt in my mind that he wouldn't judge me by the size of my breasts. He was a doctor. He must have done the procedure hundreds of times. I was just one in a million of those women.

However, I did feel a weird vibe when Dr. Michael examined my breasts. I didn't feel embarrassed, I just felt that he really was enjoying what he saw. A tiny smile formed at the corner of his lips and I could've sworn something in his pants moved. But maybe it had all been a part of my imagination.

"Now, Ms. Love," Dr. Michael said, after he glanced down at paperwork and informed me that I could put my shirt back on.

"Oh please, call me Candi."

"Candi...I don't usually say anything of this nature to my patients. Well, actually I never say this to my patients, but-"

"What? Do you think they need to be bigger?" I asked, before he could finish his sentence. "I can go bigger if you think that's best."

"No, no," he laughed. "That's not what I was going to say at all."

"Oh...then what was it you were going to say?"

He replied, "I was going to say I don't think you need this surgery."

"Huh?" I was confused. Didn't he want my money? What doctor actually cared about his patients saving money?

"Why do you want this procedure again?" he asked.

"Well, I believe having bigger breasts can get me further with my career."

"And you're an actress, right?"

I nodded, curious to see where he was taking the conversation.

"You don't need this surgery. After I carefully examined your breasts, I've found absolutely nothing wrong with them."

I started looking around the room, in search of cameras. It had to be a joke. What doctor in his right mind was about to pass up thousands of dollars just because he believed a patient didn't need bigger breasts? Wasn't he supposed to just give me what I wanted, as long as there weren't any health concerns?

"Are you serious?" I was having a lot of trouble wrapping my brain around what he was telling me.

"Yes, I am. You don't need large breasts to become a successful actress Candi."

"But it would surely help."

"Who told you that?" he asked, taking off his glasses. He looked even sexier without them. Don't get me wrong, the glasses added a combination of sexiness and smarts, but without them he looked like he belonged on the front page of a magazine.

"Plenty of people," I replied. "Directors, producers, people I've met in the industry."

"That's a load of bullshit," he blurted.

"Excuse me?" I was about ready to leave. First, he didn't want me to have the surgery, which made my mind wonder how legit he actually was. Then he began using language no doctor would ever use in front of a client. Talk about unprofessional!

"I'm sorry," he immediately apologized. "I didn't mean to say that. What I meant to say was, don't fall for that rubbish. I mean, just look at Angela Bassett. Sure, your breasts are a bit smaller than hers, but she doesn't have the huge breasts you desire and her career did great things."

I laughed. "I'm no Angela Bassett, so no need to compare us. I'm just the average chick who has a love for acting. Just like so many women here in Cali. The competition is fierce so I gotta always be on my A game."

What I told him was nothing further from the truth. As Lilly Allen stated in that song, it's hard out here for a bitch. The competition was no laughing matter. Everybody and their mama wanted a taste of fame. What pissed me off was the fact that a lot of chicks couldn't even act. They landed gigs for how good they looked, not how well they could sell the role. It was ridiculous how superficial things were.

"You don't think you look as good as Angela Bassett did when she was your age?"

"No," I laughed again. "Not one bit."

"I disagree completely."

"You do?"

"Yes, you are a gorgeous woman," he said with a small smile. "You should take being compared to her as a compliment."

I smiled even though I tried to fight it. Was Dr. Michael hitting on me? *No way*, I told myself. He was only being friendly, nothing more and nothing less.

"Thank you," I told him.

"You're quite welcome."

"So about my breasts," I began. "Are you thinking the size I want is too big? I really want to know what size you think is best."

"Did you not hear a single word I've said?" he laughed, like he couldn't believe it. "I'll leave the decision up to you. It's your money, but I honestly believe you are just fine the way you are."

I paused, then asked, "Why are you saying this to me? I know you can't possibly say that to every woman who walks in here."

"You're right," he agreed. "If I did that I'd never make enough money to keep this place open."

"Then why?"

"Do you really want the answer to that question?"

There was something about the way he said it that made me think twice about whether or not I wanted an answer. Still, I told him yes.

"To be perfectly honest with you I believe you are a beautiful woman. I've never had an issue with remaining professional around my clients. But you...you surely have changed that."

I was confused. "But what did I do? I haven't flirted with you at all. All I did was show you my breasts, but you see that every day. And bigger ones than mine as well."

"Ever heard of the saying size doesn't matter?"

I nodded. "Yes, but doesn't that only apply to men?"

He laughed. "Most certainly not. Take this situation for example. You're so hung up on fitting in society that you neglect what was already given to you. Big breasts don't make a good woman, just like a big dick doesn't make a good man. The size is irreverent. What's on the inside is what counts."

"I see your point, but honestly I'm just trying to get my breasts done, not listen to a sermon on loving myself."

"I apologize," he replied quickly. "I was out of my place to say any of that."

"Besides," I continued. "I love myself plenty. But I love my career also. And when push comes to shove you gotta do what you gotta do."

"I agree. I admire your determination. Not many people these days have that left in them."

"Yeah, well I have no choice. I'm not going to get anywhere in life just sitting on my ass. So let's get this procedure done as soon as possible!"

Finally giving up, he replied, "Okay, sounds good. Let's determine what size you really want to go with."

"I honestly think I need to at least go up to a D-cup," I replied, as I began searching through photos on my phone that showed exactly what I wanted.

"You sure about that?"

"Yes!" I said, as I unbuttoned my blouse then placed it in my lap so I could compare the photos to my breasts.

He stood, then walked over to me and sat at the edge of his desk. He stared at my breasts and then briefly focused on the photo displayed on my cell. He averted his attention back to my breasts and surprisingly I still didn't feel one bit uneasy. The way he stared at them was exactly the way I craved for my past boyfriends to gaze at them. When he realized I noticed his long stare, he looked away.

"And you're sure about this size?"

"Yes, look at how small my breasts are."

"I know how small they are," he told me, as he started to walk away from me.

"No," I said, grabbing his arm. "Look."

His eyes met with mine then fell down to my breasts. He only stared for a moment then focused his eyes on the wall of medical degrees.

"Do you have a problem looking at my breasts now?"

"No, no. Not at all," he defended. "I do this for a living, remember?"

"Yes, I'm well aware. But why is it so hard for you to look at my breasts now?"

He didn't respond. He just gave me a blank

stare.

I took his hand, then placed it on my right breast. There was that look in his eyes again. He wanted me, but was fighting it with all his strength.

"What are you doing?"

"Giving you what you want," I replied, right before using my free hand to grab his head and direct it toward mine.

Our lips briefly touched, then he broke the kiss to look into my eyes. It felt as though he was searching my eyes to see if this was indeed what I wanted. When he got the answer he was in search of, his lips meet back up with mine for an erotic lip-lock of tongues. From that moment, I knew there was no turning back. I had started something that wouldn't be over until we both were satisfied.

I closed my eyes and allowed myself to become fully engulfed in the kiss. Nothing else mattered. All I really wanted to do was to give that man a piece of me. It had been a little over a month since my last sexual encounter. And that wasn't the least bit pleasurable. Something told me this time around I wouldn't end up disappointed.

Dr. Michael broke our kiss, then lifted the heavy-duty chair like it weighed nothing and turned it so that it was directly in front of him. I giggled. Judging from his stature I had no idea he was so strong. Don't get me wrong. I could tell he definitely wasn't puny, but I was unaware of his strength.

"You like that?"

"I surely do," I smiled.

"Good," he said, as he picked me up into his arms and resumed our heated kiss.

My hands roamed up and down his arms. There definitely were some defined muscles on that man. I was more than eager to see what all he had been hiding underneath that white jacket.

Dr. Michael placed me down onto his desk and proceeded to lick me from my neck down to my breasts. He really allowed his passion to shine through once his mouth was completely covering my right nipple. I pinched the other as he made my body twitch and squirm from his hard sucks and circles from his tongue. My moans encouraged him suck to harder, which really caused me to lose my cool.

"Oh God!" I cried out.

He immediately stopped what he was doing, then brought his face directly to mine. He stared into my eyes for a few seconds before saying, "You must've really liked that."

"Damn right," I confirmed, still rubbing on his big arms.

"Well, I got something else you'll like," he said, with a sly smirk.

"Is that right?"

"Watch," he told me as he took a few steps back.

I loved it, but it kind of scared me to be honest. I'd watched plenty of men undress but no one had ever done it like that before. The eye contact had me excited and nervous all at the same time.

When he informed me he had something else I would like, he surely wasn't lying. The man looked like a king without his clothes on. He was handsome before but at that moment he was beyond breathtaking.

His arms were even sexier than I had imagined. Big, hard, and with so much sex appeal that I wanted to stick my tongue out and lick them. But that wasn't the only thing I was more than willing to lick. His abs...oh my God, those abs! They weren't the most defined set I'd seen, but they did the trick for me. I could picture myself swirling my tongue from his arms, to his delicious four-pack and down to his hard dick that stood out at full attention.

Now his arms and abs were one thing. But that dick was another. It looked to be around a good nine inches. He was uncut, which was usually a big no-no for me, but it looked so mouthwatering there was no way I could ever deny it. The veins that stood out and his heavy sack of balls made it so much more desirable.

"Wow," I muttered, as he began to walk toward me.

"So you like?" he laughed.

"Like? I love what I see!"

"Well, I got plenty more to show you sexy."

He grabbed my head with his hand and forced my lips onto his. His tongue was so sweet that I could've kissed him for eternity. No one had ever kissed me so intensely. That's terrible since a few years prior, I'd been engaged for a year and a half with a man I thought was the love of my life.

His delicious lips went down to my neck which sent chills down my spine. His thick dick poked me between my legs, although it was trying to break through my jeans and take control of my pussy. Honestly, I had no issues with allowing that shit to happen. He could take me anyway he wanted.

"You won't be needing these," he told me, unfastening my jeans and taking them off.

"But Dr. Michael-"

"Call me Alex."

"Alex...what's happening? What are we doing?"

He placed a finger to my lips. "Shh...you're talking too much."

He was right. I did tend to overanalyze everything in my life. Call it what you want, but thinking so much prepared me for any possible outcome. I'd rather be walking into something ready than unprepared, which was exactly how things were turning out. What if he had cameras placed all over his office? I'd end up on every porn site known to mankind.

"Just go with the flow and enjoy the moment," Alex continued to tell me. "Don't think about tomorrow or what will happen when this is over. Enjoy me as I enjoy your body."

I nodded my head even though I silently allowed my mind to race. I believe he sensed that since he ripped my panties off, then opened my legs and stuck a finger inside of me.

"Oh God!" I blurted out.

"Didn't I tell you to relax?" he smirked.

I wanted to respond but it felt so good that my mouth became powerless.

"Do you hear me talking to you?" he asked, as he shoved another finger inside and began to finger fuck me.

"Yes! I heard you!" I blurted out.

"Good," he told me, before removing his fingers and sucking my pussy juices away. "Mmm," he moaned, staring at me with intense eyes. "I could eat that all damn day."

"I won't stop you," I confessed, with dirty

thoughts of him setting my pussy on fire with his tongue.

"Say no more," he informed me.

Alex placed his knees into the chair, and leaned his upper body over until his elbows rested directly on the desk. His face was now staring directly at my pussy.

Usually, I have to say a silent prayer before a man puts his tongue down below. But this time around I didn't think I had to ask the good Lord for any favors. From the way he was staring at my pussy gave me confidence that Alex could blow my mind just from what he'd do with his mouth. The excitement of it was killing me!

Thank God he didn't just sit there and stare. In no time at all Alex was licking my pearl with that long, thick tongue of his. My kitty purred as that man proved he had skills that were completely out of this world.

Once he was satisfied with eating me from the front, he cleared a section of his desk off by sliding papers and folders to the floor. He then instructed me to sit on my knees as he ate me out from the back. I lowered my head onto the desk and pushed all remaining thoughts out of my head. He wanted me to live in the moment and I damn sure was about to just that.

I tried to massage my swollen clit as he dug inside of me with his tongue but every time I made an attempt, he pushed my hand away.

"Just relax and enjoy," he told me between licks.

I obeyed even though I really wanted to touch myself. Playing with my clit would always help me elevate oral pleasure to the next level. I guess Alex was just waiting for the right moment 'cause when he finally did begin to show attention to my clit, I lost my sanity.

The more I moaned, the harder he'd pinch and rub my clit. The more I cried out, the deeper his tongue traveled inside of me. I could only last another minute or so. And when I came it felt like I'd just released a year's worth of tension. It made sense though, 'cause just like my career, things hadn't been smooth in the sex department.

Usually after a great climax from a man's tongue, I'd be ready to pounce on his dick and ride the fuck out of him. But things were much different this time. I was ready to put my clothes on and hit the road so I could sleep. He had other plans though.

"Where you think you going?" he asked me when I attempted to turn around. "I'm not finished with you."

I looked down at his hard dick and eagerly turned back around. I loved a man with plenty of stamina. No matter how tired I got, I was gonna let him do what he pleased.

The next sensation I felt was the tip of his dick rubbing against the opening of my vagina. I closed my eyes and moaned as my body surrendered completely to him.

"Open that pussy up," he moaned, as his thick dick entered me slowly.

I closed my eyes as my head rested on the desk. He felt so good inside of me. The more he pushed inside, the wetter my pussy got. By the time he was all the way inside, my juices had begun to leak out and create a tiny puddle beneath me.

"Fuck me," I moaned, eager to see if he could blow my mind.

"Your wish is my command," he told me, before proceeding to fuck my pussy hard, just how I loved it.

Alex grabbed a fistful of my hair, pulling my head back toward him. His tongue invaded my mouth, escalating the already hot fire he had set off in me. I dug my nails into his arm as an orgasm poured out of me. It came out of nowhere. And it certainly wasn't the last.

He placed me on my back and spread my legs apart. Alex then climbed on top of me with his head down by my feet and ensured my legs would remain in place with his strong thighs. I looked down at his tight bubble butt and squeezed it with both hands. My head fell back onto the desk when he penetrated me and began to pump quickly. His mouth found my big toe, then sucked it as another climax rocked my body.

For big the finale, Alex slipped out of me and pulled me away from the desk. He picked me up into his arms, then stuck his dick back into my now widely-opened hole. I wrapped my legs around his waist while he bent his knees and cradled my back. In and out he went, all while kissing me and uttering out naughty thoughts.

"Fuck, I'm about to cum!" he moaned loudly.
I took control and rode him until he exploded deep within my walls. He suddenly lost his balance, which caused us to fall down onto the floor. We couldn't help but laugh as we attempted to catch our breath.

We laid there for about ten minutes before his secretary buzzed him about an appointment. Immediately, I felt embarrassed. His secretary and whoever else had been in the waiting room had to have heard our cries of passion.

Alex saw the fear in my eyes and said, "Don't sweat it. As long as you enjoyed it."

And fuck yeah I enjoyed it! I enjoyed it so much that I couldn't get enough of it. Alex and I have been fucking for the past three months. But truth be told I really don't see anything solid forming between us, except for mind-blowing sex. And hey, that's just fine with me.

Alex helped me see just how beautiful my body is, believe it or not. The way he kisses my body, licks my pussy and adores my breasts helped me see just how superficial I was to want to enhance what God had already given me. And even if Alex and I decide to call off our little fling, at least I'll have unforgettable memories and a load of confidence to last me a lifetime.

Studio Love

"Sounds great. Come take a listen," my new producer suggested from the control room.

"Aight. Cool."

I eagerly placed the headphones on the stand before me and exited the vocal booth to join her. I was so excited because everything I had done so far with Savannah had been completely on point. My latest single on the R&B charts was barely pushing toward Top 40 and it hadn't even charted on Billboard's Top 100. Things really weren't looking too good for a platinum-selling artist who scored five number one singles four short years prior. It felt like I was about to be forgotten like so many singers I'd seen it happen to in the past.

"How do you feel about the song so far?" Savannah asked me, once I had taken a seat beside her.

"I feel really confident. And to be honest, I feel like this material is actually going somewhere this time around."

My first two albums had solely been produced by my childhood friend, Tommy. My debut album was on fire! Critics worldwide fell in love with it. However, as soon as work for my sophomore effort began, I felt things were on a different course.

Tommy had been with this chick, Denise, for five

years on and off. He thought they would wed and build a family together. He had even brought her an expensive-ass diamond ring that he was waiting until the right moment to give to her.

Unfortunately, my boy found some nasty-ass text messages between Denise and one of her co-workers. Tommy flipped the fuck out. He beat the dude's ass so bad he lost vision in one eye. Luckily for him homeboy was too frightened to press charges, probably because Denise didn't want any more drama in her life.

Long story short, Tommy hasn't been the same man ever since. All of his beats are wack as fuck. He has no direction anymore. No drive to succeed either. One day I could've sworn I walked in on him finishing up a drug injection. He swore up and down he has diabetes and he was just injecting his insulin. I asked to see his diabetic meter for proof but he refused.

When the time came to release my second album I had lost all faith in the project. No singles had charted. Critics predicted I'd experience a sophomore slump. And man, they were right. My first week sales were only about 20,000 units sold. Those numbers are fine for an indie artist doing shit by themselves. But I had a major label behind me with a previous album that debuted numbers twice as big. The new album was wack and I tried to inform the label it would go nowhere. But the CEO had this vision that the tracks Tommy was producing would be epic. Hmph, shows how much his ass knows about music.

So, there I was in the studio with one of the many new producers I'd enlisted, trying to get a winner that could aid me in selling another platinum album. Hell, I was even willing to settle for gold, as long as I saw some type of status.

Out of all the producers I'd met with so far, Savannah had the most creative perspective. She was always thinking outside the box telling me to shoot for something the public hadn't heard before. I liked the new direction I was headed toward. It was a plus that she'd produced a few top ten records since she hit the scene last year.

"So what do you think? Still liking the direction we're headed?" Savannah asked, after playing back my vocals on the smooth track she'd created.

"Hell yeah, I like it!" I said immediately. "I fuckin' love it!"

She laughed. "Well, good. I'm doing something right."

Just as I was about to respond, my cell rang. It was Tommy. It had been the third phone call since I'd gotten in the studio that day. He must've seen the tweets I'd posted informing fans new music was coming and that I was in the studio with Savannah.

"Do you need to get that?" she asked. "We can take a break."

"Naw," I declined. "It's Tommy. I'll call him back. Besides, I'm working. And my career bouncin' back is more important right now."

"I bet it is," she replied. "What does he think of you working with other producers? I heard you guys grew up together, right?"

"Yeah, we did. We used to be tight back in the day. But shit changed. I told him I wanted to test the waters with a new sound. He wasn't cool with it at first, but he realizes I am an artist and sometimes you just gotta try new shit. So, I think it's starting to get easier to deal with."

"Good. I'm glad to hear that," she said smiling.

She was so gorgeous. If she wasn't a lesbian I would've kissed her right then and there. I could tell she worked out regularly by her toned arms and calf muscles. That would all work out perfectly since it meant she could most likely keep up in the bedroom.

But if I kissed her, even if she wasn't a lesbian, things definitely would've changed. I had fucked a couple interns at the label and they were always blowing up my phone tryna get some play. Females had to realize that when a man doesn't put any interest in you and only fucks you, it means he doesn't want anything of substance. I only wanted to get my dick wet. And if a female catches my eye and she's willing to put out, then let's do the damn thing!

I couldn't do that to Savannah though. I respected her. Maybe it had something to do with our passion for music. I don't know for sure. But I did know that I'd want something more than sex with Savannah. She'd be the type of chick I'd date and cut off the groupies for.

"I have this new track I've been working on," she said, bringing me out of all my not-so-realistic thoughts. "I was saving it for Usher's new album, but I want you to try it and see what happens."

"Whatttt?" I asked in disbelief.

"You interested?"

"Fuck yeah I am!"

"Good," she laughed. "The beat and chorus are finished. You just gotta come up with the verses."

"I'm down," I smiled. My day was getting better

and better.

"Awesome! Let's get started."

Almost an hour later we were finished. The lyrics just poured out of me. I only had to tweak a few notes, which wasn't new for me because I was such a perfectionist. Usually, I could spend forever and a day rerecording my vocals. That shit used to piss Tommy off 'cause he claimed he had other things to do than to be in the studio all night. But my philosophy was that hard work always paid off.

"This shit is dope!" I exclaimed, leaning back in my chair, satisfied with a job well done.

"I agree. I'm glad I gave this track to you. This has potential to get you back at the number one spot."

I was glad she'd said that 'cause currently the R&B charts were full of no-good-ass singers who sounded like shit without auto-tune. I prided myself on only relying on my vocals and not studio devices to enhance my sound. A true singer was finally making his way back to the spotlight!

"Man, I just can't thank you enough," I told her. "You are a fuckin' genius."

"Well, thank you," she said, showing me a beautiful smile that showcased her perfect white teeth. I had a thing for women with white teeth.

"You're welcome. I should've been working with you a long time ago."

"I'm flattered. I really am," she told me, before tossing back her long micro braids from her shoulder. "It means a lot coming from a man as talented as yourself."

"Hey, I'm just stating the truth."

Her phone chimed, then lit up with what I

assumed to be a text message. She immediately replied and informed me her girlfriend would be outside soon to pick her up.

"So, how long y'all been together?" I asked, as she began to gather her belongings.

"It's been almost four months," she said with a tiny smile.

"Is it love?"

She paused, then stated, "It's getting there."

"What made you start dating women?" I asked, fully aware it was none of my business. "Did you at one point date men?"

Savannah stopped what she was doing and stared at me. It kinda scared me 'cause I had no idea what was going through her head.

"What's up with all the questions?"

"I, I don't know. I guess I'm just curious," I confessed. I wanted to know what made a woman so fine give up dick.

She took a long sigh before saying, "Well this isn't the first time I've been asked that question and I know it won't be the last, so I guess I'll tell you. Promise me that what I tell you won't leave this room, Markcus."

"I promise," I told her, as she placed her purse and jacket down.

"Okay...Lynn is the first woman I've ever been intimate with. I've always had thoughts about what being with a woman would be like since I was a teenager. I even had a few girlfriends in my past but as soon as it felt like things were moving towards sex, I would back out of the relationship."

"Interesting," I laughed.

"Shut up!" she said, laughing right along with me. "Now I've always loved dick. Nothing compares to how good it feels to have something nice and thick buried inside of me." My dick began to lengthen immediately after those words rolled off her tongue. "And I love it when I climax all over a dick as it fucks the shit outta me." That did it for me. My dick was brick hard.

"Oh my God," I said, adjusting myself.

"Are you okay?" she asked, looking down at the imprint through my jeans.

"Oh, yeah. I'm just fine," I replied.

"Are you hard?" she asked, as though she couldn't believe I had gotten hard from our conversation.

I didn't feel the need to answer what was so obviously in front of her face. I really wanted her to get down on her knees and suck my dick with her beautiful mouth.

"So what made you go all the way with a woman?"

She sighed. "I guess had my final straw with men. No one seemed to want an actual commitment. Sure, they'd say that's what they wanted in the beginning, but as soon as a sista gives up the pussy, things change. Sex changes things."

"True," I agreed. I had lost a great deal of friendships because of sex. Feelings would always arise after the deed had been done and when I didn't want anything more, I'd be called a no-good bastard.

"When I met Lynn I had no issues with testing the waters. She gave me more attention than any man had. I had no doubts that after I gave my body to her, she'd still be with me. And here we are, almost four months into the relationship and she's still here whenever I need her."

"I see," I said, after she'd finished pouring her heart out. "I just think you haven't the right man Savannah."

"And what makes you say that?" I could tell she wasn't believing a word I'd said. She'd been so bruised by men that she wanted nothing to do with us.

"I just believe once you find the right man you won't have to worry about getting hurt."

"Well," she began, grabbing her things and standing up. "I'm not worried about it because I'm done with men."

"I don't think you are. I think you still crave to have a man that understands you and treats you like a queen. You want kids? Marriage?"

She rolled her eyes. "What? Are you my therapist now? Yes, I want a family and kids, but gay people are entitled to that also. I don't need a man for that. This convo is over," Savannah stated, walking toward the door. "Thanks for a good session."

"When was the last time you had dick?" I asked.

She stopped dead in her tracks and turned around to face me.

"That's personal Markcus."

"That's personal?" I asked, standing up and taking a few steps toward her. "You was just telling me how you love the way it feels to have dick inside of you and now me asking a simple question is too personal?"

"Alright," she sighed. "It's been about a year."

"Let's make a bet," I suggested, taking another step forward.

"A bet?"

"Yeah...I'll make it interesting."

She looked at her phone. "Look, I gotta go. My girlfriend's probably outside by now."

She tried to turn away but I grabbed her arm. She gave me an intense stare that threatened me to leave her alone.

"Just hear me out."

"I don't like the way this is going. I don't have to bet anything with you, Markcus. This is just business and I would like to keep it that way."

Savannah's plead didn't stop me from continuing my mission. If I allowed her to walk out that door without speaking my mind, I'd probably never get the chance again.

"How about you sleep with a man one last time and then make your decision?"

She really looked like she wanted to slap me. "You must've lost your mind."

"I'm so serious. Have sex with a guy and if you still see no need to continue doing it, stay with Lynn."

"That would mean cheating on Lynn. I may be many things, but a cheater I am not."

"Come on," I continued. "Y'all aren't even in love. You're just with her because she gives you comfort. You don't like being alone."

I saw something within her shift. I was right and she hated that I was. She couldn't admit the truth...to me or to herself.

"Fine. So, who should I sleep with?"

"Me...duh," I laughed.

"You?"

"Yes, me. What's wrong with me?"

"Nothing," she said, looking down at her ringing phone. "I just don't mix business with pleasure Markus."

"This isn't business. We're all done with business for the day," I told her, as I pulled her to me and pressed my lips against hers.

She hesitated at first, but when I shoved my tongue inside her mouth she gave in and dropped everything from her hands. Suddenly, she became the enforcer as she pushed me backward until I fell back into the chair. Savannah got on top of me and grinded her ass on my hard dick, teasing the fuck outta me. I grabbed onto her ass and smacked it.

I lifted her shirt over her head and tossed it across the room. My shirt was next to go. And just when I was about to take my pants off and allow my dick to breathe, her cell rang again.

"Shit!" I mumbled, when she got off of me and went to retrieve it.

"Let it ring," I begged. I had gotten so close…too close for it to end before it could even begin.

"She's outside waiting. I can't just let her sit in the car…while I'm in here…cheating."

Damn. Why'd she have to put it like that? I felt a little bad.

"Hello." She answered the phone without hesitation. "Yes, baby. I'm coming, I'm coming. I'm sorry. We're almost finished here. Okay, bye."

"So you're leaving?"

"I have to," she said with much regret. "I can't do her like that. I can't fuck you while she's outside waiting for me."

"I understand that," I said with honesty. "So just

suck my dick."

If she had been a yellow bone I was sure I would've seen her face turn bright red from anger.

"Suck your dick?" she spat with wide eyes. "Wow. You really are just like any other nigga."

She tried to turn away again but I grabbed her arm. If she planned on leaving, I wasn't cool with her making an exit with the belief that I was just like all the no-good men from her past.

"I'm just saying that since you're pressed for time why not just try it for a few minutes. If you don't like it just leave and I'll never mention it again."

"Never?" she asked.

"Never," I confirmed, letting go of her arm.

Savannah gave me a smirk, then unzipped my jeans and pulled my soft willie out of its cage.

"Woah!" I moaned, when she dropped down to her knees and swallowed all of my dick into her mouth.

She took it out of her mouth long enough to say, "Only for two minutes," then went back to work.

I nodded my head. If she only gave me two minutes I would've been cool with that. The way she sucked my dick proved to me that she had been born to suck dick. It may sound insane but I've received head from countless women since I was sixteen. No one's head game ever compared to what I was receiving at that moment.

Those two minutes turned into ten minutes and ten, turned to twenty. Once my dick had hardened down her throat, she really showed me how precise her skills were. My dick was covered in spit, which turned me on so much that I had to hold off my nut a couple times. I didn't know if it would ever happen again, so I wanted it to last as long as possible.

"Damn girl," I grinned, looking down at her as she jacked my dick with her hands and looked up at me with the most beautiful eyes.

"You like the way I'm suckin' ya dick?"

"Fuck yeah! Don't stop girl."

She smiled, then spat on the head, rubbed it a bit and then placed it back into her mouth. I grabbed her head with both hands and began to fuck her throat slowly. She tensed up at first but after a few pumps she was able to relax and take it without gagging.

"Yesssss," I moaned, once my pumps became quicker and she began to meet up with each thrust. "God yes!"

The moment felt so good…too good to be true. It was like a dream. Better yet it was like one of those flicks I would steal from my dad's collection as a kid.

And just when I was about to convince myself that it was all reality and I would get a chance to bust a nut down her throat, the door flew open. I looked up to see Lynn standing at the doorway with rage in her eyes.

"You lyin' bitch!" she cried. "I knew yo ass wasn't through with dick! Fuck you!"

Savannah almost bit my dick off, trying to get it out of her mouth. I yelped in pain while she tried to apologize.

"Baby I-"

"Don't you fuckin' baby me, bitch," Lynn snapped. "How dare you have me outside waitin' on yo ass and you been fuckin' this sorry-ass nigga."

"It's not like that. We didn't fuck. This was just a one-time thing," she attempted to explain. "I'm so sorry."

Lynn rolled her eyes. "Yeah, you gonna be sorry bitch. You and that muthafucka both gonna be sorry."

"Baby, please," Savannah called out as Lynn stormed off, slamming the door behind her.

Now in any other circumstance I would've been sentimental. But Savannah had nearly bitten my dick off so I wasn't in the mood to be sensitive.

"Damn, what the fuck did I do?" she asked herself, shaking her head.

She spun around to add something, probably to call me a no-good nigga, but stopped when she saw me bent over in pain. She came rushing to my side, like she hadn't just gotten her ass cursed out by her lover.

"Oh my God! Are you okay?"

"Do I look okay?" I winced.

"I'm so sorry, Markcus. I didn't mean to."

"It's cool," I told her. If I hadn't had made that bet none of that shit would've even happened. "It's my fault. Go after ya girl."

"She needs to cool off. Right now, I'm worried 'bout you."

I looked into her eyes. She really wasn't worried about Lynn. Things were in my favor and I planned to use it to my advantage. Looked like Lynn was out of the picture anyway.

All the pain from the incident with her teeth faded as I kissed her. She kissed me back with more passion than earlier.

My dick rose to the occasion. Savannah broke our kiss and began to resume her position on her knees but I stopped her. She had brought me enough pleasure that night. It was her turn to feel something. Besides, I wasn't tryna have any more injuries to my dick.

I picked her up and placed her body on top of the mixing console. I wasn't worried about damage. I would easily pay for anything that got destroyed throughout what I had in mind.

"Daddy wants to taste this pussy," I whispered into her ear, slipping her panties off.

"I'm not stopping you," she laughed with anticipation.

I sniffed her panties and inhaled her essence. I could already tell she had something sweet and juicy between her legs. And fuck yeah, I was right. She tasted so sweet I could've eaten her cherry all night. I probably would've if she hadn't begged me to fuck her.

I stepped out of my jeans with a quickness. I wasn't tryna rush things but I didn't need any more interruptions. My fantasies seemed to finally be coming true. And no lesbian or anyone else for that matter was gonna fuck that up. Just to be sure things would go smoothly, I locked the door.

"Oh, it's that serious, huh?" Savannah laughed.

"Damn right. This shit is going down!"

"Then put it on me Papi."

I grinned when she proceeded to spread her legs apart and play with her pussy. I knew Savannah's pussy would fit like a damn glove around my dick. There was no way in hell Lynn was fucking her the way she deserved to be fucked. I wasn't really sure how they got down, but I assumed Lynn strapped up and played daddy. My goal was to prove to Savannah that there was no replacement for some good dick. Toys couldn't compare to the real thing.

I moved her hands from her pussy and replaced

them with mine. She gasped and moaned, which told me I was already proving I could do things better. One hand swirled three thick fingers around inside her already wet pussy. The other rubbed her clit softly. Savannah's hand found my swollen dick and immediately began to jack it.

The masturbation together was lovely and all, but a few minutes of it was all I really needed. I was dying to get my dick inside that pretty-ass pussy. It was shaved just right with lips that spoke to me, calling out my name. I kneeled down to kiss them, then brought my wet lips to Savannah's mouth and allowed her to taste how sweet her sugary walls were.

As we kissed, I rubbed the head of my dick against her clit, stimulating it and causing it to harden. I was too ready to explore the part of her body no man had had the privilege of touching for almost a year. I just hoped she was ready.

I slowly moved my dick toward her opening, then pushed forward until it gave me permission to enter. Savannah tensed up and removed her tongue from my mouth. I held her head with one hand and continued the kiss.

When I got the vibe she'd adjusted to my entry, I pushed a little further. Her body stiffened once more, but that wasn't an issue. I had fucked plenty of virgins in my day. I knew the importance of patience.

And I continued to remain patient up until I couldn't push any further and was entirely surrounded by the tight grip her walls had on my dick. My lips roamed down to her neck and sucked, hoping to leave love marks so there'd be memories of me hours after we were finished.

I couldn't help but ask, "How's that feel?"

"Feels perfect," she replied with a smile.

That gave me the incentive to begin moving my dick around inside the sugarcoated walls I was already beginning to become attached to. Her fingernails latched onto my skin, creating marks I knew would be there for days. But none of that mattered. What really mattered was me achieving the feat of making her cream over my dick. And with each stroke, I could feel myself getting closer to my goal.

As my thrusts became deeper and more forceful, I was able to push out the beautiful sound of Savannah's moans throughout the room. It was music to my ears. I loved it so much I needed it louder.

"Markcus! Oh, Markcus!"

"Yes, baby," I replied, never ending the multitude of strokes.

Her moans were becoming more and more heavenly the faster I moved. They were increasing to loud shrieks and screams that begged me to fuck her body harder, rougher. She was hollering so loud I was sure people walking by outside could hear her. That turned me the fuck on. Turned me on so much a fire down below began to ignite.

I wasn't ready to bust yet, but I couldn't stop myself either. I didn't want to bust inside of her, but I couldn't control that shit either. The hold she had on my dick was so addictive that no matter what I told myself I couldn't pull out.

"Godddddamnnnnnnn," I yelled, releasing the nut out of me and into Savannah's cave of wonders.

I was beat but she hadn't gotten hers yet so even though my dick began to soften, I refused to cease my movements inside her. It only took a few seconds to regain my erection, probably due to how good her walls were holding onto my dick.

Pretty soon I was back at my fierce pace like I hadn't even ejaculated a few moments earlier. And there were those heavenly screams again, piercing into my ear drums and giving me motivation to continue until Savannah reached her peak.

"Markcus, I'm about to cum!" she yelled, tightly wrapping her arms around my shoulders.

"Cum Savannah. Cum all on this dick," I said, as beads of sweat formed on my forehead.

And she did just that. In fact, she came so hard she wet up the mixing console. I was to blame for that as well, since when I pulled out of her my nut came pouring out. We laughed, knowing there was a chance we fucked something up from our spontaneous escapade.

After we cleaned up to the best of our ability and I dropped Savannah off at her place, I went home not really sure what to think of the situation. I had broken up things between Savannah and Lynn. But an unforgettable session of hot, steamy sex came out of it. There was no way Savannah could ever forget that, even if she tried.

Despite all that, I pondered on whether she'd go back to women. Sure, I showed her how great sex with a man could be. But was that what she really wanted?

I couldn't sit around thinking for very long so I called her a few days later to discover she'd been waiting for my call. Turns out everything that night hadn't been in vain. Savannah found out she was pregnant a few weeks later and we've been exclusive ever since. I ensured she was well aware that I would never neglect her needs like the men from her past. I swore on my father's grave that I'd be the best provider she and my child could ask for.

And in return, I'm the only piece of dick she'll ever need. Those thoughts of marrying a woman and playing with pussy are now extinct. Instead, she happily spreads her legs for a solid piece of beef, day in and day out.

Black Butterfly

"Are you sure you wanna do this mom?" my seventeen-year-old daughter asked for what felt like the tenth time as we stepped foot into the tattoo parlor.

"Yes. I am," I reassured her confidently. "Jasmine, your father is out of my life for good now. Honey, I'm moving on and living without any regrets."

I understood why Jasmine was a bit frightened of her mom getting ink. The idea had just popped in my head fifteen minutes earlier. But I was one hundred percent certain that that was what I desired to do.

I'd been married to her father for entirely way too many years and since the divorce had just been finalized, it was time to celebrate. I had already partied with my girls at the strip club and even took home a dancer. Getting a tattoo would put the icing on the cake for my newly found freedom.

"Welcome to Precision," a masculine voice called out behind us.

We were greeted by a pleasant-looking white man who appeared to be in his mid-forties. He was dressed in a loosely-fitted white t-shirt with faded blue jeans and white tennis shoes. His attire didn't proclaim any fashion statements but it suited him nicely. If I had been into white men, I wouldn't have hesitated to give him a shot.

"How can I help you?" he asked, as he approached the front desk.

"I want a tattoo, but I'm not exactly sure what I want," I admitted.

"Well, take a look through our books and let me know if you see something you like," he told me, pointing toward a stack of books on a coffee table by the wall.

"Thank you," I replied, turning away and having a seat at the table.

"You are quite welcome," I heard him mumble.

Jasmine rolled her eyes. "I'm gettin' tired of this."

"Don't hate 'cause ya moms on point," I laughed, then nudged her in the arm.

"Whatever. These men need to keep their eyes to themselves."

Jasmine never did approve when a man would hit on me in her presence. I could understand when I was married to her father. But since I was free to do whoever I wanted, there was no need to trip.

"Men look honey," I told her, as I began to flip through pages in one of the books. "That's one thing I learned while being married to your father."

And damn, that was the truth. That man never gave a fuck if I was by his side or not. If a hot piece of tail came switchin' by, he couldn't help but stop what he was doing and take a look at it.

I made plenty of complaints about it over the course of our marriage, but he just couldn't seem to understand where I was coming from. I believed it to be highly disrespectful to check women out in front of me. He could look at what he wanted when I wasn't near, but to check women out right before my eyes was beyond infuriating. And frankly, I had put up with his ass for entirely too long.

The final straw came when he had the balls to ask me to join in on a threesome. Even though he never would admit it, I knew he hadn't been faithful to me for years. Coming home at late hours, not answering the phone and finding condom wrappers when we never used condoms were just a few of the obvious signs.

I told him hell no. There was no way I'd be able to stomach watching my husband with someone else. I was an extremely jealous lover. What was mine, was mine. And him telling me that he'd do it without me if I refused, was enough for me to put him out and file for divorce.

Now he was blowing up my cell, something he never did, asking me when he could come back home. I told him to go live with that bitch he'd been sleeping with.

"Ma, I'm ready to go," Jasmine whined in my ear almost an hour later.

Plenty of people who had been getting tatted when we arrived were gone and I was still trying to decide what I wanted. I was no dummy. The idea was last minute, but whatever I got on me would have to be something fierce if I was going to walk around with it, especially since there would be no going back.

"You can leave then," I told her, reaching inside of my purse, then handing her the car keys. "Just answer the damn phone when I call you to pick me up."

"I will!" she squealed, then planted a kiss on my cheek. "I'll be at the mall."

I was about to tell her to drive safely but I was interrupted by the guy at the front desk.

"Ma'am do you need some help?"

"Yes, I do," I stated getting up and walking toward him. "I still have no idea what I want."

"No problem," he smiled. "I have just the guy to assist you."

He walked away and quickly returned with a sexy-ass light-skinned hunk who made my pussy wet as soon as I laid eyes on him.

"This is Miguel," the guy told me. "He's excellent with helping people figure out the right tattoo."

I allowed my eyes to complete a quick scan of the extraordinary piece of meat before me. From the name, I assumed he had some Hispanic blood in him, though he appeared to be mixed a few other races as well. He was tall…at least six-foot-three, which was just right in my book. I loved a man who could tower over me. His fresh tape up couldn't be missed. Neither could his perfectly shaped goatee that I imagined tickling me while his tongue played with my pink walls. I especially couldn't bypass how his black muscle shirt showed off his impeccable chest and tattoos that covered his arms.

"Nice to meet you." Miguel smiled, while shaking my hand.

His grip was tight and his hands were strong. I could immediately picture my pussy walls gripping his dick as it moved in and out of me.

Immediately, I regretted thinking naughty thoughts. Ever since I had become single, my imagination had begun to consistently run wild. And it seemed like there was nothing I could do to tame it.

"Nice to meet you," I replied. "I'm Nina."

"That's a beautiful name," he told me, while flashing a beautiful set of teeth. There was a small gap between his front teeth and I found it to be so cute.

"Thank you," I said, smiling in a way my husband hadn't made me do in years.

"And I'm Jasmine," my daughter blurted out as she approached us.

I rolled my eyes. I loved my daughter as much as any mother would. But sometimes she tried to gain attention too damn much. Her father and I showered her with plenty of affection as a child so I had no idea why she was so fixated on getting every man to notice her.

"Nice to meet you, Jasmine," Miguel stated.

He looked at her briefly and immediately focused his attention back to me. Jasmine huffed, then stated she was leaving. I did my best not to smirk as she stormed out.

At times, I did feel sorry for her 'cause when we'd go out and she'd see a guy she liked, he'd almost always look at me harder than at her. I even tried to help her a few times by asking guys if they were interested in her. They would tell me no and that they'd prefer me. I know it was a blow to her ego but it damn sure did boost mine. It made this thirty-nine-year-old feel like she still had it.

"So about this tattoo," Miguel began, as he walked me to the back of the shop, toward his booth. "You have any ideas?"

"Nope. None at all," I stated flatly, once we reached his booth and I sat down in one of the chairs lined up against the wall. I placed my purse and cell in the empty chair beside me, since my daughter would be out shopping, instead of supporting her mother.

Miguel went on to ask me what my interests were, what was new in my life, and a few other questions to help pinpoint what I should get. I left nothing out when I shared the recent events of my life. I felt so free after feeling caged and depressed, so I had no issues in telling any and everybody my story.

"I got somethin' in mind," he said, before he began sketching on a sheet of paper.

I smiled and hoped what he'd come up with was something I'd actually want on my body. As I waited, I resumed my scan of his body. A stud earring in his right ear, a small mole on his forehead, full pink lips. I pictured kissing his lips, then licking his nipples as I made my way down to his dick. And once my mouth reached his dick, I'd suck the nut out of him.

Slow ya roll Nina, I told myself. I didn't know shit about the man besides the fact that he was fine as fuck and probably packing. He could've been crazy. Maybe even a killer. What if he was married?

I looked down at his hands. Nope! No ring. But it still didn't mean shit. I knew my ex took his ring off on multiple occasions. He never figured I would pay attention but my eyes were always on that lying bastard.

"All done," Miguel told me, putting down his pencil.

I looked down at my phone. Five minutes had passed by already.

"Wow. That was quick."

"What do you think?" he asked, once he handed

me the drawing.

I was blown away. He drew a stunningly realistic butterfly with tiny butterflies surrounding it.

"Wow. This is…beautiful," I said, as I studied it a bit more.

"Think you'd wanna get that?"

"Hell yes," I replied immediately.

He laughed, "Cool, cool. So, where would you like it?"

I paused for a moment. I hadn't thought about that part. All my mind had been fixed on was getting tatted.

"Need a moment to think about it?" he asked.

"No," I blurted out. "I want it on my right thigh."

He looked down at my thighs, smiled, then looked me in my eyes and replied, "Sounds good."

About ten minutes later, after filling out paperwork and paying for my future tat, I was laid back in the leather tattoo chair, wearing only my shirt and panties. Miguel turned the chair to face him so he was the only one who could see me. I loved the thrill of him looking at my lace panties as he inked my thigh. I wanted him to think about how sweet my pussy would feel surrounding the width of his dick.

He touched my thigh to apply the stencil paper onto my skin. I jumped a little from the chill that went through my body.

"You okay?"

I nodded. "I'm fine."

He looked at me, then proceeded to sensually finish transferring his drawing to my flesh. I wondered if it was just my imagination, but it felt as though he wanted me.

"You're beautiful," he told me, with those bedroom eyes still locked on mine.

"Thank you," I responded blushing. "And you're fine as hell."

"Thanks sexy," he told me, winking.

Before I was able to fully prepare myself, he had the ink gun up to my thigh, ready to begin. Time had slipped away from me once again as I allowed my imagination to run wild.

"Ready?"

I nodded, lying like fuck. It had just hit me what was happening. Damn him for being so fuckin' fine! There was no more time to prepare myself for the pain.

As soon as the needle touched my skin, I wanted to holler out in pain. I closed my eyes because I was too embarrassed to allow him to witness the water beginning to build up in my eyes. Thank God the chair was turned away from everyone else.

It felt like I had been in that chair for almost an hour once the outlining had been completed. I looked at my phone and frowned since it had only been fifteen minutes. I needed to woman up. People got tattoos every day. I had to keep my composure.

"Are you okay?" he asked, with a sincere tone.

"I'm great," I said, faking a smile.

"Don't act like you just wasn't about to cry a few seconds ago," he laughed.

"I was not!" I defended.

"I'm jokin'. But I need you to try and keep still. You been jumping a little bit every time I put the needle to your skin."

I hadn't even realized it. He then told me the

pain might be a bit more intense since he was about to do the shading. I silently cursed myself the fuck out. Why couldn't I have gotten a damn dog instead of trying to be sexy? My mother had always told me that was my problem in life.

When Miguel turned the gun back on, I closed my eyes, preparing myself for the pain. I waited but felt nothing. All I could hear was the annoying sound of the gun piercing my ear drums. I opened my eyes to find him staring down between my legs.

He looked at my shit like he wanted to rip my panties off and lick it. I was instantly turned on and the fact that we were in public made the thought of it so much more enticing.

"Why don't you stop looking at it and do something to it?" I teased.

"Oh word?" he asked, clearly eager to taste.

"Yeah, go for it," I encouraged.

He looked around beyond the chair to see if anyone was nearby. The coast was clear so he placed the gun down and pulled my panties off.

I sighed as he leaned in to sniff me. It was evident just how much of a freak he was and I was so anxious to see what he could do with his tongue.

Miguel proceeded to spread my legs apart slightly, just enough to get access to the goodies, but not enough to where anyone could see my legs sticking out. He locked eyes with me, never breaking his stare, as he licked my pussy. I let out a small moan, trying not to allow myself to be heard.

He stared down at my pussy like it was the most beautiful thing he'd ever seen. I was amazed as I watched him eat me out. His pussy eating skills were so advanced they surpassed my no-good ex, leaving me to believe I'd wasted too many years on a man who didn't know what the fuck he was doing.

"You got some fire pussy," he whispered as softly as he could.

"You think so?" I asked playfully.

"Shit, I know so. It tastes good as fuck too."

"Then stop talking and eat," I joked.

He smiled, then stuck his thick tongue out to lick my vagina, but I stopped him. I instructed him to hand me my purse. Silly me, I'd forgotten all about the new toy I'd purchased the day before.

When I retrieved my seven-inch vibrator from my purse, Miguel's face immediately lit up. He had a right to be excited though. I was giving him the chance to be the first to fuck me with it. All I'd done so far was take it out the box. I was waiting to use it at the right moment and by the way Miguel smiled at me, I was quite sure it needed to be used immediately.

I tossed my purse to the floor while Miguel twisted the knob until it came on. The sound of the vibrations had me so eager for him to hurry up and shove it inside me. But he chose to use a different route.

Miguel used the vibrator to lightly touch the opening of my vagina, which made me jump at first. His eyes told me I needed to remain still. If we wanted to get away with it, I had no chose but to keep still as best I could.

"Put it in," I whispered. "Don't tease me."

I was surprised he obeyed. I got the vibe he wanted to fuck with my head a little longer. I bet he would've loved to feel his dick busting through my vagina instead of that toy.

A deep sigh escaped from my lips as Miguel slowly pushed inside. I closed my eyes and enjoyed the moment. I couldn't believe I was actually getting my pussy fucked in a tattoo parlor with clients and tattoo artists surrounding me. It was definitely something I never would've seen myself doing when I was younger. Back then I had become so engulfed in starting a family and remaining true to the only man I thought I'd need. Funny how life tends to throw a curveball when you least expect it!

I opened my eyes to discover Miguel's eyes glued on me. He was so damn fine that if I didn't give a fuck about his job, I would've pulled his dick out and began to ride it until my pussy ached.

"Yoooo," a masculine voice called out from the next booth. "Miguel, how much longer you think you gonna be? We got a walk-in that needs help."

I rolled my eyes. Fuck whoever the fuck that was. That walk-in could sit and wait until we finished.

"Probably another fifteen minutes man," Miguel yelled, giving me an expression that showed me how truly sorry he was.

"Damn, yo. What the fuck taking you so long? What you doin' over there?"

Now it was Miguel who rolled his eyes. "Man I'll be done in fifteen."

Pressed for time, Miguel began to rotate the vibrator throughout my center a little faster. I started moving my hips around and squeezing my walls around it like it was a dick. He turned the knob on the highest speed, then stuck a finger inside my ass.

I hadn't had anything up my ass since my wedding anniversary the previous year. I only agreed to it because of the special occasion. Besides, my ex had been hounding me about it for years. I wanted him to shut the fuck up for good.

It was much different with Miguel. I felt no pressure, only pleasure. And although it was only his finger, I still found myself on the brink of an orgasm. I closed my eyes and imagined Miguel pumping his big, veiny dick throughout my body. As I allowed my imagination to explore the possibilities, he covered his mouth onto my clit and began to lightly suck.

The struggle had really gotten real. I opened my eyes and exploded unexpectedly just from watching how intensely Miguel sucked on my clit. My legs began to shake, causing the chair to move side to side. He didn't stop sucking until my orgasm had completely run its course and the shaking of my legs had subsided.

He grinned at me, taking the vibrator out of me. His eyes widen by the heavy amount of cum that oozed from my folds. Didn't bother him the least bit. He simply stuck his tongue to my opening and licked up every bit of cum that remained.

I took the vibrator from his grasp and swirled my tongue around the tip, then sucked half of it into my mouth. I moaned and stared at him seductively, showing him how I'd suck his dick if I ever got the chance. He adjusted his crouch, which was all I needed to see. It looked like he was hiding something far bigger than what I imagined. Maybe it was a good thing I couldn't have it that day. I needed time to mentally prepare my vajayjay for that one!

Miguel leaned up and pecked my lips. He thanked me for allowing him to witness such an erotic show, then resumed to finishing my tattoo before anyone else became suspicious.

I was much more relaxed when the needle returned to my thigh. Strangely, it didn't hurt anymore. That exquisite session between my pussy, the vibrator and his mouth had surely done the trick.

When the tat was all done, I marveled at the finished product. I promised him that if I ever got the urge to get another, I'd be back. Before walking out, I gave him a deep kiss, allowing him to taste my juices one final time. I grabbed his dick through his jeans and promised if there was a next time he'd be blessed with something he'd never forget.

I walked out of that tattoo parlor with a beautifully designed new tattoo and a super-hot escapade I couldn't wait to tell my girls about. I was single and ready to mingle. Something told me that unbelievable experience would be the first of many more to come!

A Bed Full of Roses

I wanna make love on a bed full of roses. A bed full of roses with just me and you. No one there to come between us. No one there to tear apart our union or our labor of lovemaking that goes on and on until I can't cum anymore and you end up late for work.

I haven't had you yet. I have yet to taste that sweet delectable cream that oozes from you dick when your stick becomes brick hard. I have yet to feel the flesh of your beautiful shaft in my hands. I'm eager to kiss it, nurture it, then suck it like it was made for my mouth and my mouth only.

And you can have me too...all of me, every single inch. I wanna be the one you run to whenever you get that desire to be buried deep inside of something tight and warm. I crave to be that one being you desire when you get the urge to lick and tease the wetness that comes from my love below with that long, thick tongue.

Call me crazy, but all I see is you. When I close my eyes, when I awake every morning, I'm always thinking of you and the way you make my heart skip a beat. Simulating conversations, the way you say my name, the way you get excited when you talk about your goals and aspirations in life, all make me realize that this is something far more intense than just lust.

So, call out of work today. I got something far more relaxing than what you'd be doing there.

Let me run you a hot bath, then wash you. Once you're all dried, I'll fall to my knees and shower your dick with all the love and affection I know it deserves. Just when you let me know you're about to bust, I'll stop, then lead the way to the bedroom.

A bed full of roses awaits you, my king. A bed full of roses to do to me whatever you please. Just you and me; heart beats pounding to the same drum. You and I in a bed full of roses.

Never Second Best

I've never been the type of woman to simply settle for second best. That competitive trait ran through my veins, always telling me I had no choice but to win at any and everything I put my mind to. Failing wasn't an option.

In eleventh grade when I won Miss Congeniality in my high school pageant, I wasn't the least bit satisfied. Immediately after, I conducted a ton of research, studying the women who became crowned Miss USA and women who succeeded in other noteworthy pageants. So, by the time my twelfth grade year rolled around I was prepared to bring my all. And that's exactly what I did. I wasn't the least bit surprised when I left the auditorium that night with the crown.

So naturally, you see I was born to forever be a winner. Even when I fail, which has happened from time to time, I pick myself up and try over and over until a change occurs. Eventually, something has to give. Which was why I couldn't put my finger around the fact that I was seated on a plane in coach while my husband and his mistress were seated in first class.

It all began about four months ago. Ahmir had been slack with giving up the dick. He didn't even want to touch me, which was something I certainly wasn't used to. The first five years of our marriage were comprised of sex almost every night...sometimes several times a day.

When those sex-filled nights began to occur less and less I had no choice but to find the root of the problem. I loved the consistent sex. I could only produce those toe-curling orgasms with my husband. Not having a clue what to do, one night I decided it was best to browse through his phone while he was in the shower. I found what seemed to be over a hundred texts to some woman I'd never seen or heard of before. Now usually I gave Ahmir privacy. I believed a man needed his space but after my eyes came in contact with those nude pics that bitch sent and the video my husband sent her of him jacking off, I was glad I followed my intuition.

"What the fuck is this?" I questioned, once he walked out of the shower and into the bedroom.

His body was still damp. His soft dick screamed out for me to touch it, to bring it to life with my mouth.

"What?" he asked, not really paying attention to me.

"This!" I shouted, waving his phone in his face after I pressed play on the video.

He glanced, then looked away as he sat on the bed. He then began to apply lotion to his broad chest and toned arms. My husband never had the body of a body builder, but he was sexy regardless.

"So you not gonna say anything?"

"What the fuck do you want me to say Brandy?" he yelled, staring at me.

I became silent, which was new for me since I was always running my mouth. I never thought I'd ever see the day when my husband, the love of my life, would be seeing another woman. And according to his text messages he was madly in love with her. Crazy how when we got married he promised me I'd be the last woman he'd ever love.

"I want you to tell me who the fuck this woman is!" I screamed back. "Why are you doing this to me?"

"Doin' what to you?"

"Cheating on me! Why would you cheat on me when I give so much?"

He laughed. "You give so much? Please, the only thing you give so much of is that pussy. Who pays the bills around here?" I fell into silence again. "Who gives you money to shop and get ya hair done? I do. So cut that bullshit out."

"But Ahmir-"

"Don't fuckin' Ahmir me. Don't act like you didn't see this coming, Brandy. I haven't been interested in you for a while now."

I shook my head. "I just figured you was going through a midlife crisis. I never figured you'd give yourself to someone else."

"Neither did I," he stated, now calm and even remorseful. "If this has hurt you in any way I do apologize. It was never my intention to hurt you. This just happened."

"It just happened? What? You just ended up inside her pussy?"

"Kinda," he said, shrugging his shoulders.

"You sorry-ass son of a bitch!" I cried out, swinging at him.

"Bitch what the fuck is yo problem?" he hollered, as he attempted to shield his face from my fists.

"You're my fuckin' problem. You and that bitch!"

"Well get used to it 'cause ain't shit changing about that," he informed me, before storming back into the bathroom and slamming the door behind him.

And things certainly didn't change. The only thing that changed was Ahmir sleeping in the guest bedroom, with his mistress! The bitch moved in. Yes, her lousy ass moved the fuck in.

Of course, my loud mouth had some explicit words to say to both Ahmir and that ho. But he simply ignored me and she laughed in my face as soon as she realized my power was gradually slipping away. My mother told me to move out and reside with her until I landed on my feet. But I wasn't trying to land on my feet. I was comfortable in my lavish home with an elevator, maids, indoor bowling alley, and huge swimming pool.

I'd spent six years standing by that man's side. I wasn't going anywhere. I was there when he was broke, so I damn sure was gonna be there while he was rich. Shit, it was my consistent encouragement that gave him the push he needed to become a software architect. Where the fuck would he be without me? Still living in the fucking hood, that's where the fuck he'd be.

So after that bitch moved in, sex with Ahmir transitioned from once a week to being nonexistent. While I was in my bed praying he'd come to his senses and fuck the frustration out of me, he was busy fucking the shit outta that ho.

"Ma'am would you like something to drink?" the stewardess asked me, as she approached my seat with her cart.

"No, no thank you," I replied, glad she broke me away from depressing thoughts.

Suddenly, I had to relieve my bladder. The stewardess was blocking the trail to the nearest restroom so I went straight for the one in first class. I opened the restroom door to find it was already being occupied by a woman. It clearly was my fault for not paying attention to the occupied sign.

"Oh shit! I'm so sorry," I quickly told her as I turned around, trying not to see anything I had no business seeing.

But just as I was about to make my grand exit and return to my seat, something inside told me I needed to see the face of the individual on the toilet. I spun around and my heart instantly began to thump. It was that BITCH!

"Ummm…" she whined, with wide eyes. "Could you please close the door?"

"Gladly," I remarked, as I stepped inside and closed the door behind me.

"I meant for you to get out," she said, with a major attitude.

"Oh, I know exactly what the fuck you meant."

I folded my arms over my chest, then stared the bitch down. She had some nerve. Why couldn't she just get her own man and leave mine the fuck alone? Everything had been perfect until she forced herself into the equation.

She thought she was so much better than me with her fairer skin and long blonde hair extensions. It made me sick to my stomach.

"Do you have something to say?" she asked, as

she rose from the toilet and wiped herself.

I frowned, then wondered if her nasty ass would take the time to wash her filthy hands.

"Actually, I do. Leave…Ahmir…alone. He's mine, so I'm gonna need for you to go elsewhere."

"Sweetie," she laughed, flushing the toilet and walking to the sink. "Your man's the one who wants me. I know you hear him blowing my back out at night. He just can't get enough of this young, tight pussy."

I didn't like what the fuck the bitch was implying. She was only about five or six years younger than I was. And as for my pussy, my shit was always tight. No loose-ass pussy over here!

I walked toward her until I was directly behind her. She twirled around and gave me such a disgusted look.

"Can I please have some space bitch?"

"Hell no, you can't bitch," I added. "Why can't you just let it go?"

"No, why can't you let it go? You're chasing after a man that don't want you anymore. Stop playing yaself."

I'd heard those dreadful words from my mother, my sister and close friends. But the truth didn't hit me until the words came rolling out from her fat-ass lips. What the fuck was wrong with me? Was I that naïve that I couldn't open my eyes and see the mess that was right in front of my face?

"Oh God! You're right," I cried out. "He really doesn't want me. He fuckin' hates me!"

Next thing I knew I was crying my eyes out. I placed my hands over my face so she couldn't see the tears that continued to fall. And surprisingly, she wrapped her arms around me for an embrace.

"Damn girl. I never meant to make you cry. It's not that bad," she tried to assure me.

"He doesn't love me anymore. He loves you."

"But I don't love him."

"What?" I asked, looking at her like she had lost her damn marbles.

She and Ahmir were always telling each other how much they loved each other and how they never intended to part. She sounded so believable when those words rolled off her tongue. I never thought to question her feelings. I guess I was too wrapped up in my own issues.

"Hell no," she laughed. "I'm only with him 'cause he can support me. Trust and believe I get dick on the side too. Where do you think I be going when I say I'm going to see my family?"

I couldn't believe what I was hearing. She really was a dumb-ass bitch. If I had been in her shoes I would've never confessed some shit like that. I was her enemy and no matter how down in the dumps I was, she should've been smart enough to know not to share her true intentions.

I was pleased though. Ahmir deserved to get played. After the way he treated me and stomped on my heart, I didn't feel the need to feel sorry for him. Karma was a bitch that came back around no matter what.

"This remains between you and I, right Brandy?" she asked, with worry shown over her face.

I smirked and wiped away my tears. "You gotta be kidding me bitch. Why the fuck should I help you? You can't do shit for me."

I could sense the tables turning and the ball about to be in my court. She was on the brink of tears and I honestly didn't care. She never gave a fuck when I was in my bedroom crying myself to sleep because my husband was giving his dick to another woman. She would always toss her hair and roll her eyes whenever I'd enter a room. She really wanted to believe she was much better than me. But the truth was, she was beneath me.

"Please, please Brandy," she pleaded, with her hands clasped together like she was homeless begging for a meal. "I can't go back to the way I used to live. I just can't."

I laughed in her face. "Damn, should've thought about that shit before you spilled the beans. I can be quite convincing so there's no way Ahmir won't believe me when I tell him about your little scheme."

"No, you can't do that. You can't."

The little bitch had the nerve to be crying. She needed to take that shit elsewhere.

"Watch me," I said, reaching for the door.

"Wait…I'll do anything Brandy! Anything…you have my word."

I turned around and studied her face. She was dead-ass serious. I realized I could definitely use her to my advantage. I could make her cut the grass, clean my dirty bath water…oooh, the possibilities were endless.

So, I had absolutely no idea why the words, "eat my pussy", came flying out my mouth. I had to take a second to ask myself if I had really blurted out such a command. And judging from the way the bitch's mouth dropped open, I had indeed instructed her to eat my pussy.

"Ummm, what? I ain't doing that shit," she said, rolling her eyes up to ceiling.

Suddenly, I began to crave her being between my legs more than ever. She was speaking to me as if eating my pussy would be the most disgusting thing on earth. If it made her that uncomfortable and sick to her stomach, it made me a hell of a happy camper.

I smiled, while my clothes came off piece by piece. I wished I had a camera to capture the speechless expression on her face.

Honestly, I had no shame in exposing my nude body before her. I was fully aware of my bad-ass body. Toned coco-colored legs, a tight midsection and tits two cup sizes bigger than hers were all features I was proud of.

"You're really serious?" she asked, once my naked ass sat down on the toilet seat.

"Fuck yeah. Come eat this pussy, bitch," I remarked, as I opened my legs wide to expose my shaven pussy.

Her eyes widened, which I took as proof that she still couldn't believe I meant every word that fell from my lips.

"This is my final warning. Get your ass over here before I spill the beans and your ass has to go back Hooters."

That comment really got her ass moving. She knelt down in front of me, looked between my legs, then up at me. The stare I gave her was plenty warning that she needed to get to work at that moment, or else.

She slowly inched her head toward my pussy, taking her fucking time. I instantly ran out of patience. In the blink of an eye, I grasped a handful of her weave and yanked her head toward my vagina. She yelped and attempted to pull away, but there was no escaping my tight grip.

I rubbed her face around on my pussy lips. It might've been hell for her but it was heaven to me. I hadn't had someone, besides myself, touch my pussy in…damn, it had been so long I forgot.

"Stick that tongue out and lick me," I ordered.

When she didn't do it quick enough, I forced her face onto my lips again. I was getting fed up with her bitch ass, but I was in love with the power I possessed. I was beginning to really feel like a bitch in charge.

"Okay, okay!" the bitch mumbled, struggling to breathe.

"Then act right, ho. I ain't got all day. All the fuck you're doing is sticking your tongue in there. How hard can that-"

She must've gotten fed up herself because her wet tongue moved across my pussy lips with so much force, it caused me to stop midsentence.

"Mmmmm, fuck yes," I whispered as softly as I could.

I had no idea how good she was at sucking my husband's dick, but she was a bonafide expert at eating pussy. I wondered exactly how many times she'd done it because she was proving to be so much better than Ahmir.

The cum sucker opened my folds with both hands and stuck her tongue inside of me as deep as she could go. I had to hold onto the tissue holder for some type of support. But I made sure I didn't release my grip on her head. She wasn't going anywhere until I got mine.

"Yes, eat it," I moaned. "Eat that sweet pussy."

She suddenly began to rub my clit vigorously while continuing to lick my insides. That shit had me astonished. I guess it really took another woman to do it right because that bitch was doing the damn thing!

I was about to nut but I didn't want the torture to end just yet. I ordered her to suck my nipples. She looked at me like I was insane, but after I made another threat, she promptly came to her senses.

She stuck two fingers into my pool of sticky cream and locked her mouth onto my right nipple. Her free hand became occupied when I placed it on my left nipple so she could squeeze it.

I eased my grip on her head just a tad and allowed myself to become engulfed in the magnificent sensations taking over my body. It had been too long since I'd received so much affection. It didn't even matter to me anymore that it was coming from a bitch I couldn't stand.

"Take your fingers out and suck my pussy juice," I moaned slowly.

"Ummmm," she began.

"Bitch," I began. "Stop fucking up my groove and just do as I ask."

She obeyed, although I knew it was killing her on the inside. A look of disgust appeared upon her face as she slowly sucked her fingers. That was unacceptable.

"Don't be making that ugly-ass face. You better act like you love it."

She bobbed her head up and down, moaning and slurping. Now, that pleased me. And I figured I'd tortured her enough for one plane ride.

My lock on her hair tightened again as I pushed her back down to her knees. I think I injured her from the force, but she was the least of my worries. The only thing I was pressed for was that nut.

Her long tongue reentered my domain. She applied pressure to my clit once again and that time I refused to hold back any longer. Both of my hands held onto her head while she worked harder than ever for it to all be over.

"Yesss! Oh my God!" I yelled, no longer able to remain quiet.

I came harder than I had in a while…probably in over two years. The explosion was so extreme that my body became temporarily paralyzed.

I had forgotten all about the bitch until she mumbled, "Um, can you please let me go?"

I released my hands, freeing her from the hell I'd forced her to endure. She rushed away from me, looked in the mirror and almost had a heart attack.

"Look at me!" she exclaimed. "Just fucking look at me!"

She surely did look a fucking mess. I couldn't hold back my laughter either. Two of her tracks were in her hand while a few of the others looked like they were barely attached to her head. Her face and neck were smothered in my cum, which I found to be even funnier.

I wiped my pussy with tissue, then began to put my clothes on. When I was fully dressed, I pushed her aside to wash my hands. Only God knew what kind of shit had been roaming around in her head.

"I fucking hate you," she lashed out when I opened to door.

"That's all good," I told her, turning my head around. "But know this, whenever I want this pussy licked and shown some affection, I'm calling your ass into my bedroom. And there better not be any complaints. If you're gonna live under my roof, you're gonna attend to this pussy."

I walked away as she hopelessly struggled to fix her weave. That shit wasn't going back in. What she needed to stress about was washing every trace of my cream from her face so my husband couldn't see it.

Walking back to my seat, I received plenty of disapproving stares. But they could all munch on my kitty-cat as well if they had something to say. No one was going to fuck up the remainder of my trip.

I stepped foot on the plane with so much stress and anxiety. But in the end, things had turned around for me. My revenge was in full force. That bitch was using Ahmir for his money. And I would use her for any sexual desire that crossed my dirty little mind. She had no idea what I had up my sleeve. Ahmir had something coming his way also. I hadn't quite figured out what it would be, but it would make his ass regret ever degrading my status to second best.

The boss bitch had officially returned. And she wasn't losing her crown ever again.

Pink Fortress

I whipped my Ford Fusion through the hectic LA traffic with a purpose, as my passenger talked my head off in the backseat. He'd only been in the car for five minutes and I literally could not wait to drop him off and move on to my next rider.

"I just don't get it dude," he ranted, as he stared at me through the rearview mirror. I avoided eye contact. "These chicks be so crazy about Valentine's Day. And for what? For some roses? A box of chocolates? I mean, come on! Get real! I'm not doing all that. Let's just fuck and go to sleep."

Was he serious? He couldn't be. He sounded like an idiot. I glanced back at him to find his eyes dead on me, like he was awaiting a response.

"Listen man," I began, all while attempting not to allow my emotions to show how irritating he'd become. "You're right. Valentine's Day is just another day. There shouldn't be just one day out of the year to show your partner affection and give gifts. You should show how much you care every single day."

Clearly not interested in the conversation anymore, he immediately looked down at his phone and, I assume, began to text his lady or whoever he would be laid up with that night. I wasn't nearly finished talking though. If he was gonna ruin my mood by talking a mile a minute in my ear, I'd do the same to him.

"And quite frankly, I don't understand why you're complaining about not wanting to celebrate it when you already brought all that shit." He paused for a moment, glanced over at the roses, balloons and three boxes of chocolates next to him, and then resumed to composing his text message. "It's obvious you did all of that for someone, so why complain about it? You already paid the money. And isn't three boxes of chocolates a bit much? Does she really need all that?"

I knew I'd gone too far as those words left my mouth. But I wanted to know what woman would be foolish enough to put up with his whiny ass.

He looked up at me, brows raised and eyes widened. "If you *must know*, I have three women at home waiting on me."

I couldn't help but laugh. "Three women at home dude?" I couldn't even imagine one taking him seriously, let alone three.

"Yes, *three*. And since you wanna know so much about me, how many do you have at home waiting on you?"

"Honestly dude, I technically don't have one," I said with a frown as I glanced down at my wedding band. "And I'm fine with that. But if I did I'd be out with her right now spoiling the hell outta her."

"Well that's cool, if that's what you into. But I'm fuckin' my three broads then gonna knock out for the night."

I bit my bottom lip, to prevent myself from saying the first thing that came to my mind and hurting his feelings. I still needed him to give me a good review for the ride.

"You have fun with that then," was all I could muster up before focusing back on the road so I could get that nut to his destination and the hell up outta my ride.

It was people like him that made me question why I even bothered to drive Uber in the first place. I had a day job at a major insurance company, which paid a decent amount of money. I had a good car, a nice home – I wouldn't starve without Uber. But the thought of my twins brought me right back to reality. I didn't *need* the side gig but it helped when it came to providing for my two kids.

Their mother, my soon-to-be ex-wife Tonya, was indeed still in the picture. But she barely wanted to work. She'd work a few temp jobs here and there, then quit because she got into an argument with her supervisor or she didn't like the way someone looked at her. Honestly, that was one of the reasons why I asked for a divorce. I was almost thirty-five – too damn old to be just settling when I wasn't happy. And I was emotionally exhausted from picking up her slack, let alone having to deal with her infidelity.

At six-foot-one, with muscular arms and a chiseled chest I spent hours in the gym perfecting, I could have any woman I desired. The ladies loved my bald head, smooth chocolate skin and my signature goatee. It was pretty clear to see that Tonya didn't realize what she was missing out on and when the time came for me to bounce, she'd be sorry she fucked it all up.

I believe the kids knew something wasn't quite right with us. Tonya and I barely spoke anymore unless it was about the bills, our children or one of the countless men calling her cell.

My kids were young, but far from naive. And I planned to tell them everything and to separate from Tonya when the timing was right. But with the recent passing of my mother, I just felt I needed to wait a while longer to give them adequate time to process everything.

But one thing I knew for certain was when I did leave Tonya, I didn't plan on looking back. She could have the house, all the furniture. I didn't care and it didn't faze me how she'd pay the bills without me there. She could call on one of her side dudes. She was notorious for doing that. Females loved to call us men neglectful and wrong, but my ex was living proof that women could be full of shit as well.

"Yo!" my annoying passenger called out, a bit too loud for my liking, as he answered his ringing phone. "I'll be there soon. Yeah...yeah, naw...I ain't forget it's Valentine's Day. I got chu...I'm almost home...right around the corner." He nervously glanced up at me, then uttered, "I love you too."

I smirked. I didn't know what the big deal was. Why did some men find it so embarrassing for another man to hear them utter those three words? I wasn't one of his homeboys and I sure as hell wasn't who'd be sucking his dick at night. So why did it matter?

"Wait, wait...what you got on?" I rolled my eyes. This mofo needed to get the fuck up outta my car. "Oooh, those lace panties I like, huh? Take them off...now sniff them."

That was all I needed to hear to be completely over that ride. I whipped around the corner so fast, he dropped his phone and his head hit the back of the passenger seat. That wasn't my fault though. I warned him about a seatbelt when he stepped foot inside my car.

"You alright?" I asked, trying to maintain a straight face.

"Yeah, yeah. I'm good," he said, as he rubbed his head, then opened the door. "You need to work on ya driving though. Man, somebody can get hurt from how reckless you drive."

"I'll be sure to do that. And you and ya *three* women have a good night."

"Oh, we will." He smiled, gathered up his gifts and briskly walked away.

I was beyond thankful his lying ass was out of my sight. I didn't know who he thought he was fooling but there was no way there were three chicks waiting at home for him. No way! Maybe one...and she'd have to be dumb as hell. But three? Now that was a bit absurd.

I glanced at my watch and sighed, since I still had time for at least one more drive before I called it a night. That guy had already drained all the energy out of me after having to suffer through his shenanigans.

My next venture was to the gas station to fill up my tank before I ended up stranded somewhere. I always had a really bad habit of riding around until my tank was almost empty. As soon as I stepped foot in the gas station, the only thing on my mind was grabbing a Snickers bar and a Red Bull to wake me up a bit. I picked up some gum, a bag of chips and a few water bottles as well, just in case my next rider needed anything.

"Is this all for you?" the tall middle-aged Asian

guy inquired, once I approached the counter.

"Yeah, this will be it," I told him flatly. I wasn't in the mood for small talk. He was always giving back the wrong amount of change. It never failed. It happened every single time he rung me up.

At first, I figured it was a race thing and he found humor in cheating a black man out of his hard-earned money. But he actually did it to everyone. I recall the first time I saw him behind the register and witnessed an elderly white woman become outraged he'd given her back two dollars when he should've given her fifty. After he corrected his mistake, she exited the store and warned us to watch him. I found it humorous at first, until the same thing happened to me, again and again...and again.

"It was pretty sunny out today, huh?"

Man, it's always sunny out! It's California! I shrieked on the inside.

I carefully stared as the guy rung up my items, making sure he didn't "accidentally" ring up the same item twice. He couldn't be trusted.

"Let me get 25 on pump three as well," I said, as he placed everything inside of a brown paper bag.

"That'll be $37.95."

I had a forty in my wallet but quickly decided against using it. I honestly didn't have the time or the energy to curse him out. Instead, I pulled out my credit card and swiped it on the keypad.

As soon as he gave me my receipt, I jetted out the door, pumped my gas and pulled out my phone to pick my next rider.

There was one almost a mile away that needed to be dropped off at a neighborhood about fifteen minutes away. Since I was so ready for this next ride to be over, I almost accepted it. That is until I noticed the passenger's low two-star rating. I wasn't in the mood to deal with another crazy-ass passenger that night, so I immediately had a change of heart. I decided to go with one that was much closer and with a better rating.

However, this passenger's destination was all the way in Santa Ana, which was a bit far for how long I planned to drive that night. But I figured the drive could do me some good and possibly clear my head, if he or she was the complete opposite of my previous passenger. And I saw it as a much more pleasant night being on the road, than being miserable at home with Tonya.

According to my map, the rider was literally in the same area as me. I accepted the ride and within no more than two seconds, there was a knock at my window.

"Are you Cameron?" asked the beauty standing before me, after I rolled down the driver's side window and got a good look at her.

My eyes quickly studied her up and down. The sun had already begun to go down, but it didn't prevent me from noticing every single detail about her. The beauty appeared to be about thirty – maybe twenty-nine or twenty-eight. She was dressed casually; a short sleeve white V-neck that was cut above her midriff, showcasing to the world her slim waist and flat tummy. The V-neck was cut perfectly to display her cleavage, which I must say was an amazing set of what I assumed to be D-cup knockers.

My eyes roamed down to her tight blue jeans that accentuated her curvaceous hips, giving me indecent thoughts about how even more gorgeous she'd be out of them. I could slightly feel my dick growing at the thought of holding onto those thighs as I kissed her luscious lips. I told myself there was no way she didn't have a man at home. With a body as bad as hers, she had to have been turning men down left and right.

But it wasn't just her body that made her so appealing to the eye. She had the face of a goddess. With honey brown skin that glowed naturally without the need of heavy makeup, she could've easily been a model. I licked my lips as I observed how full and sensual hers were. They appeared to be the best set of dick-sucking lips I had yet to lay eyes on. She had natural jet black hair that was pulled back into one big puff in the middle of her head, with big silver hoop earrings upon her ears.

"Yep," I replied, flashing my charming smile, then informing her that she could hop in.

"Santa Ana, right?" I asked, as I inputted her destination into Google Maps.

"Yep, Santa Ana it is."

I nodded, then maneuvered my car onto the road.

"So, I think I hear an accent," I said, after a few moments of silence. "Where are you from?"

"Alabama, born and raised."

"I knew it!"

She giggled. It was strange but the sound of her laughter made my penis thump a little. "You knew I was from Alabama just from my accent?"

"No," I admitted. "But I figured you were from the south. You just seem...different."

She stared at me intensely, clearly not certain where I was coming from. "You just met me two seconds ago, and I seem different?"

"Yeah! Come on now. I know I'm not the first person to tell you that. After being around you for just one minute, anyone can see it."

"I guess I'll take that as a compliment," she replied with a smile. "And yes, I have been told that before. I just thought it'd be funny to mess with your head a bit."

I attempted to continue the conversation; tell her how much of a compliment it truly was, but she interrupted my thoughts with her sudden excitement.

"Wait, is this Solange playing?"

I nodded.

A smile crept up on her face.

"Can I?" she asked, placing her fingertips on the volume nob, as if she was certain I'd respond with a yes.

Again, I nodded.

"This is my jam!" she exclaimed, as Solange's "Cranes in the Sky" filled the car.

"Oh, is it now?"

"Damn right!" she laughed, as her body swayed side to side with the music.

As I approached a red light, I looked over and studied her. She was the exact definition of the word beautiful. With her eyes closed shut, she hummed and sung along to the song, not noticing my lingering stare. Strangely, I found joy in seeing her so happy. I didn't know a thing about her, but could see for the moment, she was content. That is until her phone lit up.

She looked down at the screen and frowned. I

observed her open the message, begin typing, and then backspacing every word she wrote. She attempted to type a few words once again, only to erase them and then drop her phone in her lap.

"You good?" I asked, curious to see who'd gotten her so upset.

"I'm fine," she replied, as she turned her head and stared out the window.

I was silent, trying to determine the next words to exit my mouth. I didn't want to pry and put my head where it didn't belong but seeing her so upset made me uneasy. It would surely be a quiet, awkward remainder of the ride.

Finally, I turned down the music and said, "If you wanna talk about it, we can."

She looked over at me with watery eyes that appeared to be ready to flow with tears at any given moment. I silently prayed that she'd hold it together. Lord knows I've never been the best person to console anyone weeping.

"I'm fine. I'm fine," she finally assured me, wiping away her tears. "It's just my shitty ex. I just can't right now."

She picked up her phone and reread the message as though she was hoping that studying it obsessively would change its content. Finally, she sighed, placed her phone down, and looked out the window.

Once again, I couldn't summon the right words to console her.

Thankfully, I didn't have to overwork my brain with a response because she said, "I just can't believe how some men can be so trifling, selfish...damn right idiotic."

"I'm assuming that was your husband or boyfriend that texted you."

She huffed. "Hmmph! Husband? He's made it quite clear he isn't husband material." She looked me in the eyes for a brief second and although it was brief, I could see the fury and anguish she craved to release. "And no. He isn't my husband or boyfriend. As of last night, he's just my son-of-a-bitch-ex."

"Sounds like he must've really fucked up."

"You give a man eight years of your life only to find out you were never really his one and only the entire time. Eight years! Eight years and no ring! Wasted time I'll never get back!"

She went on to explain how she'd received a phone call from a woman claiming to be her ex's fiancé. The woman informed her they'd been high school sweethearts and inseparable ever since. All those years spent believing there would be a future with children suddenly came to a halt when the woman informed her she'd carried three of his children and he'd gotten a vasectomy two years prior.

She didn't want to believe...couldn't believe what some woman she'd never seen or spoken to would say. She had to be lying or jealous of the strong bond they shared. There was no way in hell he had a fiancé and three children without her ever knowing it. She couldn't listen to what some crazy woman had to say.

Still, no matter how many times she told herself it just wasn't true, she had to see for herself. She had to put an end to the voice deep down inside that she tried so desperately to ignore.

Despite feeling a rush of anxiety and distress,

she gathered up the courage to talk her best friend into following him. He claimed to have been spending time with his brother but as her friend's car neared a neighborhood she'd never even stepped foot in, she feared her worst nightmare was indeed reality.

She didn't give me exact details on what transpired after that, only that she marched right inside that house and got all the answers she'd been searching for. He confessed everything after she demanded the truth before his family.

"Now that it's over, I can process everything. I feel horrible about barging into his house while the kids were home. They saw everything. I never intended on hurting anyone."

I could hear the remorse in her tone, the sincerity enhancing her beauty even more.

"But the way that bitch smirked at me when he told me the truth, just made me want to choke the life outta her."

Not possessing the right words to say, I simply said, "I can only imagine."

She continued, "But I can't be mad at her. I really can't. *I'm the side chick.* For eight years, I was waiting on a ring and he'd already given one to someone else."

"Listen," I began, as I exited the freeway. "I don't know you, but I can already see that dude doesn't deserve you. And I for one do believe in karma. It's coming to him."

"Yeah, well I couldn't wait for karma. I slashed his tires this morning."

I laughed, not the least bit expecting to hear those words. She laughed as well, which pleased me. A woman of her standards should never have to cry or stress over a man's bullshit.

We continued to converse in small talk, slowly becoming more acquainted with one another. I told her I was born and raised in Long Beach and now resided in LA. I learned her name was Whitney and she was raised in Alabama but relocated to Atlanta, Georgia during her freshman year of high school and later to California for college. I told her what I did full-time for a living and she informed me that she was a makeup artist on the side and worked at a call center full-time. She had big dreams of someday being able to lose the nine-to-five and become a makeup artist to the stars.

"Well, here we are," I said, as I pulled up to her destination. "This your place?"

She nodded and focused her attention on the small home in front of us.

"You own or rent?"

"Rent. I don't plan on living in Santa Ana forever so it'd make no sense to own a home right now."

"It's charming, really," I stated, admiring the roses planted in front of the windows and the freshly cut grass. "You live alone?"

She laughed. "Not that it matters, but yes. I do live alone."

I was impressed. I didn't know many people in California her age who had their own place. With everything being so expensive, having roommates or living with family was necessary most of the time.

"Well, I guess I'll be going," she stated, reaching down to grab her purse from the floor. "Thanks so much for the ride."

I immediately found myself disappointed. I still wanted to know so much more about her. I still had no idea what she enjoyed doing in her free time or why she even allowed herself to deal with a man as stupid as her ex. She had to have sensed what I was feeling because the next thing she asked was if I'd like to come inside.

Without hesitation, I replied yes, and quickly exited the car.

"I know it's small, but it's all mine," she stated, as she locked the door behind me and led the way to her living room. "Have a seat. Make yourself at home."

"Thanks," I replied, as I sat down upon the sofa with my eyes glued to her round ass as she walked into the kitchen.

"Would you like something to drink?" she asked, opening the refrigerator as I observed the scenery.

A small round table was stationed in front of me. The contents on the table included, multiple television remotes, pink nail polish, a comb that badly needed to be cleaned, and the Holy Bible. Even if she didn't read it, it brought a smile to my face to know she owned one. My wife wasn't big on religion and I wasn't the most holy person either. But there was something alluring about a woman who had faith in God.

"I've got some wine...tequila-"

I laughed. She might've been a believer in Christ, but she clearly loved to drink. "Let me stop you right there. I still have to drive home. I'll pass on that drink."

She paused, as if she had something on her mind. I imagined her preparing to ask me to spend the night with her. Instead, she asked, "So what's the deal with you? You're married, with kids? How many?"

"What, are you psychic or something?"

She laughed. "No, but the wedding ring on your

finger gives it all away."

I looked down at my ring finger and cringed.

"Ahhh...it's that bad, huh? You and your wife not together or something?"

"You really are inquisitive, aren't you?"

"Well, you know so much about me. I just poured my heart out to you in the car, so spill the tea man!"

I chuckled. "If you must know, me and my wife...we aren't together anymore. Well, we're together, but not together." I paused when I noticed the confused expression written all over her face, then figured I'd spill the entire truth. "My wife and I haven't been in love for a very long time. The only reason we're still together is because of our kids."

She sat next to me, took a sip of her drink, and replied, "And are you happy? I mean, being with a woman just to keep your kids happy? Don't get me wrong. I get it! I really do. But I know I could never. I'd just have to find a way to break it to my kids softly."

"You know, before all this happened I figured the same thing. I did, but going through this first hand is different."

I could feel myself getting choked up and tears developing at the corner of my eyes. She touched my arm and gazed at me with concern.

"Are you okay?"

I nodded and stared at the walls. "My mom passed away a few months ago. It happened right when we were prepared to tell the kids. It devastated them. They still cry every time they think of her. It's just too much to put on them right now."

She nodded, as if she understood every emotion

I'd experienced within the past few months.

"Yeah, that does sound really tough. I'm so sorry."

"Thanks."

"So how old are they?"

"They're six years old...twins. Cameron Jr. And Camile." I couldn't help but beam with pride as I said their names. "Those two are my everything. If I lose everything in this world, I know I'll always have them."

"That's so sweet," she said, with a bright smile. "I can't wait to have kids and be able to talk about them like that..if that ever happens."

I took her hand. "It will. I'm sure of it."

She looked at me and in that moment, all I desired to do was kiss the hell outta her full lips. They appeared to be as soft as silk. I just had to have a taste!

"What are you thinking about?" she asked me, after a few moments of us lustfully staring at one another.

"How much I'd love to kiss those lips."

She appeared to be shocked by my words. And even I was a bit taken back by my boldness.

"What are you waiting for then?"

I took a second to process her words, but when she gave me an expression that begged the question her words had just asked, I leaned in and joined lips with hers.

Her lips were sweet. Maybe it was the taste of her fruity lip gloss, but whatever it was, I knew I wouldn't mind savoring her flavor on a daily basis.

"Take off your pants," I commanded without thinking.

"What?"

"I said take them off. Take off your underwear too."

"Boy, you really don't like to waste any time, do you?"

I shook my head. "I just need to taste you."

If those lips between her legs were as sweet as what I'd just gotten a taste of, then she was in for the night of her life.

And the night of her life was simply an understatement because the moment I got whiff of her sweet cherry scent, I lost my sanity. I spread her legs as wide as they could go and buried my head and tongue deep into paradise.

She cried out my name as she scratched up my bald head.

My tongue darted in circles inside of her yummy, pink fortress.

She shook uncontrollably.

I sucked her clit and fingered her walls until her body sprinkled a rain shower.

That didn't stop me. I continued for what had to be at least an hour, maybe two. I wasn't sure how I'd suddenly become such an oral freak but something about that woman brought it out of me.

All I wanted at that moment was to please her body. And from the looks of it, the guy she'd been wasting her time crying over clearly didn't know a thing about eating a box with precision. I had her crying, literally in tears with each climax that escaped from her ravishing body.

I removed my mouth from her folds and licked my lips, savoring her sweet fruit. I'd never tasted anything as delectable as the mouth-watering, finger-licking-good dessert staring back at me. I gazed in awe as her sugary essence trickled out from her opening, taunting and teasing me to continue licking until my tongue ached.

I proceeded to slurp up her dripping nectar, then said, "You won't be needing that shirt either."

"Anything you say," she giggled, as she swiftly removed her shirt and tossed it to the floor.

I drooled when my eyes roamed toward her breasts. Even with her bra still attached, I was certain they were firm and perky. I struggled to fight off the urge to rip off her bra and smother them with kisses they rightful deserved.

"Lose the bra as well, baby," I whispered, as I inserted a finger inside her vagina.

She tilted her head back and moaned loudly.

Just hearing her moan was like a blessing and I needed an abundance of more, so I slid in a second finger.

"Shit," she whimpered, attempting to catch her breath while my fingers played inside her tight walls.

"Take the bra off," I repeated, growing a tad bit impatient. Her boobs already appeared to be ready to burst out of her bra and as each moment passed, I grew more and more eager to feast upon them.

Whitney tossed her hair from her shoulders and reached toward her back to unsnap her bra. She winked at me as the bra fell down to her lap, exposing her juicy, enchanting breasts. They were even more jaw-dropping than I had imagined.

As I predicted, her breasts were bouncy, yet firm. They were much bigger than I imagined, which I didn't see as an issue at all. That just meant there was so much more I could play with.

But what really put the cherry on top were the nipple piercings that highlighted the middle of her honey brown mounds. I'd always had a fetish for nipple piercings. At one point, I'd even attempted to persuade my wife into getting hers pierced. But she wasn't into piercings and she never had been big on me playing with her tits.

But that beautiful rack before me was about to be serviced and pleased in a way I'd never executed before. With my mouth salivating and dick harder than a brick, I just couldn't hold back any longer.

I stood up far enough for my mouth to reach her left nipple and began sucking away like a malnourished man who hadn't eaten in weeks. Whitney wrapped her arms around my head and her legs tightly around my back as she whispered my name. She begged me to continue. Begged me to suck harder. Begged me to nibble more.

I complied with her wishes, ensuring I showed the same amount of affection to each nipple. Anything she needed sexually, could and would be done that night.

"Wait, Cameron, wait," she panted, like it was all beginning to be too much to handle.

"What?" I looked up at her but couldn't subject myself to put an end to the threesome taking place between my mouth and her breasts.

"I want you to put your dick right here."

My mouth unwillingly let go of her right nipple and I watched her grab ahold of her tits with both hands.

"Put my dick where, baby?" I was out of breath

already, but I could continue throughout the night as long as she needed me to.

"Between my breasts," she slyly remarked with a wink.

I grinned and without uttering another word, opened my legs wider and slapped my erection between her breasts. Whitney then pushed them together so they could cover my dick entirely.

I looked down into her lustful eyes. Her lips remained still but allowed her eyes to do all the talking. They told me to do as I pleased – get mine and damn sure ensure she got hers. And I made it my mission to do exactly that.

My body slowly begin to move forward. I closed my eyes while enjoying the feel of her soft breasts against my hardened stick. I made up my mind to take my time with this position. My wife had never been up for a little titty fucking either, so that night was all about exploring and enjoying what I would have never gotten at home.

I placed my hands on top of hers and moved her breasts slightly to the side, just enough to lather up my dick with spit. As soon as my dick was once again covered with her mounds, I began to thrust back and forth with more speed.

I moaned as she began to talk dirty to me.

She smacked my ass, while I held onto her chest praying to the heavens above that the moment would never end.

But it did.

A bit too soon for my liking.

"Fuck! Here I come!" I cried out, ready to release my load at any second.

"Oh hell nawwwww nigga! You ain't shooting that shit on my face!" she yelled, as she pushed me off of her just in time for my nut to shoot across the floor instead of upon her face.

She laughed as she watched me jack my dick until every ounce of cum had made its exit. I shook my head once I'd gathered my composure. She didn't want the cum on her face but laughed at it being all over her floor.

"Don't worry about the mess. I'll call the maid in the morning," she reassured me.

I nodded. "So that means we can make things as wet and X-rated as we like tonight?"

Whitney smiled and patted her pussy. "I see nothing wrong with that."

I took that as an incentive to resume the lovemaking my mouth had begun earlier with her one-of-a-kind vagina. I quickly kneeled down and stuck my face where it desired to be most. I couldn't help but smile as she cried out my name only moments after my tongue slipped inside.

With each lick, her pussy got wetter and wetter, quenching my thirst while making my dick even harder.

I ate her box like a man who craved to be the first thing she thought of in the morning and the last thing she thought of before bed. At that moment, that pussy belonged to *me*! By the end of the night I wanted her to have fallen madly in love with the many talents of my tongue.

"Okay, okay, you gotta stop," she eventually told me, after climaxing for what seemed to be the fifth time that night. "You're gonna make me be sore tomorrow."

I grinned. "I thought that was the point."

Whitney shook her head, then ordered me to go inside her bedroom. She told me to strip my clothing before lying down onto the bed with my eyes closed, assuring me that something very special was coming to me.

I followed her orders without thinking twice. I hadn't been this on the edge of my seat in what felt like forever. And by the way my dick sprang out of my underwear, it was evident I was long overdue for some erotic thrills in my life.

I laid there in the darkened room with my hard dick in my hand and eyes wide open. Despite her rules, I wanted to be able to see her body even if it was pitch black.

She returned to me in a matter of moments.

"Are your eyes closed?"

"Yes," I lied.

"Liar," she laughed. "Close them or you're going home."

I sighed then obeyed, all while curious at how she knew they were open in the first place.

"Now, that's a good boy," she stated, while removing my firm grasp on my dick and replacing it with her tiny hand. "Let me reward you for all you've done thus far tonight."

The next thing I felt was a cold liquid that made my body shiver.

"Shit!" I mumbled, as the liquid ran all the way down my chest to the tip of my dick.

"You know," she continued, as she cupped my balls and wet them up with the liquid as well. "As a girl who's always loved sweets, chocolate has for sure always been my favorite. And since it's all over your body, I can't resist the urge to lick up every drop."

I opened my eyes and in the darkness, I saw her lower her head and slowly slurp my balls into her warm mouth. I shut my eyes once again and enjoyed the moment as she sucked away, making my dick jump in excitement.

She slurped at my balls a bit longer, then started with my chest by sucking each nipple then working her way down. She took her time and even though I couldn't see her movements, I knew she was trying to lick up every ounce of chocolate from my body.

She didn't warn me or prepare me the slightest bit for what came next. Her open mouth began to usher my dick inside with open arms. Before I could count to five, she'd managed to slide my entire shaft down her throat. But that wasn't what surprised me the most. My dick was at least six inches, maybe seven if I was excited enough. But what I had really been blessed with was girth. With my dick being the size of a soda can, I at least imagined her to struggle at first, maybe choke a tad bit. But she worked my shaft like a professional... as if she'd been born to wet it up and pleasure it.

"Ahhhhh!" I moaned. I found my phone and turned the camera and flash on so I'd be able to see her every move as she coated my dick.

In the heat of the moment, I pressed record. She looked up at me, winked, then began to suck on me in ways I never imagined were possible.

With the camera on her, she transitioned into someone else and became the star of the show. She proceeded to glide her head up and down, with no hands. Despite my current situation at home, I wanted to marry this girl. I needed this every night! My wife had never been the best at oral and Whitney was performing circles around her.

I hoped that I could endure the entire night. With head that awesome, I knew it was a once in a lifetime opportunity. But no matter how hard I tried to hold on, it was just too good to maintain my composure.

"I'm 'bout to bust!" I uttered as a warning. With the heavy loads I could milk out, I always felt inclined to say something.

She worked that pretty mouth harder and as I came, she opened her mouth and stroked my dick with a quickness. As I watched everything take place on my phone, I was amazed at how even more stunning she looked taking my load. I came into her mouth like milk and she greedily swallowed until it was all gone.

"Whew!" I exclaimed, once I set my phone down and closed my eyes. "You really know how to make a guy feel good."

Okay...good was an understatement. It felt like I had died and drifted off to heaven. But I didn't have to tell her all that. She must've been fully aware of how exquisite her talents were.

"I thought you didn't want any on your face."

"I didn't...I took it all, Daddy."

She kissed me on the lips, then disappeared into the bathroom and returned with a wet rag. She wiped my dick and any remaining evidence of the chocolate from my chest, then placed the rag on the dresser and joined me in bed.

We laid on our backs, side by side, staring at the ceiling. I wanted to reach over, grab her waist, and pull her into me so we could cuddle. Wasn't sure if she was the cuddling type though.

"You smoke?" she asked, after turning on a lamp and pulling out an already rolled blunt from her nightstand.

I shook my head. I hadn't done that in years. Before I met my wife I saw nothing wrong with a little puff here and there. It relaxed my nerves and for some reason, helped me perform like a jack rabbit between the sheets. But my wife wasn't feeling it. She was too worried about what her father would say if he discovered she'd fallen for a pot head.

I did sneak a few hits here and there without her knowledge but after my kids were born I really did put an end to it. I put an end to everything. The smoking, drinking, staying out at night with the guys, even though I never stayed out past two. I hadn't realized it until that moment, but my wife really had influenced the way I lived my life...and I didn't like it.

Watching her puff and blow from the blunt teased me until I couldn't resist any longer. I needed a hit.

"Pass it over."

"Oooh, change of heart, huh?" She took one final puff before passing it to me.

"Hell yeah," I mumbled through puffs.

"You have any condoms?"

I coughed, taken completely off guard. She laughed as she took the blunt from my grasp, inhaled, and then exhaled into the air.

"You good?" she asked, once I'd regained my composure and my coughing had ceased.

"Yeah, I just didn't see that question coming."

I gave Whitney her props for even asking. A lot of people get so caught up in the moment that they don't worry about all that until it's too late and the woman's missed her period. I for one, didn't want or need any more kids at the moment. And I was certain Whitney felt the same, at least not by a man she'd just met.

Her curiosity gave me a hint that if I wasn't packing any protection, there would be no sticking into her wet sea. I was cool with that. We'd both already came and explored our bodies. If the remainder of our time together would be just smoking and enjoying one another's company, it was alright in my book.

She took another puff, then handed it back to me. "You should've. We already did oral. Frankly, I should've asked you that before we even started messing around."

I nodded as I puffed away, fully aware I was being stingy with what wasn't mine. Who knew when I'd get the chance to do it again.

"So is that nod a yes? You have some?"

"As much as I would like to say yes, I don't have any," I admitted, blowing out smoke and passing the blunt. "I honestly don't just have random sex. You're the first woman I've been with since...well, since I met my wife."

"Wait, what? You're telling me there's been no one else since you got with your wife?"

I nodded. "That's true."

"Well, why'd you have your face buried in my pussy like you do this shit all the time?"

"I don't know," I admitted, staring intently into her pretty brown eyes. "There's just something about you."

She allowed herself to smirk, then fixed her face as though she didn't want me to know she was digging me. I understood it. She didn't know how to trust what a man said anymore.

"Do you go down on your wife like you just did to me?"

I couldn't contain a sigh as I held out my hand for another puff. "No, we aren't together, remember? We don't have sex. We don't even sleep in the same bed. I tell the kids I prefer the mattress on the bed in the guest bedroom."

"Okay, let me rephrase that question then. When you and your wife were together, did you ever go down on her the way you just did? I mean, you didn't just eat the pussy, you demolished it! Like you had something to prove."

As I laughed, I replied, "Naw, I don't think I ever did. Like I said before, there's just something about you."

Whitney stared at me in a way I always dreamed my wife would have. The lust that had been in her eyes minutes ago was replaced with compassion, and at that moment I could sense her walls coming down a bit.

"So, I don't normally allow anyone to film me."

"Huh?" I had forgotten all about that little porn star filming session we'd done only moments before. I told myself to definitely watch it thoroughly when I got back to my car.

She nudged my shoulder. "Boy, you know damn well what I'm talking about. And now that I think of it, you need to delete it. I barely know you and who knows what you'll do with it. My ass might end up on

XTube or World Star."

I laughed. "I wouldn't do that. If anything, I'll just jack off to it from time to time."

"That might be true. But still, I don't know you. Give me your phone," she commanded, taking what was left of the blunt and putting it out.

"What?"

She sat up and stared at me. "I said give me your phone."

"No. You're not taking my phone."

"You must be ready to go home then. Give me the phone or get out."

With that being the second time she'd given me a choice to do as she said or hit the road, I was beginning to think she got a thrill out of throwing people out.

"Fine, fine." I pulled up the video on my phone and handed it to her.

"Come on, be honest," she said, as she stared at the still shot of her mouth fully occupied with my dick. "If this were a video of you eating me out, you'd be thinking the same thing. You'd want to delete it as well."

I shook my head. "I honestly wouldn't care if someone saw it. I was in the moment with you and you taste so good, you were worth every lick."

She smirked and said, "Of course you'd say that. You're a man."

She pressed play on the video and resumed her previous position on her back, as we both studied the most magnificent blow job I'd ever received.

I glanced down at my dick and smiled as it grew to its fully erect length. My eyes focused back to the phone and became entranced at the sight of how wet she'd gotten my dick just from her mouth. And the way she sucked and swallowed! That girl was unbelievable. There was no doubt in my head that I'd be watching that video every chance I could.

"Looks like you really enjoyed that," she stated, once the video had ended.

I grabbed onto my still erect dick. "Well yeah, I'm a man, remember?"

We shared a laugh, then things became serious as our eyes connected and got lost in one another. She took my hand and moved it over to feel the warmth coming from her vagina. She then used one of my fingers to slowly push into her opening.

She closed her eyes, sighed, and said, "See...I'm all hot and bothered too."

"Damn," was all I could say when I removed my finger from her box and witnessed how wet she'd gotten.

I rubbed her sweet juice over her nipples, then sucked it away. She rubbed on my head as my tongue flickered across each nipple and two fingers slid inside of her folds.

She moaned as I finger fucked her, making her wetter with each thrust. I worked my fingers even faster when she yelled out that she was about to cum.

She attempted to remove my fingers and run from the eruption preparing to exit her body. But I pinned her down and continued to move my fingers in and out of her until she jerked her body back and forth and climaxed her most intense orgasm that night.

I grabbed the rag from the dresser, rinsed it out, and then returned to wipe her body down. The bed was soaked so I helped her remove the sheets from the bed as well.

"Do you need to shower or anything?" she asked, which gave me the cue she was ready for me to leave and have her home all to herself.

Just as I prepared to respond yes, with intentions on eating her one last time before my exit, my phone rang. I cursed when I noticed it was my wife.

"Go ahead and answer that. You never know, it could be important."

"I seriously doubt it," I remarked, before swiping to answer.

"Where are you? Do you not know what time it is?" Tonya angrily spat into my ear.

"Who do you think you're talking to? Last time I checked we weren't together."

She paused, like she had to think of a good comeback. "Well, I personally don't care but your kids have been asking for you. What am I supposed to tell them, huh? Where are you anyway? Are you out with some woman? I know you can't be driving this late."

"What I'm doing is none of your concern. And the kids shouldn't even be awake to begin with. It's a school night."

"Look, all I know is, you need to be home instead of out with-"

Click.

I just couldn't take it any longer. She was such a bitch! How could I have possibly fallen for someone so selfish and self-centered?

"You gotta leave?"

I shook my head. "I'd rather stay."

She smiled. "I think we both know it's best you

go home. You have kids and a wife." I opened my mouth to protest, but she silenced me with her finger to my mouth. "I know, I know. Y'all aren't together. But legally you are still married. You gotta go home."

I nodded, despite every urge to disagree and say fuck Tonya. She didn't compare to the woman I had standing right before me.

"I'll walk you out."

She locked her arm around mine and walked me to the door. We kissed a final time and this time it was even more heart pounding than before.

With my dick still erect and thoughts racing about when and if we'd ever meet again, I exited her place. But before I made it halfway to my car, turned around to see her mouth the words "thank you". I smiled as I waved goodbye.

As I got into my car, my phone lit up.

It was a notification from Uber. I opened it and smiled to see a five-star rating from Whitney, along with her number.

I copied the number, then texted her and told her to have a good night. A few seconds later she replied back with a kiss emoji and how she was looking forward to possibly seeing me again.

I started up my car and prepared to drive off, but stopped myself to ponder on if everything that had just transpired wasn't a dream. I referred back to the video of Whitney worshipping my dick and immediately came to terms with how real it all actually was. I was thrilled it was still dark out. I didn't want anyone to see me as I drove out of her neighborhood with a smile as big as Texas upon my face.

A Valentine's Day that had been lonely and

annoying turned out to be one that gave me hope. And it was all thanks to a pretty brown honey with a sugary pink fortress, who took the time to listen to me and give my body something it'd been long overdue for. It wasn't love but everything that had transpired that night helped me realize it was possible to move on and maybe, just maybe, find happiness once again.

Thanks so much for reading, "Silk: The Complete Trilogy"! If you enjoyed reading this book, as much as I did writing it, please feel free to post a review.

You can also follow me on social media and express any thoughts about the book, or inquire about upcoming projects!

Facebook: @daryljarod
Twitter: @daryljarod
Instagram: @daryljarod

COMING SUMMER 2017